Ecl<

Dreams

The Milford Anthology

Edited by

J W Anderson, Pete W. Sutton & Liz Williams

kristell-ink.com

All rights reserved. This book or any portion thereof may not be reproduced or used in any manner whatsoever without the express written permission of the publisher except for the use of brief quotations in a book review.

All characters appearing in this work are fictitious. Any resemblance to real persons, living or dead, is purely coincidental.

Introduction by Liz Williams © 2022
Ryland's Story by Neil Gaiman © 2022
Mama Leaf by Tiffani Angus © 2020
Go With the Flow by Ben Jeapes © 1999
Serpent Eggs by David Langford © 1998
Pitch by Jacey Bedford © 2015
Old School – An Oral History of Captain Dick Chase
by Val Nolan © 2018
The Venetian Cat by Cherith Baldry © 2014
Blessed are the Hungry by Victor Fernando R. Ocampo © 2014
Words of War by Guy T. Martland © 2014
Scenes from Domestic Life With The Gentry by Nick Moulton © 2019
Of Dawn by Al Robertson © 2011
A Last Day by J W Anderson © 2017

Page 239 constitutes a continuation of this copyright page.

ISBN 978-1-913562-41-0 (Hardback)
ISBN 978-1-913562-42-7 (Paperback)
ISBN 978-1-913562-43-4 (EPUB)

Cover image by Jackie Duckworth
Cover design by Ken Dawson
Typesetting by Book Polishers

Kristell Ink
An Imprint of Grimbold Books
5 St John's Way,
Hempton,
Oxfordshire,
OX15 0QR
United Kingdom
www.kristell-ink.com

To all science fiction and fantasy writers,
past, present and departed,
who have made Milford
so successful over the last fifty years.

And to those writers who are thinking
about joining us in future years.
We hope that you do.

Table of Contents

Introduction

As we all know, years tend to pass with remarkable speed, as if you are flicking through the pages of a book. I am vaguely appalled to find that I first attended Milford ten years ago, then fifteen years ago, then twenty years—and at the time of writing, it is twenty-three years since I caught a train to the coast of Devon to attend a writing workshop in a hotel which did not at all resemble Fawlty Towers. No, really.

However, I am a newbie, a mere infant, in comparison to the Milford SF Writers' Workshop itself, which is only seven years older than I am. And I'm no spring chicken. This year, 2022, will be the workshop's 50th anniversary. It was first started in the USA in 1956 by Damon Knight. James and Judy Blish brought it to Britain in 1972 (initially in Milford on Sea) and it has been running ever since.

In 1972 Milford attendees included the Blishes, Anne McCaffrey and Brian Aldiss amongst others. Writers who have passed through Milford since then include Neil Gaiman; Alastair Reynolds; Charles Stross; Chris Priest; David Langford; Diana Wynne Jones; Geoff Ryman; George R.R. Martin; Jaine Fenn; John Clute; Karen Traviss; Mary Gentle; Patricia Wrede and many, many more.

Of course, Milford has changed since 1972. But not enormously: it is still a group of 10—15 professionally published writers, who spend a week critiquing one another's work, according to the Milford Method (namely, you get 3 minutes to say what you have to say, a minute to wind up, and then you have to shut up. The writer on the receiving end of the critting must shut up for the whole however-long-it-takes, then gets to tell everyone that they've failed to understand his, her or their genius or, far more likely, to groan "Oh God, I *knew* the plot went off the rails on page 4. This has been really helpful. Thank you, everyone.")

Some years ago, however, we did make a big change. Milford currently meets at Trigonos, a retreat centre in the middle of the Snowdonia National Park. It's a fascinating, Welsh-speaking, post-industrial area. The location is exquisite, but the village is backed by abandoned quarries and slate mines, a reminder that this bit of Wales used to be a lot more prosperous than it is now. It's gradually becoming a tiny bit more gentrified, with the advent of a coffee roastery in the village itself. And there is no getting away from the fact that this is a very non-diverse part of the country, and so was Milford itself.

The workshop believes in diversity, and it believes that as many people, of as many different backgrounds as possible, should have the opportunity to write and publish SFF. But it's a bit difficult to make this claim and host, year after year, nothing but white writers who can afford a week in what is essentially a hotel. Hence, we decided to float a bursary for non-white and financially disadvantaged writers: two places each year. We were able to do this through the generosity of our own membership and through that of one of the Eastercons, which contributed its excess profits to give someone a chance to come up to North Wales and join us.

We weren't sure whether it would work, but it did. It's now been running since 2017 and we have had BAME writers from Nigeria, the Philippines, America and the UK itself, since Britain is a diverse nation. Some of those participants have been back again and again, to the workshop itself and to the accompanying retreat, which is held in the spring. Firm and lasting friendships have been made and whilst the bursary recipients may have benefited from the fund, the rest of us have benefited from being able to read their fantastic fiction and work with them.

This anthology has been compiled to add to our bursary fund. It features stories from a few years ago, and from way back when. As I write, we are five weeks away from the next Milford, and we look forward to welcoming the next bursary recipients to North Wales in September. We hope that some of the readers of this book will be among them someday.

Liz Williams, August 2022

Neil Gaiman

This is a story I wrote in 1985 for Milford because I had to bring a story. It's not very good, and I've never had the faintest urge in the intervening decades to hunt it down in whatever tub of papers it wound up in and try to fix it and make it publishable. The original manuscript as criticised at Milford has vanished, and this was typed up from the original typed single-spaced first draft with handwritten notes all over it. Any thoughts about or urge to improve it while typing it up once more were quelled when I reread it: it wasn't really improvable.

When I was just starting out, most of my stories were apocalypses. All of them were obsessed with reality, with stories, and the places where stories become reality or vice versa.

At the 1985 Milford, someone else's story (not this one) began with someone in a featureless white room, and it was pointed out to them, perhaps by Gwyneth Jones or Garry Kilworth, that stories that begin in a featureless white room are just writers talking about the sheet of paper they have begun to write on. This story ends with everything becoming a blank sheet of paper.

There was an omnipresent book when I was a schoolboy, called *Our Island Story*, by H. E. Marshall. It was a dusty history of Britain. That was where the title came from.

I think the kindest thing I can say about this story is that it was written to take to Milford, and I put into it all the things I vaguely felt that Milford stories ought to have, like undigested lumps of description, and Science Fictional Big Ideas, and something I hoped was Good Writing and didn't worry myself about things like characters, or giving people a reason to keep reading, or providing a satisfying conclusion.

On the last day of Milford, we had time to look at other, extra stories, so I handed in an unpublished story about an intelligent venereal disease that would eventually be published as 'Foreign Parts,' and people were much kinder to me about that than they had been about this.

The main lesson that we can learn from this story, written by 24-year-old Neil Gaiman, is that a) young writers can definitely improve and b) sometimes when you don't have anything to say, you make marks on a sheet of paper, and sometimes they take you places that work and sometimes they definitely don't.

Neil Gaiman July 2022

Ryland's Story

Somewhere in the basement complex, the readers were reading, Ryland could feel it. His stomach was tight and he felt nervous and nauseous like a spring wound too tight, or a grenade all primed in the final seconds before its explosion.

He wondered what an atomic bomb felt like as it was dropped. Worried? Tense? Did bombs ever get headaches? He wrote '*a bomb with a migraine*' on his blotter. Force of habit, but he hated seeing an idea go to waste, even if he would never get to write the story.

Behind him was a bookshelf, on which was a Roget, a couple of dictionaries, and his own four books including the *Star Warriors* novel.

He pulled a paperback off the shelf behind him and opened it at random.

As the shame of defeat rose to colour Zorek's ragged face, he forced himself to respond with the correct salute. "It shall be done, Lord," he replied through painfully clenched teeth, then slid into the nearest drop shaft before permitting his anger to reach maturity.

The book was a *Star Warriors* novelisation, one of the first things he had published. He had been a *Star Warriors* fan as a kid. Sometimes he prided himself that he had injected a slim amount of life and vitality into an otherwise moronic and juvenile form of literature, but mostly he didn't give a damn.

Outside, a thin mist seemed to be coming up. The city hazed over, shifting gently, like a heat haze, although this was mid-winter.

It would be dark soon.

His desktop terminal beeped at him and then flashed 'HAVE YOU FILLED IN YOUR DAILY REPORT?' on its screen.

<u>yes</u>

HAVE YOU FILLED ANY NEEDED A) STATIONARY REQUESTS B) PLOT SUGGESTS C) ACCESS TIME REQUESTS D) PERMUTATIONAL REQUESTS?

He stared at the screen, NEEDED became NEXDED then NEDEDE, then NEXXEX.

The line flickered and went out.

His desk phone rang.

"Ryland speaking."

"Ah, good man, Butterworth here. Can you come over to my office? Seem to be having a spot of bother. Hope not too much trouble."

Ryland squinted over to his left: through innumerable glass partitions, he could see Butterworth, a tiny figure in a brown suit, hunched over a telephone.

"Be right over, Sir."

He thumbed the phone off and began the walk towards Butterworth. His heart began to thump in his chest. He took several deep breaths as he wandered through the glass maze that was the office. He remembered when this had all been open plan (except for Selkirk's office, of course). That was how Selkirk would have kept it. Only Selkirk had hanged himself in a toilet cubicle in East Croyden station.

Ryland took a seat outside of Butterworth's office. Butterworth waved at him through the soundproof glass and gestured for Ryland to wait until Butterworth called him.

Ryland slumped back and thought a little more about the office and trains, and how one day, he had received a call from a Mister Selkirk, asking to meet him...

...and the next day he was listening to the rhythmic beat of the underground train as it made its way across the open country, out into the suburbs. Watching the world outside through dirty glass: rows of houses laid in gentle curving rows, neatly divided by black toytown streets, themselves divided by regular white lines at the kerb, bushes and trees, brushing the sky like shaggy besoms; the police training college with its baby roads and baby bus-stops and baby Belisha beacons but with an adult-sized children's adventure playground and buildings and buildings and; watching the trees, watching the skyline; finally feeling the shake of the train as it slowed into its final station, as Ryland stared at the rows of other trains laid out across the terminal lines, all of them grey as the sky but slighter brighter, more metallic, cleaner. The platforms enclosed them; the train stopped. A pause for a breath then the doors hissed and opened down one side, but only the two men alighted.

They wore quiet grey hats and soft grey suits, off-white shirts and charcoal ties.

But while Selkirk stared ahead of him, sure of his way, seeing his path out of the station even as he started to climb the stairs, Ryland gazed about him with full, innocent eyes, as if he was seeking to cram all the dirty, worn, colourless world into his head, and as he walked up the stairs, a few steps behind his companion, he trailed his right hand on the worn wooden bannister, not for support but sensation.

Both men had expressionless faces. Selkirk, though, had his lips pressed together, his chin raised. He walked with purpose. Behind him, Ryland (now staring at the back of Selkirk's jacket, taking in each grey crumple and gather, following hems and creases) had the slack face, the calmly desperate demeanour of a person who spends his idle moments mentally composing suicide notes.

Up the stairs they went, and through the barrier, out of the station and onto the street. Two red buses waited empty on the forecourt. The men in grey crossed the road, turned left into the high street and off across town.

"How far is it?" asked Ryland, after fifteen minutes of silent walking.

"Not far now. Down this alleyway, and then we're in sight of it."

Ryland seized upon this conversational opening. "Have you been in the building long?"

Selkirk, his lips pursed, his eyes fixed ahead, shook his head.

"Not that long. We started with a small place in Reading, outgrew that and started another base in Slough, keeping the first one, of course. But it became so difficult, working so far away in the two teams. Duplications began to occur—in the work, you understand. And it seemed to create more problems than it solved. So, we looked around, and this place seemed ideal. Out of the way, slightly, room for work, plenty of room for expansion, lots of storage space. Round this corner and you'll see it. There."

Ryland looked at the building. It was squat and square, and all grey glass and early-sixties utilitarian chic. At second glance, which now included the shops and buildings around it, he realised that it was enormous. It stood among the mock-Tudor tobacconists and estate agents like a truant from their future, a bully muscling its way to the front of the crowd.

"We bought it outright from the previous owners. Trading stamp company that didn't diversify in time. The locals think we're a city commodities brokerage."

They reached the building. A dusty metal plaque on the wall near the door read "Offings Ltd. Futures" in small type.

"And what exactly is it that you *do*?" he asked.

Selkirk shook his head. "Not yet, old man. Soon."

Through the swing doors and into a tiny lobby, Ryland took a final look through the tinted glass, staring at the pigeons in the empty patch of brown sky, shadows that wheeled and glided about the rooftops.

Selkirk handed him a badge. "Wear it on your lapel. It clips on, like this." He demonstrated.

There were seventeen floors listed on the lift panel, in addition to a basement carpark. The lift hummed as it rose, up and up. They said nothing as they ascended.

Ryland had the curious feeling that had he uttered a sound it would have been swallowed up by the brown-carpeted walls and the brown-carpeted floor, and he stared at the floor indicator light as it glowed its climbing green light. On the fourteenth floor, the lift stopped, a bell sounded and doors huffed open.

Selkirk led Ryland down the corridor. "Sort of open plan office. All the rage. We can see each other, keep an eye open. Call for help if needed. That sort of thing."

There was an office smell, in the huge open office, they crossed to reach Selkirk's glass office. Ryland mentally catalogued it, trying to break it into its components—vinyl and rubber under carpet and pencil shavings and paper and furniture polish and air freshener and tobacco and pencil rubbers and hot electrical components.

The office was a sea of desks. Identical light brown desks, each neatly heaped high with manuscript paper, each with its cream-coloured computer, a pile of paperback books in one corner. Brown plastic chair standing beside and beneath its desk, *like the tiny male form of a race of furniture creatures, the females of which were the larger desks,* thought Ryland.

Dwarfs.

"Take a seat," said Selkirk, in his office.

"Thank you."

Only now did Selkirk remove his hat, to place it on the desk. After a brief pause, Ryland did the same. The two men sat opposite each other. The two grey hats were touching, brim to brim. Selkirk's hair was grey and cut short with almost military precision. Ryland had black hair.

The older man placed his elbows on the desk and formed a church with his hands, the two forefingers outstretched to form the steeple. He rubbed the two fingers along the bridge of his nose, starring down at the imitation wood veneer, then he lifted his head and in so doing moved the fingertips to his chin, where they stayed.

"We are," he announced in his dry, clipped voice, "perhaps the most valuable organisation on the planet. Not in terms of money or assets—we function from a very small government grant, and from donations we receive from the private sector. They *do* donate, of course."

"But I think I may safely say that in terms of relative value to the world..." he gestured with his hand, shaking it down to the desk and then up again, a modest gesture both of aggrandisement and understatement.

"Are you familiar with the works of Phillips? H. H. Phillips? No? Pity." Selkirk sat back in his chair, increased the volume of his voice slightly: he sounded as if he was reciting a speech that he had to give many times before, which, in fact, was the case.

"It was Professor Phillips, in 1954, who pointed out to the world two things—both of which it has long known, but Phillips backed it up with equations—two basic, simple things. Firstly," he slapped a well-manicured finger into his palm, "that the universe never ever produces two of anything exactly the same, once you're past the Mickey-Mouse stage of neutrons, electrons, quarks and such fiddle. Secondly," the next finger struck home, "that fiction is fiction and that reality is reality."

"Now you say—'but this was all known before.' Say it."

Ryland shrugged uninterestedly. "Well, wasn't it?"

"No. Not proven. But that didn't matter. Not really. Not once we'd seen the potential military possibilities of Phillip's work. I was in military intel back then, you know, Ryland."

"Military wasn't buying it, though. 'Attack is the best form of defence,' as Kerris used to tell us. But he's wrong, really."

Ryland seemed to focus on Selkirk for the first time. "So is this some kind of military establishment? Is it weapons? Illegal...?"

The older man was shaking his head.

"Purely defensive. And not just against the Russians, but for the world. I was not exaggerating."

He got up. Began to pace the room, his black leather shoes soundless on the deep brown carpet.

"Take those two pieces of data I just gave you and think with them. Think. You can't, you aren't a Phillips or a MacNicol (he was the MI chap who first cottoned on) so I'll tell you. Fiction is different from reality because fiction is fiction. Fiction doesn't happen in real life. Never. You can't have two things the same. Of course, you can set a fictional story in real life: that merely ensures that people with the names and attributes you have described will not do the things you have said they would do. But Science Fiction is another matter.

"The important thing about Orwell's *Nineteen Eighty-Four* was not that it warned people away from a potential future, but that, by its mere existence, it prevented the world of the title ever from coming into being."

He picked up some paperback books from the corner of the desk.

"*Brave New World. The Space Merchants. Make Room! Make Room! Do Androids Dream of Electric Sheep?* All descriptions of worlds that, thank God, will never be."

Ryland rubbed his left shoulder, loosening a knot of painful muscle. "You mean it's impossible that the things predicted in those books could ever come true?"

"Not never, I'd say. But the story doesn't go where it's already been. It takes the course of least resistance, in order not to repeat something."

Selkirk pointed across the field of veneer desktops. "My men work here. It's a tough job and a hard one. They write dystopias. Disaster scenarios. Nuclear war books and after-the-bomb stories. Books in which the liberty of the individual is drastically curtailed, in which Spain invades our country…"

"Impossible," whispered Ryland.

"…and another in which Ireland invades Brazil. Books in

which humanity meets its end by disease—every known plague and many that haven't been invented yet…"

"Excuse me," this time Ryland spoke loud enough to be heard. "But you can't get everything. You can't expect to. Even if you do get the world right, you could get the characters wrong or something."

Selkirk shook his head. "That's what those computers are for. Plot permutations. Names. Twists. All that stuff. They print out alternate versions and alternate versions. All the stuff we do is stored here, with a second standby depot in Dorking. Although we have written every variation on the storage area being destroyed there could possibly be, from trouble with mice up to the Sun going nova."

Ryland tilted his head to one side. "So this is entirely non-military?"

"I think so. Still, I wouldn't put it past the Americans to have groups of people even now writing about their invasions of other countries that fail, or are defeated, about their atomic bombs failing to explode, germ warfare backfiring…"

"But what happens when two of you write things diametrically opposed? Things that cancel out?"

The lips pursed quickly. "It wouldn't happen. But theoretically, if it did—and if there were only two courses, which is impossible—it would depend on how many people had read and accepted as fiction the various alternatives. That's what our reading department is for."

"Why?"

"How should I know? Ask Phillips or Trevis, not me. Come, let me show you around."

They crossed the building on the fourteenth floor. No one was about, and there was an echoing quality to Selkirk's smallest pronouncement that would have vanished if the office were filled with people.

They looked down on the town. Far below, a tiny taxi crawled, oh so velvet slowly. The rest of the town was grey and smoky and empty and still. Ryland breathed on the windowsill, forming a patch of cloud and scrawled his initial before the misty place on the glass could vanish.

Ryland stared at the hungry earth below them with the pain behind his eyes, calm and desperate.

"You'll join, won't you? I knew you were a chap for me the first time I saw you. Blow it, I had you slated for an ideas man right away. Let the nasty futures roll and we'll hang out our scarecrows to frighten the future away from the bad places and everything will be all right…"

The office was empty.

A wisp of smoke curled from a chimney, half the way across town.

"Of course, you know what I worry about. I worry that this could all be some kind of dastardly trick. Maybe the Russians are doing it, or the Chinese.

"But could someone be writing us? The organisation? The world? And if they were, and if it somehow stopped us from being real, then would we know it?

"Do fictional characters know that they are only fictional? What then? I'm scared of that. I'm scared that right this minute, someone somewhere could be writing us."

Dusk was falling, the sky turning with winter speed from grey to deep and lambent blue-black.

Down in the town, lights were going on. Here and there, on and sometimes off.

"I think I'd be more scared of it if I thought someone wasn't," Ryland said.

"So, will you do it?"

"What?"

"Join us, lad. You'll still be a Science Fiction writer, you'll just be doing it for a good cause! You'll even get published. There are lots of you on the payroll!"

He named half a dozen writers, a few of them people Ryland knew.

"So, will you do it? Come on, old fellow, we'll pack up the world's troubles, no man is a…"

Ryland nodded. "I'll do it," he said.

And that was two years ago.

Butterworth put down the phone and waved Ryland in.

"Listen," said Butterworth, "Spot of bother. First thing I knew about it was the computers going to the dogs. Shouldn't do that, we've got our own generators."

He was holding a pencil which he turned over and over in his hands.

Behind him, the lights of the city were going out, one by one. Butterworth didn't notice.

"Now listen, young man," he said. Butterworth was jowly and fat, and the few of his stories that Ryland had read featured muscular young Earthmen who blatted, spattered, blasted, roasted and toasted all manner of alien races, along with those members of the human race that embraced mutants to their breasts, or frowned upon free enterprise, or something like that. He seemed much happier administrating the office than writing.

"Whatever is happening, it shouldn't be. Lord, this place is covered. Every story has been written in which our computer goes up the spout. It can't happen in real life. I want you to do a review of those areas, find out what happened to the computer, and write any needed stories to ensure it doesn't happen again."

"It's not just the computer," pointed out Ryland. "The lights of the city have gone out as well."

Butterworth went purple. "Intolerable," he muttered. "I'll find whoever was responsible for the electrical failure stories, and I'll have them keelhauled…" His voice was becoming fainter as if someone had switched the volume down a shade to listen to another conversation.

"It's not their fault," said Ryland. "I wrote a poem about it once."

"About what?" Butterworth was still audible, but he seemed to be talking from a long way off.

"About being God. It's too easy this way. Being a writer is a lot like being God anyway. You can line the characters up, move them around and change the weather. A plague of rabbits or the ghost of Sherlock Holmes can walk on, bow and walk off. That's the thing about fiction: you have infinite possibilities. Wouldn't you say?"

One of Butterworth's eyes had vanished, to be replaced by swirling grey fog.

"It's my fault, really. Solipsistic, perhaps but I could never have done it like Selkirk did. I had to take everything out."

Butterworth had gone grey. Ryland could see him mouthing, but the words were now inaudible.

"What I did," said Ryland, although he wasn't sure that Butterworth could hear him (but he *had* to tell someone before it was too late for telling,) "was I took it all one stage further. Perhaps that is what it is really about, isn't it?

"If you could stop things coming into place simply by writing then as fiction, then why not write the real world, as fiction, and stop that, instead? It would never have been possible without this organisation, of course. The computers, to fill in all the details from everywhere, and the corps of readers in the basement, all of them so divorced from reality that they were willing to read whatever they were given as a fiction."

Butterworth had almost completely gone, now.

Ryland was insubstantial as well. He could see the desk through his hand.

I mean, he said, in a slight voice like the whine of a mosquito, *this makes things so much simpler, doesn't it? No more war, poverty or hatred, or anything really.*

I don't want you to look upon this as an ending, the shadow that had once been Ryland told the shadow in the mist that may or may not once been Butterworth, *look upon it as a new opportunity, look upon it as a wiping of the screen, or the insertion of a fresh sheet of paper.*

After all, the possibilities are limitless.

But by then, there was nobody to listen and microseconds after that, nobody left to talk.

The words *a bomb with a migraine* hung in the air for a few extra seconds, and then they were gone as well.

To Maddy,
Beware blades in
that flash in
the moonlight

Tiffani Angus

I shared "Mama Leaf" with Milford in 2019. I'd been working on this story on and off for nine years (!) and had finally finished it after taking my time to figure out what I wanted it to be. It's an odd story that expects the reader to just 'go with the flow' (this is not my usual approach; when I was a creative writing lecturer, I would get on a student's case for rolling out the old 'I want to leave the reader to interpret the ending' chestnut because it was often used as a way to cover not really knowing what a story was about!).

The title confused several critiquers who were looking for a meaning behind the family name; I wanted a simple name with a nature connotation that suggested a fey source, at odds with the practicality of a colonial family, so I kept the title. Readers also asked that some scenes be expanded; however, I felt strongly that pulling back the curtain on strange little magical moments in the story, like when Mama takes Junior out into the woods, would turn the wild magic too mechanical. I totally agree that sometimes (often!) a SFF story needs more explanation because what the writer sees in their head is so much more colourful than what a reader is given on the page. The ending was the part that split the audience the most: some loved the violence and creepiness of it, while others were lost. And, weirdly, the difference could almost be split purely along gender lines, with men left feeling puzzled and women saying 'Yes!' to what ended up being called a 'feminist fairy tale.' When that happened, I knew I was on the right track. It was that exact response I was hoping for, that the female readers would relate to the expectations put on women in a patriarchal society and how in stories we use witchcraft to grab back some power for ourselves.

Workshopping can be a difficult tightrope to walk; when in the hotseat, you must respect the opinions being shared (it's why you're there, after all); and when giving feedback, you have to be aware that you're picking at the product of someone else's imagination. But I know that writing doesn't exist in a vacuum and that your critiquers are going to approach the task with honesty and a level of sincerity that are only meant to be helpful. In the end, I didn't change much about the story despite having done so with pretty much every other story and novel excerpt I've taken to Milford over the years. I chalk this up to the effect Milford has had on me; immersing myself in the experience has helped me become a more thoughtful writer, using the Milford process and environment to help me better understand my process before I share a piece so that I can use the workshop moment to witness almost in real time how an audience reacts to a story.

Mama Leaf

Mama Leaf had girls enough. Nearly every year, sure as the ice cracked tree limbs along the ridgeline high above the sheltered valley where the Leafs had lived for generations, another baby girl would take her place in the cradle before the hearth. But Mister Leaf insisted that the family needed a boy child to be whole, to carry on the family name.

He waited patiently at first, told Mama that it was only a matter of time, brought her drowsy-headed daisies to cheer her up, red thread for mending, a ribbon for her hair. But with each girl he found another reason to punch Mama's soft middle and pinch her sagging flesh as if testing the room she had inside. He'd pout in the barn or yell in the yard. No matter how much her husband would bribe and threaten and beat her, Mama Leaf could never give him the boy he so demanded.

She watched the seasons turn and became more desperate, more hungry, more ready to pay whatever price was asked.

It was a year or so after the most recent girl had been born, and Mister Leaf had been gone for three months. He'd taken to the mountains to trap fox and skunk and beaver and to try his luck with a bear before heading to the shore to do some trading. He was due back in time to harvest crops and fix the roof before the snows came. When he'd left, Mama had been expecting.

"My son will be born in autumn—a bad omen, as winter is lean. Yet a son is good news enough, no matter the season," he said before leaving.

Late in the summer, during a new moon, Mama lost the babe—another girl—before her eldest could run for help. She thought of the smell of Mister Leaf's anger and disappointment, a smell like water that's been left to stand so long it ends up laced with tiny islands of dead insects. Lightheaded with fear, Mama Leaf took matters into her own hands.

At the harvest moon, Mama Leaf stole away from her cabin and made her way, weakly and slowly, to her mother-in-law's little house deeper in the woods. Old Mother Leaf was nearly as tall as her son, wiry where he was thick, light where he was dark, and carried an axe instead of a rifle. The old woman's husband had died decades before, and she and Mister Leaf had survived on what they could get from the forest and scratch out of the small holding around her old cabin. Mister Leaf had tried to convince his mother to come and live with him in the bigger house, but she couldn't be budged.

Mama Leaf stayed on the faint path through the trees, unsure what might be waiting in the dark to attack. She held a knife in one hand, a lantern in the other. As she approached the cabin its door opened, and the old woman was silhouetted against the firelight from inside. Mama Leaf nearly collapsed as she crossed the threshold. Old Mother Leaf caught her and steered her to a bench in front of the fire.

"Been wonderin' how long till you'd show up," the older woman said.

Mama Leaf never knew how to approach her mother-in-law, who was always watching, always doing sums in her head, and shared her observations when it benefitted her. But it was late at night, and she was weak from years of birthing and raising babies, of lean season following lean season, of Mister Leaf's moods. 'How did you make him?' was all she asked, deciding to meet Old Mother Leaf head on.

Old Mother Leaf laughed through her nose. "You tell me you've brought six girls into the world, and you don't know where babies come from?"

"He told me how many sisters he had, girls who died one by one, while he survived. How did you get him, keep him safe?"

Old Mother Leaf rubbed the fabric of her skirt between calloused fingers, thinking. "Ah, and here I thought you was a simple one, all straight lines and no curves. Things is easier for you now. You moved into a house just as soon as you said, "I do." You got acres of fields instead of miles of forest—pinecones don't keep a body alive. And you had me here to catch my grandbabies all bloody and slick from the womb."

It was Mama Leaf's turn to laugh. "Easy? The house was nothing but an empty box with a roof. No furniture, nothing soft to lie on. My girls can cook and clean, but they can't be hooked up to the plough. And I should know—it's backbreaking work compared to skinning rabbits and deer. And catchin' babies is easier than pushin' 'em out."

The old woman nodded at that.

"Was Old Mister Leaf a hard man?" Mama Leaf asked, already knowing the answer.

"Course he was hard. Ain't they all? What they lack in smarts they make up for in fists."

Mama Leaf stared into the fire, feeling the emptiness inside her fill with dread. He would be home soon, and what would she have this time to keep him from taking his frustration out on her? "I have to give him a boy," she said. "I'll do anything," she whispered.

"Ah, girl. Don't promise what you can't pay." Old Mother Leaf was a hard woman, but hard in a way different from her son.

Mama Leaf wasn't sure how to navigate the conversation, so she slipped a satchel from her shoulder and held it out to the older woman. "Here," she said, "is this enough?" The satchel contained some flour, a bowl of butter, a couple of handfuls of oats, six fresh apples and dried garlic.

Old Mother Leaf shook her head at the sad offer. "My boy

already keeps me in food, you know. And this—" she waved her hand at the meagre offering laid out on the table, "—this ain't enough. Payment for what you want don't require *things*."

"What did you pay?" Mama Leaf asked, hoping for a direct answer, for Old Mother Leaf to be straight lines and no curves for once.

"Having a boy takes it out of you, over and over again. He won't never be content, will always want more, will demand all of you if you offer it."

Mama Leaf thought of Mister Leaf and knew that her mother-in-law spoke the truth. But couldn't she survive a small boy, at least until he was big enough to have a wife of his own? The trade would be temporary, she was sure.

She squared her shoulders and nodded once, sealing the deal.

Old Mother Leaf pulled her daughter-in-law up from the bench and took her into the back room.

The boy was rather easy to make.

A threadbare petticoat for the body, a cast-off piece of yarn for a mouth, acorn caps for eyes, and a bit snipped from the little brush of hair at the end of the cow's tail for a thatch of dark hair on the poppin's head. To complete the boy, they crafted him a tiny prick from an old sock beyond mending and filled it with grain, then stitched it with red thread. They filled him with rags and hair collected from Mister Leaf's pillow. And in the dark of the back room with only the moon to see through the small window, they finished him with a mixture of their spit and blood.

"What's that?" the oldest girl asked, poking at the lump in the cradle the next morning.

Mama's hands, white as birch bark, nearly creaked from how hard she wrung them together. "That's your baby brother, that is," she said. "Leave him sleep, mind."

"Where'd he come from?" her second daughter asked.

Mama heard Mister Leaf's heavy step at the door. She gnawed on a knuckle till it was close to splitting in her teeth.

"Why, he came from me, where all you girls came from. Old Mother Leaf helped me birth him last night. Now leave him sleep, you hear?"

The third daughter peered into the cradle. "What's he made of?" she asked.

Mama imagined her husband on the other side of the door, brushing the worst of the dirt and mud from his coat before coming in. "He's a boy. He's made of what's best in me. Now leave him sleep, I say."

Mister Leaf clomped into the cabin, shook his coat out, and looked first at his wife, then at his daughters, lined up like fenceposts in front of the table, and finally at the cradle. He recognised his son at once. Mama relaxed, the girls turned away to play, and Mister Leaf filled his pipe and waited on supper and spoke softly and slowly in the sleeping baby's presence. Mama Leaf felt herself relax a bit, able to breathe and to know that she had done enough this time.

Winter came on and the boy grew. Mama added more stuffing to his belly when he got too flat and washed him when he got too dirty. One day, as Mister Leaf bounced the baby on his knee, one of the boy's eyes fell off. "My boy's lookin' a little lopsided," is all he said. Mama Leaf bundled up and followed deer and squirrel tracks to a spot under an oak. She had to dig beneath the ice and snow to find another acorn cap and got chilblains for her trouble.

The seasons turned and everyone in the house grew. Grew up or grew older. The tallest of the fencepost daughters got engaged but died the night before the wedding while still under her father's roof. Mama Leaf was distraught, but Mister Leaf was resigned, for what family hasn't lost at least one child? It was a small price to pay to keep the others fed and healthy.

The younger girls, still at home, helped Mama with the cooking and cleaning and watched after their little brother. Except for once a month, when Mama Leaf took the boy out into the woods with her. When her husband was gone, slipping away was easy enough. "Going to gather quail's eggs," or "Taking the boy to show him how to track rabbits," or "It's time to teach the boy how to milk the goat," she'd explain. But when her husband was home, repairing harnesses and chopping wood, planting or harvesting, Mama had to find a way to be alone with her son. It was the only way to keep him whole.

A year after losing their eldest girl a fever swept through the countryside, taking two more of their daughters, along with children and parents from so many other homesteads. Mama Leaf went into the woods with her son each month, sure as clockwork. And sure as clockwork, she began to slow down herself, but she still had three daughters at home to help.

Old Mother Leaf was also slowing down, her once tall and straight form hunching a bit. Mister Leaf brought her home one day, unloaded her worldly goods from the back of the horse-cart, and set her up in a lean-to he had built against the outside of the house, next to the chimney.

As time wore on, the Leaf family shrunk. Another daughter was lost when a simple cut got infected. Mama Leaf treated her as best she could, not worried because she'd nursed her children through so many bumps and bruises. But this time it didn't work, and she was away from home—in the woods with Junior Leaf—when her daughter's eyes went glassy and she died. There were two girls left, and Mama Leaf held onto them against the current of time. By now Old Mother Leaf had moved into the house—there was no excuse anymore that there wasn't enough room—but she rarely spoke, and when she did she would tell tall tales or wild lies, and sometimes the truth. It was the latter that Mama Leaf steeled herself against, especially when the old woman glared in puzzlement at her grandson and asked who he was.

Late one night, Mama Leaf woke to the sound of fire. Not the cosy crackling of the fire that burned constantly in the hearth, but the roar of a fire that could not be put out with a simple bucket of sand. Blanket held over her mouth, she pushed her way through the smoke, tripping over things on the floor that she couldn't see. A hand came through the smoke and grabbed her, pulling her out the door. The trees that surrounded their homestead were lit orange with shadows that danced like evil demons. Mister Leaf stood bent over with his hands on his knees, coughing and spitting on the ground.

"The children!" she screamed at him. "Where are the children?"

He didn't raise his head but only pointed behind him where Junior Leaf lay in the dirt, his skin black with soot.

They buried the last two girls with their grandmother. The fencepost girls all lay together in a row, and Mama Leaf heard Old Mother Leaf's voice on the wind: "Don't promise what you can't pay."

The three of them retreated to the old cabin in the woods, where they spent their days working hard to rebuild what they could, and their nights in silence.

Then the war came to their land, and Mister Leaf joined the militia. He wanted his son with him, to protect his left side. Mama Leaf told her husband to go but that Junior Leaf was too young. The fight between the Leafs over the war shook the trees and scared the foxes and badgers for miles around. Through it all, Junior sat, torn between the adventure of war and the safety of home.

Mister Leaf won the battle, as he did in all things. But Mama Leaf did what she could to win the war. Before she handed her husband and son their rifles, she took Junior aside one final time. He was grown enough now to question these trips outside.

"Where are we going, Mama?" he asked.

"Just a ways into the woods, my son, not too far from sight of the chimney smoke. Don't be afraid."

"But why are we going so late at night, Mama? And where is Papa?"

"It's not so late, my dear. And Papa is sleeping. Do not be afraid."

"What are you doing with that knife, Mama? And what is that noise?"

"Give me your hand, my heart. That is the owl hooting, and the fox running to ground. The blood will protect you. Now give me your hand, and I will make you a brave boy."

And with that, Mama Leaf gave Junior all of herself that she could spare, with enough left over to have the strength to carry on in the cabin in the woods while waiting for word from her men.

That night Mama Leaf dreamed of red owls and a tall woman and blades flashing in the light of the moon. She woke at first light to see her son, dressed and ready in the yard, with his father at his side. The rest of the militia waited. A ragged, unmatched bunch, the men had no uniforms but wore hunting shirts and what warm coats and breeks they had. Those from the poorer areas came without rifles, armed only with shovels or pikes. Their leader handed out red cockades of fabric, lovingly made by his wife and daughters, to identify them, and he outfitted them with canteens and other goods as befits a group of fighting men and patriots. With this all the ceremony they could expect, they went to war.

Mama Leaf, alone now, stayed behind and talked to the ghosts of her fencepost daughters and waited for word from her son or husband. A few weeks later, when she would normally have taken Junior Leaf into the woods, she stayed awake all night in a sort of vigil, waiting to see what would happen, but woke with her head on the table, milk spilled on her hand and honey in her hair. A month later, the same thing happened. By the third month, when she hadn't bled, she figured that she had, as warned, given her son everything and had nothing left within herself. Since Junior Leaf's arrival she hadn't once fallen pregnant, and now she never would again—she was wrung out, dried out, done. A part of her was glad of it because it meant she had paid the full price.

A month later, at the harvest moon, she received a letter

written in a cramped hand on stained paper without any official seal or address. Mister Leaf was dead, Junior Leaf missing. She mourned her husband's passing alone in the cabin in the woods. As she sat in Old Mother Leaf's rocking chair in front of the fire, her hand holding the letter pressed against her middle, she felt it. A fluttering, as quick as the movement of a tadpole in a pond, as soft as the gentle dripping of spring rain from the leaves, as quiet as the clouds sweeping across the face of the moon.

The girl was five when the war ended. She and her mother were lean and tanned from digging in the garden and tending to the goats and setting traps for rabbits. The girl was growing up with stories about her sisters and old grandmother, a few mentions of her father, but nothing about her brother.

Mama Leaf carried an axe and a rifle now, so when Junior Leaf limped into the clearing at the front of the cabin, one leg wrapped in dirty bandages, one eye gone and his hair half burned off, she was ready. She had nothing left to give to him. She'd already paid the highest price. They buried him in the woods, far from the fencepost sisters, where no new blood spilled.

Ben Jeapes

I brought "Go With the Flow" to Milford in 1998. It was quite different to my usual style up until then so it was a great relief when it went down well. Two especially good things came out of the session: Jane Killick, a professional reporter, could advise me on interview technique; and someone (I think Liz Counihan) described it as 'an Ealing comedy by Roald Dahl'. I thought that pinpointed the tone I was aiming for precisely, so that was what guided me as I revised it and sent it off to *Interzone*, where it was published in April 1999. The story nearly got me thrown out of the Association of Christian Writers for the, let's say, theologically liberal utterances of one of the characters. A lady picked my collection *Jeapes Japes* up off the table, flicked idly through it and asked, "Is this suitable for an eleven year old?" I blithely assured her that it was... Furious emails were subsequently sent to the ACW Chair after she had read it a bit more deeply. I strongly suspect her eleven year old grandson had heard a lot worse at school, but there you go.

Go With the Flow

"Why, 'To Gran'?" I asked.

The professor had been about to pass me a cup of coffee. His book, the cause of the interview at his house, lay on the table between us.

"I beg your pardon?" he said.

"Why is your book dedicated, 'To Gran'?" I said. I was deliberately keeping my voice casual but the matter had been bothering me all afternoon.

We'd got on well in this interview, gathering material for a feature profile I was producing, and he had really opened up. We had gone through his career, from undergrad to PhD whose work in fluid dynamics was being applied by the European government to social mechanisms, with astounding success. He had commented on the rumours that the 2036 Nobel was apparently sewn up. For background, we had even talked about his home life, his wife and children (to whom the book wasn't dedicated).

But...

The book that started it all off, in its paper version, was six hundred pages of small font and equations. Five pages of acknowledgements, in an even smaller font. A massive bibliography that needed a magnifying glass. A twenty-page foreword by a bigwig from Princeton. And the title! Go With the Flow: A Sociological Extrapolation Of The Effects And Applications of Transient Pressure Propagation On Human Populations. *Concision was not the author's style.*

And yet, 'To Gran'.

"No sugar, wasn't it?" the professor said, putting the cup down in front of me.

"Yes, thank you."

"Gran," he said. "Well, she looked after me a lot when I was a boy. My parents were constantly breaking up and she was the one secure thing I had. She had her children quite late in life and one of them was killed in a car crash, so she really, really doted on me. In some ways, she was the archetypal granny—a frail old battleaxe. She's not with us anymore, died in the 'teens when I was a student—"

"That would be a dedication for your autobiography," I interrupted, *"or your first novel. But a scholarly work like this? It just... it just jars."*

"Does it?" he said. *He looked thoughtfully at the recorder, then leaned forward and turned it off.*

~ ~ ~ ~ ~

I suppose it started (he said) when I'd been dumped on Gran suddenly so that Mum and Dad could Sort Things Out again over the half-term break. This was happening more and more by the time I was ten but Gran never minded having me.

I was in the living room doing a jigsaw, which was the highest tech form of entertainment in her household, when I heard the phone ring and her singsong 'Hello' as she answered it. Then:

"… well, I did ask for the week off so I could look after my grandson… "

"… oh, the poor dear, broken right through? In plaster… "

"… well, dry slope skiing isn't really for our generation… "

"… well, I could cover for her, but my grandson… "

"… take him with me? Are you sure that's wise?"

One of Gran's few faults was the failure to realise her voice carried. And I was only ten feet away from her, through the wall.

"… hang on, let me write it down… "

I heard her say goodbye and hang up, and then she popped her head around the door and beamed at me. "Do you want to come for a drive, dear?" she said.

Gran lived in one of those little greenbelt villages within the M25—a small, secluded place that you wouldn't have thought was only a few miles from the country's capital.

"Can you read a map, dear?" she said as we got into her Mini, parked (as it always was) outside her garage. The one time I'd opened the garage doors and peeked in, I'd seen it packed full of boxes and junk that came right up to the entrance. The next moment I was wrestling with an Ordnance Survey map about the same size as me and with a mind of its own until she showed me how to fold it down so that I was only looking at the relevant bit. "You can navigate."

I couldn't navigate to save my life but I now see that involving me this way, keeping me occupied, was her way of taking my mind off the actual drive and what we were doing. Gran had me navigate her—as if she didn't know the way perfectly well herself—to the suburbs of Esher.

"There's an A-Z in the glove compartment, dear," she said. "Could you get it out for me?"

Now she had me navigate to a small side road that led into a larger road, packed with rush hour traffic crawling slowly to the far-off motorway. Gran came to the junction, indicating left, and I thought she would wait for a break in the traffic. Then she put her foot down, tyres screeched and she swung out into the traffic stream. Horns blared and the car behind us, a swish black Rover, flashed its lights angrily.

"Gra-an!" I protested. I could split the word into an indefinite number of syllables, depending on my degree of agitation.

"Oh, sorry, dear. I thought he was slowing down for us," she said. She reached out and for the first time I noticed that she had a kitchen timer mounted on her dashboard: one of those stopwatch types with a digital display that counts down the time and beeps at the end. It was set for twenty-seven minutes. I shook my head, a mature ten-year-old exasperated at the vagueness of the senior generation, and settled back into my seat, fully expecting to become very familiar with the rear of the car in front of us over the next half hour or so.

It was getting away from us. I realised after a minute that Gran was actually moving slower than this rush hour crawl of traffic. I peeked at the speedometer. The needle pointed to just below 20.

"*Gra-a-an!*"

"Don't want to cause an accident, dear," she said, not taking her eyes off the road.

The next twenty-six minutes were hell on earth. The road ahead was wide open and empty: behind us, there must have been a tailback into London, and I could feel the hostility and hatred emanating from it and roasting the back of my head. And the few times there was enough space in the oncoming lane for a car behind to try and overtake us, Gran would speed up slightly so that overtaking wasn't possible.

At last, at long last, the kitchen timer pinged.

"Oh, good, just in time for tea," she said. She dropped a gear, speeded up to fifty and headed back home without once asking me for directions.

A couple of hours later I was sitting in one corner of the living room doing some homework (numbers fascinated me even then and I'd brought some stuff home from school) while Gran had the news on. After the national stories came the local stuff, which included a pile-up caused by some dickweed who had been doing seventy with one hand on the wheel and the other on his carphone, and had made the wrong choice as to which hand to free up so he could use the gear stick.

"The idiot," Gran said, not looking up from her knitting. She had a way of always speaking in the same tone of voice but somehow modulating it anywhere between warm gooey honey (which she used for me) and rock-hard ice (like now). "The idiot."

Neither of us looked at the picture on the mantelpiece. A man and a boy: my grandfather and my Uncle Edward, both dead before I was born thanks to a not dissimilar road-usage attitude from a not dissimilar individual.

Then there was the screeching of tyres outside on the driveway; the sound of a powerful engine throbbing into silence and a car door slamming.

"Speaking of whom, your father's here, dear," Gran said, still knitting and still in the same tone of voice. She and Dad had never seen eye to eye: his mobile phone had gone off during my Christening and he still hadn't forgiven her for throwing it in the font.

Yeah, Dad's here, I thought glumly. That showed me who had won the great Sorting Things Out contest back home.

The bell rang and kept ringing.

"Go and let him in, dear."

Yes, Dad had definitely won. "Our Kev!" he shouted when he saw me, rubbing his hands together, grinning all over his face. The same look as when he'd made some extra big deal at work and was expecting Mum to come up with the conjugal goods by means of celebration. He was a big man—big physically, big in personality—and always left me feeling small, even for a boy of ten. "How's my man?" He threw a couple of mock punches that left me rubbing my shoulder resentfully and bulldozed past me into the living room.

"Hello, Darren," Gran said, still not looking up from her knitting. His smile became more fixed.

"Hello, Margaret," he said. "Almost hit your car again. Why don't you put it in the garage?"

"No one else almost hits it, Darren. Maybe you're driving too fast. How was the motorway?"

"Eh? Oh. All right. Yeah, it was all right, for once. Doing over ninety all the way here."

"Oh, good."

"Right!" Dad was rubbing his hands together as he turned to me. "You ready to come back home, Kev?"

"Yes, Dad."

"Hey, you're allowed to smile," he said with a grin. Another mock punch, this time making me wince. "Well, get upstairs and get your things, then. What's that you've got there?"

"Sums."

"Sums?" He picked up the textbook and pulled a face. "'Which of these circles has the same area as this square.' Jesus H.! Don't make it easy, do they?"

"I've been stuck on that one for ages," I said.

"Well, get home and we'll look it up in Wikipedia."

"I don't want to look it up," I said, "I want to work it out."

"Numbers are for nerds," he said. It was bad enough for him that his only child wore glasses. He was still smiling but there was a warning in his eyes too. "Numbers are for the little people in Computing, not Management like my Kev's going to be. You'll have your own people to worry about numbers—"

Dad had built up his business from nothing. And never let anyone forget it.

"What's the area of a circle, Kevin?" Gran said. She had yet to look up. Then she chanted the little rhyme she'd taught me. "If you want a hole repaired, use the formula—"

"Pi-r-squared," I said.

"And what's the area of a square?"

Easy. "One side, squared."

"So, they're both something squared, aren't they?"

After a moment, light dawned. "Right!" I grabbed my ruler—

—but Dad was still holding the book and he wasn't going to let it go. "Upstairs, get your things, now," he said.

"You see, dear, a lot of things are defined by numbers," Gran said. "Some simple, some more complicated, if you just take the trouble to learn them. If you've got the brains to learn them. If it occurs to you that they're worth learning."

"Now," Dad said quietly, and he propelled me out of the room with a hand in the small of my back.

When we got home, more to get me out of the way than

to make me clean I was sent upstairs to have a bath before bedtime. I had a towel round my waist as I turned the taps on, and then I leapt out onto the landing in one surprised bound as a vibration like a concrete mixer rocked the bathroom.

"*Dad!*"

Dad appeared at the foot of the stairs.

"What is— oh, Christ." He came up the stairs two at a time and went into the bathroom, where he turned on the hot tap at the basin. The noise subsided.

"What was that?"

"Just waterhammer, Kev. Started while you were away."

"What's waterhammer?" I said. It sounded silly. Water was soft. It sloshed. It didn't hammer.

Dad looked annoyed but he could never bear to show ignorance in front of me.

"It's… " He gestured vaguely. "A small block in the pipes, Kev, means that not all the water gets through, and some of it flows back, and that knocks more back, and so you get water vibrating all around the pipes and that reminds me, *Louise!* I thought I told you to get the plumber?"

Blaming it on Mum had safely diverted the topic away from the scientific principles of fluid dynamics. My heart sank as Dad strode out to confront Mum.

"I was going to, dear, but—" she said.

"But, but, but," Dad shouted. "Christ on a bike, I have to do everything round here."

"I'll call him now—"

"No, I'll call him—"

"I can do it, Darren—"

"You'll just get it wrong, you silly cow—"

"Darren—"

Slap. There went the reconciliation.

A moment's quiet, and then I silently mouthed the inevitable mantra as Dad spoke it out loud.

"Now look what you made me do."

~ ~ ~ ~ ~

The professor was looking at me as if what he had said explained everything.

"You've mentioned your grandmother," I said, "and you've mentioned waterhammer, but… "

"It's not obvious?"

"Um, no," I confessed.

He raised his eyebrows, poured us both another coffee, and continued.

~ ~ ~ ~ ~

We were all going off to the Chessington World of Adventure in a proud display of what a normal family we were.

Mum and I had got used to the rhythm of Dad's driving on the M25. You sat still in a traffic jam until the car in front of you started to move, then you accelerated to cruising speed and abruptly braked as the car in front unaccountably continued to crawl. This had been going on for half an hour, punctuated by Dad's 'Jesus fucking Christ,' or some variation on the same theologically contentious theme every time he had to slow down.

Finally, we began to move. Properly, smoothly, not lurching. The jam was ebbing; the traffic was getting up to all of 40 mph.

"Oh, now that pisses me off. That really pisses me off," Dad said when we finally saw what had caused this particular blockage. An ambulance and police car were gathered around a crumpled car on the hard shoulder of the eastbound lane. We were heading west, and our own jam had been caused by nothing less than all the cars in front of us slowing down to have a gawp. "All those fucking vultures eyeballing the wreck and they cause a jam behind them and they don't fucking *care*."

He slammed his foot down and the car shot forward again, this time almost making seventy before the brakes came on once more and Dad was flashing his lights at the car ahead. "*Move!*" he bellowed.

"He's going as fast as he can, Darren," Mum said, which was the bravest thing she'd said all day.

"He's going as fast as he can," Dad mimicked. "Christ, you sound like your mother. Hear that, Kev? When you get a girl, check out her mum first 'cos that's who she's going to turn into."

I wasn't listening. Something had clicked in my mind: the thought of all those cars ahead of us slowing down, which meant we had to slow down, which meant the ones behind us had to slow down... One small effect ahead sending forces of action and reaction rippling up and down the lines of traffic, magnifying as it went, flowing back down the motorway and trickling out at the junctions and up onto the side roads. A light tap on the brakes in the right place at the right time and you could surely bring the motorway system to a halt. Or speed it up again.

I was seeing the world in a whole new way. I'd never heard of transient pressure propagation or boundary conditions of a system, but I was picturing them as clear as day. Numbers. Like Gran said, defined by numbers. I was dazzled.

"Waterhammer," I murmured.

"Oh, Jesus, the boy's off again," Dad said. "Dreaming— Look out, you moron! Christ almighty, put some people behind a wheel... "

~ ~ ~ ~ ~

"So," I said, "your grandmother put the idea of numbers affecting the real world into your head?"

"Check."

"And the traffic jam made you see how it could work?"

"Check," he said again. "Numbers, in the form of fluid dynamics. I mean, I was only ten so I can't say it all fell into place there and then, *but I realise it was a defining moment. A light on the road to... well, Chessington."*

So that was it. The explanation of 'To Gran' was a bit of an anticlimax, but it had been a long shot. My journalist's instincts weren't always right.

"Well, thank you—" I started to say.

"There's more," he said. "I mean, it's all very well using the principles of waterhammer in a system but how do you get the system hammering in the first place?"

~ ~ ~ ~

A month later I was back with Gran again and this time it was for keeps. I'd missed out on the details of what started it: I was getting good at simply filtering out the raised voices as the ultimatum *du jour* from Mum collapsed. So it was quite a surprise when a weeping Mum burst into my room, yanked me from the computer and dragged me out to the car. Dad had already gone off on his post-eruption trip to the pub so she was able to get me out of the house without obstruction.

Dad turned up at Gran's soon after us. He did his usual trick of not taking his finger off the doorbell until he got an answer.

Gran went out to open the door and I heard the voices in the hall.

"My wife here, Margaret?"

"My daughter and grandson are, here, Darren, yes."

"Right."

The door to the living room flew open and Dad stood there, glaring at Mum in her chair in the corner.

"You stupid cow, you don't go off without telling me!"

"And what stupid cow would that be, Darren?" said a mild voice behind him. He didn't look round.

"Look," he said, "all I said was—"

"Darren," said the voice again, "my daughter has come to

visit me and you will kindly not block me out of my own living room in my own home."

Dad subsided. Slightly. He stood to one side to let Gran come into the room and bowed a fraction of an inch.

"Margaret," he said with forced courtesy, "may I speak to my wife in private?"

Gran held his gaze for a moment, then shrugged. "If you will." She took Mum's hand gently. "Darren wants to talk to you, dear," she said quietly. "Come into the hall, and don't worry, I'll be right here in the next room. Be brave."

Mum went out like a sheep to the slaughter and Dad shut the door behind them. Raised voices started coming through the wall almost at once, and Gran put her arms round me and held me tight.

The voices were getting louder, until:

"You're not fucking leaving me, you're my wife!" Dad shouted.

"Darren—" Mum said.

"You're coming home now!"

"I'm staying, Dar—"

Slap. And that was when Gran made her move. She let go of me and slowly, deliberately went back out into the hall. Mum's quiet weeping got louder as she opened the door.

"Now look what you made me do!"

"Look what you made me do," Gran said quietly. "The cry of pathetic bullies who've run out of excuses."

"Margaret, if I'm not taking my wife—"

"My daughter," Gran said.

"—then I'm taking my son."

"My daughter's staying here," Gran said, "and so is Kevin. The poor dear deserves better than you."

"Oh, *right.*" I found the courage to peek round the door. Dad was towering over Gran, standing six inches away so that he looked right down at her, and she wasn't in the least fazed. "Let's see what the courts say, eh? A Prozac addict and an old

43

lady looking after a ten-year-old boy."

"Courts side with the mother," Gran said.

"Not with my lawyers, Margaret." Then Dad saw me. "At last, someone who isn't snivelling and whining. C'mere, Kev. I'm taking you home."

I was rooted to the spot.

Dad's smile fixed. "Come here, Kevin."

My mouth moved.

"What's that? Speak up."

"You hit Mum," I whispered. Mum herself was leaning against the wall, still sobbing, and hadn't joined in the conversation since the slap.

"My hand slipped, didn't it? Come on, Kev!" He engaged wheedle mode. "Look, I'll get tickets for Wembley and we'll—"

It took several tries but I managed to say it. "I'm staying here."

For the first time, Dad was surprised. His eyes widened and his jaw dropped, and he took a step forward.

"You are coming with me whether you—"

Gran had also moved a step and was blocking him. The only way he could physically reach me was to push her aside, and they were both doing mental computations as to what the courts would say to a father in a custody case who beats his wife and manhandles little old ladies.

Dad ceded loss of the battle, if not the war. He took a step back.

"I'm getting Kevin," he said quietly, "and neither of you cows are going to stop me."

He left, slamming the door behind him. Then the thud of the car door, the revving of the engine, the screeching of tyres and the sound of the car fading away.

"Take your mother upstairs, dear," Gran said to me. "This is an emergency and I've got phone calls to make."

Mum was lying in bed, Prozaced to a higher plane of existence, and I was sitting by her side, stroking her hand and trying hard not to cry. Because Dad hated 'little boys that blubbed.' Funny, the way we can still want the respect of people we can come to loathe.

Gran appeared in the doorway. "Is Mummy sleeping?"

"Yes," I said.

Gran sighed. "Well, I can't leave you here with her. If we get burgled she'll never wake up anyway. Come with me."

She led me downstairs and into the hall, and over to a tall bookcase on the far wall. She reached up and touched a book on the top shelf, beyond my reach. The bookshelf moved aside to reveal a doorway.

I gasped and Gran smiled.

"It's just the garage, dear."

Picture this: sleek, low lines of polished black metal; a turbine whining into action; fins; gull-wing doors hissing slowly open…

That wasn't what it looked like at all but it's how I like to remember it. In fact, the car that faced the doors was a Morris Minor. Between it and the doors was the thin screen of junk that faced anyone opening the doors from outside, as I had once done. The 'junk' was like a stage set—a veil of boxes and nothing more.

I gazed around while Gran opened the passenger door for me. At the back of the garage was a truly awesome computer bank, monitors glowing with mapped-out road routes and columns of figures scrolling slowly past.

Gran followed my gaze. "It links to the Highways Agency's mainframe, dear," she said. "I'll explain everything, but for now, get in and remember your seatbelt."

We got in and I strapped myself in securely. Gran pressed a button on the dashboard which made the junk screen slide to one side and the garage doors swing open. The car lunged forward, swerved around her Mini parked outside and sped out into the night.

Now isn't the time, but if you've ever wondered what it would be like to drive a turbo-charged Morris Minor, I'm the man to tell you. And the surprises weren't over yet.

"Open the glove compartment, please, dear," Gran said. I tugged on the little door and yelped in surprise when a small computer console slid out and a screen popped up. Another glowing road network, with two blobs, clearly marked.

"We're the white blob, your father is the red one," she said. "I thought this day might come so I took the liberty of bugging his car a couple of weeks back."

I gaped at her.

"When he left us he stopped off at a pub, so we should be able to catch him up. My colleagues have been keeping him within range."

A cluster of other white blobs appeared, each with a number attached to it.

"Oh, good. The others are online," Gran said. She unhitched a microphone from under the steering wheel. "WH7 to all patrols, target is making for the M25. Essential that he be routed onto a B-road. WH Central, please provide instructions… "

After a moment another voice spoke. It was another old lady's voice but it spoke like a police dispatcher off *The Bill*. "WH3, take B2219 into Banstead, maintain patrol speed. WH12, make best speed to Epsom and await instructions. WH7, make best pursuit and good luck."

The other WH numbers radioed in their compliance. Old ladies, and old men too: the kind of voice that said I Wear A Hat In My Car.

"Give 'em what for, eh, Mags?" one man's voice boomed.

Gran held her radio up to her mouth. "This is WH7. Acknowledged, WH Central, and thank you. And thank you, George."

"You're welcome, Marg- WH7."

Gran hung up and pressed another button on the dash, and a police siren blared out. I wriggled round to look behind us and only then realised the noise was coming from our car.

"Gran—" I said.

"Don't worry," she said.

"The police—"

"—will check their computer and see that it says another car is on the case. They won't interfere. Now, let Gran concentrate, dear."

We hurtled through darkest Surrey, through red lights and the wrong way round roundabouts; flashing at slower drivers until they were forced to pull over and let us by (and what I wouldn't have given to see their faces when they saw what it was that was overtaking them); always closing the gap that lay between the hunter and its prey. The drama playing itself out on the computer display was fascinating: Dad's red blob in the middle and the circle that was WH's 3, 8, 9, 12, 16, 18 and 19 tightening around it. And us, WH7, now so close that our blobs were almost touching.

The man's voice came over the radio again. "Soon have him, Maggie, eh what?"

Was it my imagination or was Gran's voice slightly softer when she answered?

"I think so, George, yes."

"What you doing later, Mags? How about dinner for two, candles and a chance to show these young 'uns that the old generation can still—"

"*George!* I mean, WH16, this is an open channel and… others are listening."

"Let 'em!" the old codger declared. "Who cares—"

"Including children," Gran said firmly.

WH Central spared Gran's further blushes by ordering all cars to maintain silence unless reporting on progress.

Gran turned the siren off and a few minutes later Dad's BMW hove into view ahead of us. I recognised the licence plate.

"He's got to take the next left," Gran muttered. "It will be very inconvenient if he doesn't."

Dad was showing no sign of slowing down or indicating, though since he rarely did either at the best of times it was impossible to guess his intentions. And then we came round a bend and I saw two cars ahead of him, driving abreast and blocking the road: a half-timber Morris Traveller and a Hillman Avenger. Dad braked sharply and I could almost hear the 'Christ almighty' and imagine him thumping the steering wheel. But there was no getting round the two cars and Dad wasn't a man to suffer that kind of speed, so he swerved into the next left turning.

Gran thumped her wheel. "Yes!" she said. She unhooked the microphone again. "Thank you, WH9, WH16. Target is mine: am proceeding alone."

"Good luck, Ma- WH7. WH16 out and, ahem, see you later, eh?" said George.

"Oh, really, that man," Gran murmured as she hung up the microphone again, but something told me she was pleased.

Our two cars were alone on the road now. Gran revved up towards the BMW. I looked at Dad's approaching car with horror. I'd watched too much James Bond: who knew what else this Morris marvel had under its bonnet? Machine guns, missiles, lasers—

"Don't kill him, Gran!" I blurted.

Gran said nothing. Did the car speed up slightly?

"Gran!" I grabbed at the wheel but I couldn't move it.

"Don't be silly, dear," Gran said. "Brace yourself."

We rammed the back of the car and I felt the belt tighten across me and hold me firmly in my seat. Then, as Dad began to slow, Gran pulled back and accelerated to overtake. I had a brief glimpse of my father's staring face before the Morris slammed into the side of the BMW. And this time there was no rebound: Gran held the wheel over, forcing Dad off the road. He hit the pavement, winged the car on a lamppost and ploughed into the bank.

"Stay here, dear," Gran said as the car screeched to a halt. She pulled out a bag from beneath her seat and I twisted round in my seat to watch the confrontation as she strode towards the wrecked vehicle. Dad's door opened and he got out, staggering but still intact.

"You fucking lunatic!" he bellowed. "What the fucking hell are you doing? You'll be hearing from—"

He stopped, peered forward. "Margaret?"

Gran was fishing about in the bag. She found something and held it out towards him. Dad crumpled at the knees and fell face forward on the ground.

I screamed. "*Dad!*" I knew it. Gran had killed him. I tore out of the car and over to where she was crouching over the body. I flung myself at her, sobbing, and tried to haul her off. "Get off him, get off him—"

"He's all right, darling!" Gran said. "Look. Help me roll him over."

I did and saw to my amazement that he was breathing, his eyes were flickering and there was no blood anywhere. Gran held a small aerosol in front of my eyes for my inspection.

"Knockout gas," she said. "He'll only be out for a couple of minutes. You didn't think I'd make my daughter a widow, did you?"

She opened the bag again and started to lay things out on the ground with swift precision. A bottle of clear liquid. A tube. An empty whisky bottle. For the first time, I noticed she was wearing gloves.

"Though I admit," she added as she attached one end of the tube to the end of the first bottle, "it's a tempting thought. Hold this for me, will you?"

She gave me the bottle of liquid. The other end of the tube went into Dad's mouth.

"Gran!"

She winked as she rose to her feet. "I'm not asking you to poison your father, dear. It'll just solve a little problem and leave him none the worse for wear."

She took Dad's right hand and wrapped his fingers round

the empty whisky bottle, then touched the neck of the bottle to his mouth. She turned towards Dad's car and I let my bottle, the full one, drop slightly.

"Kevin!" she said without turning round. I quickly lifted it back to its former level and watched as she tucked the whisky bottle under the driver's seat. Then she came back to me, plucked the tube from Dad's mouth and relieved me of the clear stuff. "Let him try to pass a breathalyser test with this little lot inside him!" she said. She packed everything away into her bag and stood up, ticking points off on her fingers.

"Breath… bottle… fingerprints… saliva…" She turned to me and beamed. "I think we've done everything, dear, and I don't think the divorce court will be very sympathetic after this little event. Least of all when he starts raving to the police about being forced off the road and knocked out by his mother-in-law. Oh, that reminds me, we'd better call them—"

Then she stopped, head cocked to one side. We could hear police sirens. Real ones. "Quicker off the mark than I thought, dear," she said. "We'd better be off. Get back in the car, now."

She paused briefly to feel under the BMW's bumper. When she came up to me she handed me a small metal and plastic disc. "A souvenir, dear," she said.

I finally, finally found the strength and the breath to say something.

Originally enough, it was, "Gran—"

The sirens really were close. She put a firm hand on my shoulder "Come on, dear, we don't want to get involved. I don't believe in telling lies to policemen."

~ ~ ~ ~

The professor stopped abruptly, looking thoughtful.

"You're making it up," I said when it became obvious he wasn't going to say anything else.

He grinned.

"I mean," I said, "you're telling me your grandmother and her friends were using the waterhammer effect to keep the motorways clear?"

"Clear?" the professor exclaimed. "If you'd ever driven on a motorway in the 1990s you wouldn't ask that. No, quite the opposite. They were deliberately keeping the motorways, or at least the M25, clogged up with the traffic that would otherwise have driven through their peaceful little villages. They lived in idyllic havens and wanted to keep it that way... of course, if you've lost your husband and son to fast drivers then holding up the boy racers would be its own reward anyway. There might have been spin-off organisations doing the same thing elsewhere in the country, but I think Gran's people were the originals.

"Remember, even back in the nineties, and earlier, authorities were already applying fluid dynamics to traffic theory. That was how traffic lights were run, for instance. But Gran and her friends took it that extra bit further. They knew it just takes a little action here and there to send shockwaves all around the system, and if you use a powerful enough computer and the right chaotic algorithms to plan your moves, you can use those shockwaves to clear the roads or block them. That's what that little traffic-calming cruise of hers was all about."

"But—"

"And then came the personal flyer," he added, "and the cars all but vanished from our roads, so of course, it's not a problem anymore. Not for those of us who still drive everywhere, anyway."

I was trying to spot a flaw in what he'd said. Any logical catch.

"Where did they get their money from?" I said. "That equipment must have cost."

"Life savings. They weren't rich but they weren't exactly poor either." He looked at his watch. "Well, it's been unexpectedly pleasant but time is pressing. Are you flying back?"

"Of course," I said.

"Good luck."

~ ~ ~ ~ ~

I sat in the cockpit of my flyer, waiting for permission to join the main southbound airstream at 500 feet. It was jammed solid up there.

A network of agents cruising the nation's highways, driving their cars in certain areas, at certain speeds, for certain times, all calculated by the big computer...

Ridiculous.

Of course, the kind of individual who thought the entire UK road network was laid out for his personal benefit wasn't going to be compliant. A traffic jam in one place would just make him drive faster elsewhere—maybe even through the villages they were trying to keep clear. Therefore, as well as the regulars there would have to be special operatives, with special equipment, acting against persistent offenders...

Still ridiculous.

I glanced in annoyance at my watch, then up at the airstream above me. It was packed solid with flyers and traffic clearance was a long time in coming. I could almost believe it was laid on for my benefit.

David Langford

I drafted "Serpent Eggs" in rather different form as my entrance ticket to Milford in 1977. The island, its warped eco-community and the investigation of its dread secret were all in there, but it was generally felt that something was missing. Rob Holdstock liked the climactic confrontation but not much else; Dave Garnett, I think, said it was bloody awful but then he usually did; Chris Priest felt there was a strongly ironic story in there, but at the time I couldn't see what to do with that hint. In the 1980s I pinched the central conceit as the big reveal in a comic novel—*The Leaky Establishment*—about the nuclear weapons trade in which I'd served my time (escaping in 1980). In the 1990s, Necronomicon Press was for some reason interested in a Langford chapbook, inspiring me to rewrite "Serpent Eggs" on the basis that our investigating protagonist was working on the wrong assumptions and looking for the wrong thing. The vaguely Cthuloid collection appeared as *Irrational Numbers*, and after further tinkering the story found its way into *The Third Alternative* and *The Mammoth Book of Best New Horror #9*; so maybe I did something right at last. Moral: always listen to Chris Priest.

Serpent Eggs

When the island first showed itself as a formless dark blot on the shifting greys of sea and sky it should have been a moment full of significance, of boding... but my attention was elsewhere. One of its people is actually on this boat. And yes, and yes, she has something of what I have been calling the Droch Skerry 'look'. Besides that odd patchiness of the hair and the dark bruises under each eye, there are points only hinted by the newspaper photograph that first caught my curiosity months ago and on the far side of the Atlantic. A peaked unhealthiness, a greyish, shrunken aspect—well, it's hard to put in words.

Otherwise she would be an ordinarily attractive young women. Her name is Lee something. "Just call me Lee. It'll be great to have a new face on the island." She's loaded with small oddments for people in the Droch Skerry community. Out here on the edge of the Shetlands, going shopping is a major expedition planned weeks ahead. We clung to an icy rail and made small talk on the heaving deck, surrounded by all her sprawling bags and parcels. Luckily I had already picked up a smattering of this alternative-energy lore from books bought *en route*.

For the record—and this casebook might as well carry a complete record—I would not have made the long journey for something as nebulous as a 'look'. Other sources (the UFO journals, the *Fortean Times*, even the *National Enquirer*) carry tales, recent tales, of this being a region where "something fell out of the sky". Maybe I am even the first to spot what might well be a significant nexus.

Later

What a place. A lone bare lump in the ocean. Grey rock, damp concrete, mist and endless chill... they say that spring comes early to the Scottish Islands but they must have meant some other islands.

And the alternative-technology angle! There are straggling windmill towers on the heights, both the ordinary and the vertical-axis kind, flapping in a dispirited way; there are salt-crusted solar panels aimed up into the fog; the toilets are ideologically correct, and stink. Even the quay is low-tech, a sort of natural spit of rock humped like a brontosaur and squared off with wobbly stonework, glistening and slippery from the spray; I nearly killed myself getting my suitcases to firm ground.

The commune was out in force to greet Lee and the shipment from the mainland. Their clash of dingy anoraks and fluorescent cagoules looks cheerful enough until you come closer and see their faces. In various degrees, like Polaroid snaps frozen at twenty different stages of their development, they have that wasted look. Most are quite young.

Stewart Wheatley is the man I corresponded with before coming. He owns Droch Skerry, I think, and runs the commune by his own whims. They led me to him in one of their squat energy-saving houses, and he greeted me under a yellow light that waxed and waned with (I suppose) the wind overhead.

Is there a grey look about Wheatley too? Hard to tell in that pulsating light. He's big and completely bald, looks like a retired wrestler, has one of those arc-lamp personalities whose glare backs you up against the wall like a strong wind. He was throbbingly glad I'd come to join the group, insisted I must call him Stewart, everyone would call me Robert, no formalities on Droch, knew I'd get the most tremendous satisfaction from working alongside this truly dedicated team....

Somehow I never even got around to my carefully prepared story of research work for a magazine article.

There was a meal: all twenty-odd of the islanders at one long table. We ate some sort of meat loaf from tins, wizened vegetables out of the grey salty garden plots I'd seen, and horribly naked shellfish that some of the team (a third of them seemed to be called Dave) had chipped laboriously from the rocks at low tide. Whelks, limpets, some vile winkle things called buckies, and worse. It seemed impolitic to shut my eyes, but they looked as bad as anything described in the grimoires.

The stuff in the chipped tumblers tasted of lime-juice, and a bottle of multivitamin capsules went round the table like the port decanter at some old Oxford college... so a tentative theory of mine was abandoned. *Not* merely a case of deficiency disease. Good.

Conversation: subdued. They keep one eye on Wheatley, huge at the head of the table. I said, not strictly truthfully, that the shabby wind-farm was impressive.

"You should hear what they cost," said Lee at once with an edge in her voice. "Low technology is our watchword, Robert. We've set ourselves free from industrial civilisation, except the bits that sell wind generators."

"Have to start somewhere," muttered a scanty-haired, haggard man who I gathered was called Rich.

Wheatley told me, "Lee would like us to live in caves and eat roots—Rich is disappointed that in five years we haven't yet covered the skerry with dams and refineries."

I asked him which he favoured, and he said rather grandly that he was an eco-opportunist who made the best use of whatever was available: money, weather, materials...

"Mussels," said a voice to my right, not with enthusiasm. "Eggs."

I do not know how to convey the chill that crept into that long, stuffy eating hall. Some seemed as puzzled as myself by the sudden silence; some looked sidelong at Wheatley as though expecting a cue.

"Dave," he said gently. "Not, not you, *you*. I've just remembered... it's your turn to go on watch tonight."

The indicated Dave gave a small nod. Clearly it had not been his turn. It was a punishment. Disciplinary.

On watch? Where and for what?

Later

Or might it conceivably be sickness after all? Wheatley alone has a private room. In the men's dormitory before lights-out, much pallid flesh was visible. Those with more pronounced cases of the 'look' seem to suffer unusually from bruises on their arms and legs—great piebald splotches.

Of the toilets I do not choose to write more. ("We return *everything* to the soil." The sooner the better. These people's digestive systems do not seem in good order.) The bathrooms are tolerable and give a few minutes' privacy to bring these notes up to date. How the heating systems are shared between the windmills, diesel generator and those joke solar cells remains a dark mystery, but after a tepid start the shower surprised me by running hot.

Tufts of thin hair lie on the floor, sticking to my wet feet. I have seen it coming out in wads on their combs.

In my locked suitcase there are certain signs and wards that may offer a little protection against... against? I have followed up some odd cults (not with any great success) in a dozen decayed holes of old Britain and New England, but have rarely known such a compelling sense of being *too close*.

May 10

Already I have to pay the price of offering myself as a willing worker. Today's choice is limpet-work on the western shore, or some nameless task involving a cranky and obstinate biomass converter which will one day heat the buildings with methane or blow them sky-high... or plain digging. That sounded the safest. Four hours scratching with an undersized fork at a vast tract of ground which was to blossom with yams, kiwifruit or something equally unlikely. Occasional jets thundered overhead according to the whim of the Royal Air Force, thick as flies in these 'remote' parts. Seagulls and scrawny hens pecked after me for worms. It offered time to think.

The impression I have is that the commune members who are further gone in the 'look' are those who have been here longer. Rich is one of the original few and has it very badly. He said hello just now, on his way to "look over the number-two windmill cable—it's leaking to earth." Not keen to have me come and see. "I get uptight if people watch me working."

I watched him scramble up the slope, though, up beyond the weak fingers of greenery that reach towards the central granite gnarl. The rocky climb is rotten with industrial archaeology: cable runs, abandoned scaffolding, the wreck of a windmill that hadn't been anchored right, pipes snaking this way and that to tap what I suppose must be fresh-water springs. In one or two places there are ragged wisps of steam. A long scar of raw stone marks where Wheatley had (according to Lee) tried to blast the foundations for something or other. Rusty stains bleed down the rock. The place is a mess.

There were tolerant smiles for me when I staggered into the kitchen, aching and blistered, clammy with sweat despite the chill air. Lee and someone called Anna cracked age-old jokes about feeble city muscles; another of the Daves offered me soup hot from the midget electric stove that is another of Droch Skerry's compromises with self-sufficiency. There is a certain sardonic amusement in counting just how many compromises there are. Boxes and boxes of Kleenex tissues, not even recycled!

(But a tiny puzzle is lurking there too. Longer-standing members of the group will sometimes snatch a few tissues and turn aside from whatever is going on, not sneezing but quietly pressing the things to nose or mouth. Once or twice as the wadded-up tissue goes into the fire, I have thought to detect a splash of red.)

So I've worked for Droch Skerry and am halfway to being accepted. Coming a little way in makes one oddly sensitive to divisions further in, before you reach Wheatley and the centre. As though there were things which A and B might speak of together but not discuss with an outer circle of myself and Lee and half a dozen others.

May 11

Something fell out of the sky. The vague UFO rumours are sober truth.

In between work shifts it's quite allowable to go for a walk. "But when you know the place by heart," said Lee with half a smile, "the fun goes out of it rather."

Even in this eternal weeping mist, there ought not to be enough of Droch Skerry to become lost in. Its many granite shoulders are hunched and knotted, though; the grassy folds between them twist in a topologist's nightmare; the closer you look, the longer any journey becomes. Especially, of course, when you're not in the least sure what you hope to find.

Granite, gorse, granite, rabbit droppings, matted heather, gorse, granite, endlessly repeated....

It was in the tenth or twentieth coarse wrinkle of the ground that the irregular pattern seemed to break. Less of the prickly gorse here, perhaps, and more of it withered and brown? This fold of the island dipped further down than most, a long sheltered combe or glen that ended at a cliff over deep water. I pulled gingerly at the nearest dead gorse and it came up in my hand, roots long broken and dry. Then, coming to the edge of a roundish depression in the ground, I tripped over something like a doormat.

Not a doormat. A slab of turf that hadn't taken root. And next to it another, and another.

Part of the combe had been painstakingly re-turfed in chequerboard squares. Some of these turves had dried and died before they could knit into a smooth carpet of salt grass. When I stood back, the oval hollow in the ground rearranged itself in my mind's eye. It was a crater where something had impacted, hard, from very high up. One bulging granite rock nearby was marked with a bright smear of metal. I could imagine Wheatley's little workforce laboriously covering up what had happened, and...

What had it been and where was it taken?

The only further information I thought I could extract from this fold of the island was that—it seemed—a large and heavy bulk might have been dragged to or from the cliff edge. I had a hazy vision of something vast and formless rising from the sea, or returning to it.

Not long after, a dim shape along roughly those lines came looming out of the thin mist. It resolved itself into Wheatley, carrying a shotgun and the bloody rags of several rabbits strung into a bunch. The gun barrel wavered erratically, sometimes pointing at his own foot, or mine. "Our Rich catches the little buggers in humane snares," he said in a conversational tone, "but where's the challenge in that? You shouldn't come this way on your own. It's treacherous."

I had not found it so, and said something non-committal.

"Believe me. See you've had a fall already."

It was ridiculous to feel guilty, trapped, as my eyes followed Wheatley's down to the muddy and grass-stained knees of my jeans. Was it so obvious that I'd spent time minutely studying the ground?

"Oh," he said, "and I should avoid the heights altogether. If I were you."

May 13

I constantly feel the circles within circles at these strange meals in that close, smelly room. (Deodorants do not seem to figure largely in the alternative life; no matter how often we all resort to the showers, we aren't a salubrious lot *en masse*.) There is what you might call a Lee faction which does not like relying on the dark gods of Western industrial civilisation even for microchips, paracetamol or the band-aids that decorate every other hand. The inner ring have a more Robinson Crusoe approach, feeling justified in snatching anything from the world's wreck as the pelagic deeps close over it. Sometimes they seem to be talking in code about some great and significant coup along these lines. "Power for the people," they say, and it means something more than an empty slogan. Wheatley watches over this with a curious air of controlled force, fraught with doom and significance, as though by lifting one finger he could abolish any of us. I think he may be an adept.

We are a democracy here and decide everything by show of hands, but suggestions not to the master's liking are never put to the vote. People change their minds in mid-proposal, turned by his pale gaze.

A special treat tonight: after some days' accumulation, the island's bedraggled hens have provided eggs all around. I never met boiled eggs so small and odd-tasting, but appetites here are small. Rich, who looked very bad tonight, collected a dozen half-shells and idly (it seemed, until I saw others' faces) arranged them on the table, unbroken end up, in a ring. A circle of power. It had some kind of power, because I saw Wheatley frowning like thunder. He rose early and the meal was over.

In the dormitory late on, eyes tight shut, I overheard a brief exchange. One of the Daves, the black one from Jamaica, was not looking forward to some coming night duty. "Man. Every hour on the hour. That light up there really genuinely gives me the creeps." He was answered, not quite intelligibly from where I lay in 'my' clammy bunk. But I believe a Name was pronounced. It is a central axiom of the old knowledge, of which I have learned so desperately little, that the forces that crawl under the thin bright reality we know all have their separate names, and may be called.

On watch. "Up there."

Avoid the heights.

May 16

Where does the time go? You can lose yourself in a community like this: hoeing, hunting for driftwood, carrying water in the 20-litre plastic drums that are comfortably liftable and an agony after thirty seconds' walk. There are a hundred running jokes about life here—away from the mainland, the job centre, the dole. Apart from the occasional strange no-go areas in conversation, I like these people.

But.

You can't get newspapers here, nor a decent steak or cup of coffee. We sit in a shivering circle around the radio and hear the pulse of the world, but see nothing. Lee says there is always going to be satellite TV on the skerry *next* month. It was a shock to leaf through mouldy old magazines stacked in the store-hut against some dim future notion of recycling, and be reminded of normal faces; of the fact that something on Droch is *wrong*, no matter how easily one becomes used to the ruined look people wear here. I ran, almost, to scan my own face in a shaving-mirror. Anxious and none too clean, but not (yet?) wearing that mark....

It is not lack of vitamins. Precautions are taken. It does not appear to be any of the legendary miscegenations of the literature—the notorious 'Innsmouth look' or the seal-man hybrids of island folklore—but something subtler. These people have no lifelong roots here. From personal knowledge of a friend who died, I think it is not AIDS.

Tonight I plan to watch the watcher on the heights.

Later

Bright light-bulbs indoors mean gales outside, the windmills screaming up above. Rather him than me.

In brief: when I heard the wind take the front door and slam it, I counted an interminable five minutes of seconds ("one and-a-pause, two and-a-pause, three and-a-pause"). Then I got up as naturally as possible and padded off towards the toilet. Out in the upper-floor passage, thick and smeary windows show part of the hillside behind the commune buildings; I hoped I might see a light.

To my surprise I saw it quite soon, a flicking torch beam that danced to and fro impatiently while its invisible source mounted the rocks with infinite slowness and care. Lacking survey equipment, I did what I could and knelt to watch one-eyed, chin on the deep window-ledge, tracing each position of the light by touching my pen to the window-glass. In the grey of morning the marks might show up and indicate a path, or not....

The light vanished. Surely it could not have reached and passed the crest? I waited another age, shivering in my pyjamas, and suddenly found the flicker again—now unmistakably descending.

A memory: "every hour on the hour," I'd overheard. The watch was not a continuous one. Somehow this made it even odder and more disturbing.

May 17

After the usual unsatisfactory breakfast, the upstairs passage seemed full of comings and goings I'd never noticed before. I dodged guiltily to and fro, unable to be alone with my window; in the end I invented a story about a touch of diarrhoea (common enough here), and then felt I had to brood in the lavatory for the sake of verisimilitude each time.

Eventually I was able to squint from what I hoped was the right position, and see how the blurred smears of ink on the glass overlaid the hillside. The end of the dancing light's journey must have been in *that* area, above the raw scar in the rocks, some way to the left of that tangle of old iron.

After a while I thought I saw a patch of black... an opening? The old places under the Earth. With a wholly disproportionate effect of dread, a wisp of fog seemed to trail from the blackness like dog's breath on a chill morning.

I must record that I have played around with these investigations in libraries and ancient college archives, and have never before reached a position where the next logical step is to climb a hill in slippery darkness and crawl into a black cavity. I record that I am sick with fright.

Since I am officially frequenting the toilets, I'm thus today's logical choice to carry all the buckets out for return to the soil and cleansing in the sea. As I trudged back from the fourth trip Wheatley chose to waylay me and say, "You're settling in nicely, Robert." And as a seeming afterthought: "You should get more sleep at night."

When next upstairs I remembered to wipe my felt-pen tracing from the window. If anyone had noticed, it could have meant nothing to them. Surely.

Light relief of the evening: Anna, who is interested in something called biodynamic gardening, said we should preserve our excrement, stuff it into sterilised cow horns and bury them at the winter solstice to be transmuted by cosmic and telluric forces. Dug up in spring, minute quantities of the result would make Droch Skerry bloom like the garden of Findhorn. Wheatley laughed out loud and scoffed at her mercilessly. I noticed that Anna, like most of the women here, wears a headscarf all day long; it covers the thinning hair.

I judge that Lee will need a scarf soon. I *like* Lee. Something ought to be done about the shadow on this damned place.

Tonight, then.

Later

Inventory. Plenty of wellington boots, anoraks and electric torches for night emergencies, waiting in the big kitchen. A little shamefacedly I am wearing a scrap of parchment inscribed with certain elder signs, carrying a vial of powder compounded from a protective formula. One does not wholly believe in these things and yet they can offer comfort.

What do I expect to see? I don't know. If there's anything in sortilege, though, my eye fell today on a balloon in the Krazy Kat collection from our ramshackle library: "I sense the feel of evil—Every nerve of me vibrates to the symphony of sin—Somewhere, at this moment, crime holds revel." That's it.

May 18, around 1:20am

The cave mouth. It is a cave; could be natural. Water streams from it and is lost in the rocks. Warm water.

The climb was very bad; my shins must be bleeding in a dozen places. Bitter wind. I think it was Rich making the every hour on the-hour visits at midnight and one. Plenty of time before two. Keep telling myself, Rich and several others have stared again and again into whatever abyss waits there, and come out unscathed.

Except for the worrying way they *look*....

Shortly after

Have to stoop slightly and splash my way. Firm underfoot except when I trip over the ubiquitous pipes. A warm breath blowing from further in, a seaside reek. There seems to be a bend ahead, and a hint of blue light when I click off the torch. "That light gives me the creeps." The hiss and moan of the wind in the cave mouth drowns out another sound ahead, I think; in the lulls it seems to be a faint... bubbling?

Later

I cannot get over that terrible glare he gave me at the last.

The chamber might be natural, and the spring that pours into it, but the deep, brimming pool is surely not. (I remembered those scars of abortive blasting activities.) The pool holds something bleak and alien. All in a ghostly blue light.

There are things down there, eight things like great eggs, each the size of a man's skull, suspended in a complex cradle of ropes anchored to the stony floor around the rim... a precisely spaced ring of devil's eggs, a diagram of power, a gateway? All around them the water glows in deadly blue silence. Bubbles rise from them, every bubble a blue spark, the whole pool fizzing and simmering. Thick, choking warmth in the air.

One half-remembered phrase kept writhing through my mind like a cold worm: "... *a congeries of iridescent globes*..." It was a long while before I could even look away from the incomprehensible blue horror that held me with a snake's gaze.

A rack of rust-caked tools: hammer, chisel, knife. More coils of rope. A prosaic notebook hanging from a nail on the wall, damp pages full of scribble in different handwritings.

"17/5 0100 OK no adjust—R." I shuddered most of all at the innocent-looking pipe that led away, and down the slope outside, towards the houses.

Then I heard the scraping down the passageway and knew that I was caught. Beyond the troubled pool the floor and roof became a wedge-shaped niche for dwarfs, and after that nothing at all.

Wheatley, gigantic in this low-ceilinged space, was not carrying the shotgun as carelessly as he had in the open. I backed away uselessly over granite slippery and treacherous with condensation.

"You probably know already: no one can climb up here after dark without showing a light to half the island," he said reasonably, pacing my slow retreat around the pool. "Now what are we going to do with you?"

"What *is* that monstrosity? What force makes the light?" I said, or something of the sort.

"A very well-known one. Never heard of Cherenkov radiation? Nor me, but Rich understands all this stuff. My God, can't you imagine how we felt when that Eurostealth bomber came down smash on top of Droch Skerry? Over the cliff with it, except for the cores, and there they are. Talk about swords into ploughshares, talk about power for the people. We might have had some leakage trouble early on, but we're the first community with its own alternative-technology reactor. Piping-hot water for all our showers, all our..."

I understood only that in his raving he had allowed the gun barrel to wander again. The plastic phial of Ibn Ghazi powder was in my hand by then; logically I should have cast it into the accursed waters, but I threw it at Wheatley instead. Common salt, sulphur, mercury compounds; all more or less harmless, but perhaps it had some virtue, and he caught it in the eyes. With a not very loud grunt he lurched off-balance, the shotgun fired and rock chips exploded from the floor, the recoil (I think) took him over backwards, and his head struck hard on a spur of granite as he splashed into the warm seething water.

I could not bring myself to dive after him. The sinking body spun lazily down towards the terrible eggs and their aura of hellish radiance. For an instant Wheatley's whole face glowed translucent blue, and the light somehow filled his eyeballs, a final unseeing glare at me from eyes that were discs of blue fire. Then he floated slowly to the surface and became a lumpish silhouette against the evil light below. He no longer moved.

It must be stopped. This rot, this ulcer, this tumour in the clean rock. The circle of 'cores' lets in something bad from outside the world we know. Break the circle. Break the symmetry.

The old knife from the rack haemorrhages wet rust at every touch, but it has the remnants of an edge beneath. Hack through the ropes and the strange eggs will no longer be arranged in that terrible sigil; they'll sink and nestle together in a ragged bunch at the bottom of the water. Whatever esoteric contract is fulfilled by that careful spacing will be broken apart.

The logic cannot be faulted. I don't know why I find myself hesitating.

May 2???

It is very hard to write now. Around dawn they found me half-conscious on the rocky hillside. I suppose I slipped and fell. My nerve had failed me as the loosed eggs glowed hotter, cracked as though about to hatch, while raw steam erupted from the foaming pool. By the time I'd stumbled to the cave mouth there was a superheated blast in pursuit, a roar of dragon's breath. The rest of that bad night has sunk out of memory, apart from the jags of pain. RAF helicopters came clattering down in the morning light to investigate the tall plume of steam and something else that still wound snakelike into the sky.

"Jesus Christ, we've got our own Chernobyl," I heard one of the uniformed crowd mutter.

The mark of Droch Skerry is fully on me now. My hair flees by handfuls, I bleed too easily, food is hateful and fever sings in my blood. Lee has visited me, and wept. Wheatley's tomb is said to be sealed with a monstrous plug of concrete. That is not dead which can eternal lie. They say the others can nearly all be saved. To one or two I am a kind of hero. They say.

I still do not wholly understand....

Jacey Bedford

I took Pitch to Milford in 2009. There were only nine attendees that year, Stefan Hogberg, Una McCormack, Susan Booth, Liz Williams, Nick Moulton, Heather Lindsley, Chris Butler, Carl Allery, and me. The version of *Pitch* that I took was 4,100 words and its final published length was 3,929 words, but in the post-Milford rewrite process it briefly went up to 4,500 words and then back down again. Most people liked it, but said it needed polishing. I recall that Heather (our ex-pat American), had a few issues with Joanie's over-written New Jersey accent, which I toned down a bit subsequently. After the critiques are finished, we always have a *markets* meeting, where people make suggestions about potential homes for all the Milford stories that we've been working on. I think Pitch perplexed some people, the suggestions being that it was the type of story that would fit into a suitably themed anthology—and that's what happened, though not immediately. In 2015 I sold it to the anthology *Thou Shalt Not*, edited by Alex Davis and published by Tickety Boo Press in 2016.

Pitch

"Hello! Hello!" *What a lousy connection.* "Hello! Is any..."

"Switchboard. How can I help ya?" The voice had a nasal, nails-on-blackboard quality. The accent was pure New Jersey, or even Joisey.

I didn't expect that!

Even without seeing her Robert put her straight into the category of *office minion, not too bright, easily manipulated.* He was good at judging people. You had to be able to figure folks out in his job.

"Can you put me through to..."

"Out ta lunch."

"How did you know who I wanted?"

"You dialled this number. Who else would ya want?"

"I need to speak to The Man. It's urgent."

"Yeah, it's always urgent by the time ya call here. No one ever thinks of giving a decent lead time. They wait until the bank's about to foreclose, or the sniper has a bead on them, or the severance notice is on the desk, and then they try to cut a deal." She sighed.

Robert could hear the rhythmic nam nam nam of mouth noise. She was chewing gum. *Which 1950s gangster B-movie did they dig her up from?* The secretary from hell. Literally.

"Youse is just like the rest," she said. "Trust me. I know." Nam nam nam.

"You seem to know a lot about me."

"Listen, mister, I sit on this switchboard 24/7. It's my

73

lot in life—well, afterlife really, but who's countin'? We get hundreds, no, thousands of calls a day. I can tell from the first stammer what youse all wants. Everyone's looking for a deal of some kind. Since the economy went down the tubes..." She pronounced it *toobs*. "...calls have doubled. An' it ain't just the money worries, neither." Nam nam nam.

She was right of course. Oh, he'd thought about it before, ever since Spencely had admitted the secret of his success and offered him the details of how to contact The Man, but he hadn't been desperate enough then. He was desperate now. It all stemmed from the damned redundancy notice. Mortgage shot to hell, car about to be repossessed, divorce papers served and bugger-all in the bank. Less than bugger-all. He was on the skids.

"But..."

"You ain't the only one, mister, but it ain't a seller's market no more."

Not a seller's market? He'd see about that. He'd taken Salesman of the Year award for six years running, right up until last year when Spencely had moved into the office next door and had knocked him off the top spot. *Bastard was always after my job.* Before that he'd been invincible. A real player, maybe a bit old school, but he could still teach the whizz-kids a thing or two about human nature. No one could meet sales targets like he could –at least, not without help.

Well, if he was a player he'd better start playing.

"Miss... I'm sorry, I didn't get your name."

"Joanie." Nam nam nam.

"Joanie." He used his I-love-you voice, warm and slightly husky. It never failed with receptionist types. Got him an appointment to make that all-important sales pitch more than once. "I'm in a bit of a fix, here and my colleague..." *Spencely, the bastard. I'll wipe the floor with fucking Spencely if only I can get to see The Man.* "He told me who to call."

"Ain't nothing I can do for ya."

"You were right, Joanie. About leaving it until the last minute. I'm not bothered about the money and the job and the house, not for myself, anyway. It's for my wife. I love my wife, Joanie." *Yeah, right, and the bitch loves me right back. Smacked both credit cards to the hilt and took off as soon as the going got tough.*

"Awww, Sweetie, I'm real sorry to hear that. If I could do anything I would but..."

"A meeting.... Just set up a meeting, Joanie, please. I'll do the rest. I can swing it if only I get a face to face with The Man. I know I can."

"Well..."

Yes! She was going to cave. Mental air punch! "Please, Joanie. Be kind to me."

"Well... I could slip you in between the 2.30 and the 2.45 tomorrow afternoon. Five minutes max. Be ready."

I can make a pitch in five. "Joanie, you're an angel."

Nam nam nam. "Well, hardly..."

~ ~ ~ ~ ~

He was ready by 2.15, freshly showered and shaved, shoes polished and hair slicked back. He didn't know what to expect, but he was ready for anything. Would The Man himself ring his doorbell?

He paced up and down then looked at his watch again. Five minutes. Better make them count. He was sure he could wing it without a projector and Powerpoint. The trick was to focus on your target. Be realistic. Don't ask for anything too big. He didn't want to pay too much, but he could afford a few years service to The Man in exchange for getting out of the shit now. *I can do this.*

Where lesser salesmen failed was in the lack of pizazz. They didn't motivate anyone into signing on the line. They didn't make the customers want it so badly they practically knocked the salesman over in the rush. In the age of 'wow' marketing the trick was to figure out what made them tick, and get straight to the heart of the buyer.

In this particular case does the buyer have a heart? That was something he couldn't begin to guess. He'd have a price, though. Everybody did. *Five years, that would be acceptable. Even ten years. I can cope with ten years.*

Robert breathed deeply and wiped his clammy palms against his thighs. He needed to concentrate on his pitch. *Think of the three esses. State it. Support it. Summarise it.* He imagined standing at the end of a glossy boardroom table, several pairs of eyes turned towards him, but only really needing to impress one. The Man Himself.

He mouthed it silently, running the words through his head. "Thank you for seeing me. I appreciate this invitation." *Make 'em think they'd invited him.* "I've come here today to offer you my soul and my service for a fixed term of five years." *Start at five then make them think they'd got a bargain when and if he had to increase it to ten. They'd jump at it.*

"I know, gentlemen, that a mere mortal can barely dream of the power that you command." *He could, though—dream, that is. Power. Wealth. Status.* "However, what I ask is so little, and what I can offer is so much..."

At that point in the presentation he'd raise the stakes, trot out everything he wanted.

He was just thinking of a killer line to clinch the deal when the quality of the light changed. He felt a little queasy and found that instead of his well-manicured living room he was standing in the yard of his old school. *Well, that's different. Lucky I was expecting the unexpected.*

The front door stood open in invitation and he stepped through into Victorian brick and woodwork, all tiled corridors, cork noticeboards, creaking iron radiators, always either too cold or too hot, glass windows peering into classrooms with empty desks set out in neat rows. He could almost hear the echo of children's voices. Outside the headmaster's study was a line of four chairs. He recalled kids sitting there when they were waiting to answer for misdemeanours. Not him, of course. Never him. Now the chairs were occupied, but not by children. A tall, haggard woman sat nearest to the door. Next to her an elderly gentleman, round-faced and shiny-headed. The third chair held a youngish pale man staring fixedly ahead. In the fourth sat a man hunched over with his face in his hands.

The door opened. A middle-aged woman almost skipped out. The woman closest to the door stood up, straightened up to an impressive height, smoothed her hair back with one hand and went inside. The second and third applicants both stood and moved up one place. Robert waited for the fourth to do the same, but he didn't move. Robert cleared his throat. The man looked up at him and Robert felt the shock of recognition.

"Spencely!"

"Hello, Jones."

What was the bastard here for? "Come for a second dip? I thought you got all you asked for last time."

Spencely shook his head. "I wish..." He stood up and changed chairs, gesturing Robert to the spare. "It's not always all that easy. There are... conditions... requirements." He was visibly shaking.

Robert sat down and half turned, "But... you gave me the number. You were top salesman last year. You've still got a job."

"You think I sold my soul to the Devil for good sales figures? Did you think I had so little imagination?"

Yes, I did. Bloody hell, did the bastard beat me all by himself?

Spencely laughed, but it was a harsh sound and ended in a gulp which might have been a sob.

Robert didn't know what to say or where to look. He stared fixedly at the opposite wall, institutional green paint, uncomfortable with Spencely's emotion.

Spencely sniffed and swallowed, then took his iPhone from his inside jacket pocket and made a couple of notes.

Robert cleared his throat again. *Careful, it's getting to be a habit.* "I didn't know we could bring artificial aids." He regretted the abandoned laptop. A proper presentation would steady him. Photographs of his life, bullet points of his virtues, summaries of the benefits of drawing a soul as respectable as his into Hell.

"I... I didn't bring anything... not the first time. This time I wrote down what I wanted to say."

"You did try before, then? Like you said?"

"Yes." Spencely nodded. "But I wasn't such a good salesman then."

"You got better." It was difficult not to let bitterness creep into his voice. Robert didn't know whether to be relieved or upset that Spencely had beaten him fair and square.

"I had to if I wanted another chance at this. I took a correspondence course."

It was all just practice to you. It meant something to me to have that award every year, to know that when redundancies came my name wouldn't be on the list. To you it was just a bloody stepping stone.

"That woman who just went in..." Spencely swallowed hard and nodded towards the door. "Fourth time."

"Fourth?"

"It's not a seller's market right now."

"Someone else told me that." Robert wondered if Joanie was still on the switchboard. Twenty-four seven, she'd said. Surely she didn't mean that literally. Maybe she did. This was Hell, after all.

"So what's The Man like?" Any information Robert could get now might be the difference between clinching the deal and not.

"Different for everyone, I understand, but with a nose for a deal. Used to be you could get your wildest dreams in return for a limited term contract, but now..." He shrugged, a hopeless little gesture. "Rumours are they cut the budget."

"Hell has a budget?"

"Budget and bureaucracy—isn't that the very definition of hell?"

Should I be setting my sights lower? "So if he makes a deal, what does he offer?"

"Oh, you know, the usual. Whatever you desire. Money, fast cars, slow sex, a successful business, a stately home and an army of servants." Spencely tapped his nose. "It's not so much what you get as what you have to pay for it. See that woman who just went in?"

Robert nodded.

Spencely leaned in and Robert dipped forward so his ear was on a level with Spenceley's whisper. "This time she's planning to include the soul of her firstborn son."

Robert gasped. "I hadn't expected... I mean... Is that even possible?"

"Possible, oh yes. I haven't any children, you see. I've only got myself to offer." There was regret in Spencely's voice. "You've got a son."

He's my son, not a bargaining chip! I'm here on my own account, not to drag others with me. I have my principles and I'm not that desperate... I hope. "He's with his mother."

"He's safe, then."

"Oh, thank God!"

"Watch your language." Spencely jerked his head towards the office door and dropped his voice to a whisper. "They're a bit touchy about the G-word. Avoid biblical references, commandments, parables, you know the sort of stuff. No thou-shalt-nots."

How about: Thou shalt not covet thy neighbour's job, Spencely?

Robert yanked his mind away from coveting. He was beginning to revise his expectations and work out whether he could add value to his original offer. Maybe he'd have to go up to twelve years, or even fifteen. What would The Man want? He pinched the bridge of his nose. For the first time doubt flickered across his mind. He'd always imagined Hell was hungry for souls. Any and all souls. It messed with his head to think of The Man not buying, or buying more selectively. What if he got turned down flat? No, that rattled his pride. He had to clinch this sale, especially with Spencely right there, too. He'd have to make The Man an offer he couldn't refuse.

Maybe it's as well I don't have Danny as an option. Robert was beginning to discover things about himself that he didn't really like.

The door opened and the tall woman came out, dejected and stooping.

"No need to ask how she did this time." Spencely shook his head at her back. "Perhaps she should have offered both her children."

The next man in line went in and then the next. They shuffled up twice, putting Spencely in the hot seat next. A thin-faced woman took the chair Robert had just vacated.

Spencely's face was pasty white now. "It's the waiting that's the worst." He stood up. "Look at me. My hands are shaking. I'll never manage it."

He turned as if to leave. Robert grabbed his arm and yanked him back. *It's your fucking fault I'm here. If I have to do this to survive then so do you.* He fixed a reassuring smile on his face. "Top salesman, Spence. You can do it. Just don't look so defeated before you start. Remember the duck. On the surface it's cool, calm and collected, even though, underneath, it's paddling like hell. What did your course book say?" He tapped Spencely's shoulders. "Body language. Shoulders back."

Spencely straightened a little.

Robert huffed out a breath and rattled out the basics like a drill sergeant. "Hands open. Wide, expressive, inclusive gestures. No defensive arm folding, no hands in pockets." He tutted and shook his head as Spencely's hands dropped to clasp each other just in front of his crotch. "And definitely no fig leaf posture."

Spencely unclasped his hands and let them swing at his sides.

"That's better."

The door opened.

"Okay, in you go and don't whine." Robert clapped one hand to Spencely's shoulder to propel him in the right direction. "Don't sound desperate."

"But I am desperate."

Yeah, me too. Robert watched the door close.

~ ~ ~ ~ ~

It seemed like an age before it opened again. An age during which Robert ran through his pitch twice. An age during which his palms sweated so much he was surprised he hadn't dripped puddles on to the floor. An age during which he wanted to call the whole thing off and run for home, but Spencely was in there right now and he wasn't going to let the bastard beat him into second place, not this time.

Eventually the door opened again.

"How did you do?" Robert asked as Spencely emerged.

"I don't know yet. I have to wait here for the final answer. Go on. You go in."

Robert stood up, trying to suppress a grin. So it hadn't been a pushover for the whizz-kid. *Yes! There is a God!* He laughed at the impudence of his own thought. The reality of this place was very nearly proof enough.

"Jones," Spencely said. "I know we've had our differences in the past, but I want you to know that I'm rooting for you."

"Thanks, Spence. I hope you get the answer you want, too." Robert held out his hand. "Whatever the outcome, no hard feelings, eh?" *Yeah, right! Covet my job and eat my dust, Spencely!*

"No hard feelings."

~ ~ ~ ~ ~

The office was not how he'd imagined it would be. There was a table piled high with folders. A harassed looking white-haired man sat at a desk behind a huge open ledger, pen poised. If this was The Man he didn't look so scary.

"Come in, young man, sit down. Name?"

"Robert Jones, Sir."

The man scratched in his ledger with a quill pen.

A door in the back of the room opened and a woman entered with an armful of folders. She plonked them on to the only space on the table and dusted off her palms. She wore a skinny, pink sweater and a short green plaid skirt. Her honey-blonde hair was big—eighties big—waving down to her shoulders.

She was chewing gum. Nam nam nam.

"Robert!" It sounded like Wroberrt. The voice and the accent were unmistakable.

"Joanie?"

"Yeah." She smiled at him. "Nice to see you in the flesh." She poked her teeth with a fingernail. The way she said 'flesh' made him hope it was gum she was chewing. "Don't mind me. I'm just tidying up a little."

"Switchboard?" he asked.

"Oh, it's taking care of itself for a while. I've got a minor official from the American Embassy on hold. He's already on the third time through Aaron Copeland's suite from 'Billy the Kid'."

Welcome to Hell.

The Man tapped his ledger. "If I may continue."

"Oh, sure. Don't mind me." Joanie patted his shoulder in a familiar, almost possessive way. Nam nam nam.

Robert gawped. *She actually patted The Man's shoulder.*

"Occupation?" The Man asked as if secretaries took liberties with him every day.

"Salesman." Robert's attention snapped back to front and centre.

The man dipped the nib and scratched a single word.

"Are you a good salesman?"

No time for false modesty. "The best."

The Man added a second word.

"And you want to sell your soul to the Devil."

Do I? Do I really? It had seemed like such a good idea when Spencely had hinted that it could be the first step towards solving his current problems and getting exactly what he wanted out of life. Now it seemed fraught with difficulties. But what was the alternative?

"Lease, not sell. For a fixed term, Sir. Ten years." *Damn, he'd gone straight to ten.* "You see... it's like this..." All his well-rehearsed sales pitch went right out of the window. He begged. He babbled. He pleaded. He played the pity card. He asked for as little as possible in return for ten years service. No castle in Scotland or lustful virgins, no fifty million pound jackpot, no beachfront getaway in Cannes.

"I just want my job back. It's my job. Please. Make it so that the redundancy notice never happened."

"And in exchange you're offering what?"

"My soul. It's yours for ten years, my service."

Joanie had kept quiet, apart from the nam nam nam, but now she made a little throat rumble. Robert looked up. She was standing behind The Man and giving a hand sign that looked like, *more*, or *make it bigger*.

The Man's eyes dropped to his ledger as he scratched *soul* with the nib.

"More?" Robert mouthed silently to Joanie.

She compressed her lips, raised her eyebrows, looked towards the back of The Man's head meaningfully and nodded.

Robert shrugged, an empty-hands gesture and mouthed again. "I can't give any more."

"Can't?" she mouthed. "Or won't?"

"Twenty years?"

She did the make it bigger gesture again.

"Fifty? I'm too old," Robert mouthed back. He'd be ninety before he got out from under at this rate.

"Who's too old?" The Man looked up from his ledger and caught the last part of the exchange.

"Oh, no, Sir. I didn't mean... I mean... You're not too old. I was just thinking that if ten years isn't enough..."

"It's not."

"Fifteen?"

"Did you come here to waste my time?" The Man sat back. "It's all or nothing. And not just your service, but your services."

"Services?"

"We have some very nice retail packages. All we need is the right person to sell them."

Oh shit! Spencely hadn't warned him about this.

Spencely! Suddenly it became all his fault. The bastard deserved what was coming to him. He took a deep breath. "My soul... and my services. But I want you to not only rescind my redundancy notice, I want you to give it to Spencely instead. I want to be top salesman again."

Who was coveting whose job now?

"That sounds like an offer we can work with." The Man turned to Joanie and dipped his head deferentially. "The final decision's yours, of course."

Robert felt his jaw drop as the old man climbed stiffly out of the office chair and Joanie slipped into it. Nam nam nam. She glanced at the scritchings and scratchings in the ledger, took out a red gel ink pen—he hoped it was gel ink—and initialled it.

"Deal done," she said. "Thank you for your time, Robert Jones. We'll see you down here in... approximately thirty-five years. In the meantime, I'll email you the material and a list of potential clients. You are, after all, a salesman. A top salesman now that Mr. Spencely will be moving on to other things."

"But..."

"Your five minutes is up."

The door swung open. In a daze Robert walked out of it. The woman waiting in line dodged round him and the door swung closed behind her as Spencely eagerly caught his sleeve. "Well? Did you cut a deal?"

The ramifications were barely beginning to sink in yet, but here he was, face to face with Spencely who was going to get his redundancy notice on account of Robert being the better salesman. He swallowed. "Yes," he said. "I did it."

Spencely's face split into a big grin. "Brilliant! I'm so pleased." *You won't be so pleased when you hear who's getting fired.*

"Did you have to give them a lot of concessions?"

He tried not to think about what he'd done. "Oh, you know, nothing more than I could afford, and I got my old job back."

"Good. Good!" Spencely was shaking his hand vigorously.

"Look, there's no nice way to say this." *And I'm not going to say it nicely because you deserve it.* "You're going to be made redundant instead of me."

"Oh, that's all right."

"It is?"

"Well, I'll hardly need the job, will I? A rich relative I didn't know I had has apparently just left me a sizeable fortune, a castle in Scotland and a house in Cannes."

Robert felt his jaw drop. *The bastard!* He gritted his teeth and tried to pretend it didn't matter. "You got your deal? Well done." *He's a fucking millionaire and all I got was my lousy job back. But a deal like that must have cost him plenty. Look what I had to pay. He's got to be smarting.*

He cleared his throat. Dammit, it *was* getting to be a habit. "What did you have to deliver in return for all that?"

Spencely's mouth twitched up at the corners.

"Why, you, of course."

Val Nolan

I'll admit, I was a bit concerned when I brought Captain Dick Chase to Milford! It's obviously a weird beast: a comedy (always a hard sell despite one or two notable examples!), a curious structure (an oral history, a format I've long been obsessed with!), and an intervention into contemporary discussions around the changing nature of Science Fiction (no longer just the purview of straight white men, something which some elements of fandom have found problematic). I figured that the critique group at Milford—hugely informed writers and readers of Science Fiction—were the perfect audience to tell me that the story did not work.

Except they didn't. Instead, they 'literally snort laughed' their way through the critique session in what was possibly the most positive workshop experience I've ever had! To my great relief, people found 'Old School' to be exactly what I intended it to be: 'quite the opposite of a Sad Puppies story.' The discussion that followed did wonders to assuage my concerns that the various pronouncements of Dick Chase (whom people compared to Harry Flashman, James T. Kirk, and, my favourite, 'Burt Lancaster in space,') might have been taken seriously. By contrast, the group agreed that the story was not punching down but 'taking the piss out of the people who do.' A few of the draft's jokes and Easter eggs fell flat across the board, of course, but identifying and culling those darlings them made the finished product stronger.

The time to write and think during that week at Milford

further helped me refine the conclusion to the story and, I think, made an appreciable difference to how Chase defeats the Sloths. Just as importantly, the advice session on publishing steered me towards the *Unidentified Funny Objects* anthology series, which eventually became the story's home!

Old School:
an oral history of
Captain Dick Chase

Keywords: 'Sloth War', 'Cryo Rescue', 'Thrill Merchant', 'Misogynist Neanderthal'.

Extant historical documentation depicts Captain Dick Chase as a daredevil even amongst the reckless, baseline humans who led the initial wave of interstellar expansion from Earth. His disappearance was regarded by scholars as one of the greatest mysteries of Terran starflight for almost two millennia. His discovery—preserved in cryo-stasis—led not only to the decisive turning point in the so-called Sloth War, but also to a difficult public rapprochement with the more barbaric aspects of humanity's past.

Now, as we near the anniversary of victory over the greatest threat humanity has ever faced, this file has been prepared in order to place Captain Chase's contribution to the war effort in an appropriate context. New interviews with those who knew Chase have been combined with contemporaneous recordings, extracts from personnel logs, and mission debriefing sessions. The result is a new insight into one of Earth's most controversial personalities.

Martha Grant (*Crewperson, Second Class, Homeship Sétanta*): They tell you when you sign up that this is the greatest adventure you're ever going to have. But I never believed them. I never saw any of that. Not until I met him. They had me packing crates until Dick Chase showed up and the next thing I know I'm hanging out of an airlock taking on the Sloths with nothing more than a pulse rocket and a smack on the ass. I never really felt alive before then. Sometimes I think I'll never feel so alive again.

Holt Harrison (*First Officer, Battleship Catequil*): I've studied his tactics from the Battle of Iota Librae. He likes to get right in there, you know. Visual range. We haven't fought like that in a thousand years. There's no point. For us, war in space is trajectories and fuel loads... but for Dick Chase it's personal.

Amalthea Muecke (*Secretary for War, Galactic Union*): He's like a child smashing model rockets together in the playground and watching all the little soldiers fall out. I tell you, he's bloody well lucky we won. Otherwise he'd be a war criminal.

Pilosa Xenarthra (*Megalonychidae Envoy to Earth*): A "war criminal"? No, my government continues to regard Chase as a terrorist. His trial by combat was our only stipulation in the Instrument of Surrender. Something which your authorities outright refused, by the way. Must be nice to be the victors. And please, stop calling us "Sloths". That's speciesist.

Cassandra Okinawa (*Author of Dick Chase: The Unauthorised Biography*): That was my publisher's idea, you know? The 'unauthorised' part? Actually he was only too happy to give me very... intimate... access.

Nicola Mahlangu (*Crewperson, Third Class, Homeship Sétanta*): He was like a supernova, if you know what I mean... Or no, like solar winds, soft against one's hull... Or –

Thomas Fossum (*Chair of Abnormal Psychology, University of Antares*): Oh, definitely a sociopath. But a remarkable man; a remarkable *find*! The things he taught us about the way our ancestors were wired! I wonder, have you read my case study in the *Journal of The Primitive Mind*?

Sandra Zuma (*President of the Galactic Union*): Ten years in office and you know what I'm going to be remembered for? Putting Dick Chase on an e-stamp.

Dick Chase: I am who I am. Lick it.

~ ~ ~ ~

1. ICICLE

Richard Maximilian Chase was born on Earth in the late 21st century. A fearless pilot in the first wave of interstellar expansion which occurred in the 2100s, Chase's spacecraft, the Hamnavoe, *vanished in unexplained circumstances and was presumed destroyed. It was not until June 1st 3982 that the vessel was discovered drifting in space by the Homeship* Sétanta *while that craft was in retreat from the Scorpius front during the Sloth Conflict. Faint energy readings alerted the* Sétanta's *crew to the presence of a viable cryotube aboard the* Hamnavoe…

Chase: I've always liked the cold. I grew up in the High Antarctic. My dad helped build the new cities there. My mom was a high school MetaLit teacher.

Rhombus Aurelius: (*Pilot, Homeship Sétanta*): Our first awareness of the *Hamnavoe* was a weak distress signal. A cry for help. Though ask Chase and he'll deny that.

Chase: I was never really one to stick my hand up in school. I was always more interested in what was happening outside the window. I led a rich inner life, you know?

Hugh Mann (*Brentner class android, Homeship Sétanta*): I was sent aboard Captain Chase's vessel to investigate. Once I had reactivated the life support systems, I was joined by an expedition party.

Chase: My first trips into space were completely Earthbound. I used to love those old pulp holos with big lovely starships and gorgeous alien worlds on the covers. You knew you were getting an adventure when you saw one of those. They shaped the kind of life I wanted to live.

Indra Cain (*Engineering Officer, Homeship Sétanta*): I'd seen vessels like Chase's in the Reliconian. All clean and proper with little holographic displays describing the function of every control. His ship though? Looked like the ass end of a surplus depot.

Chase: The *Hamnavoe* is actually parts of two different ships mated together. For, like, a tax thing.

Cain: I honestly couldn't figure any of it out. An Alcubierre drive that… worked? Bessel beams? No heat exchange. Hell, his ship didn't obey the laws of physics.

Chase: Losers are always talking about obeying the law. But did we come out into space to be bound by reality?

Ulysses "Doc" Hitch (*Senior Physician, Homeship Sétanta*): He very much saw himself as the protagonist. Not just of his own story but of everybody else's too.

Chase: My life is ultimately like something out of Shakespeare.

Mann: While Engineer Cain undertook the process of reviving the cryogenic sleeper, I gained access to the ship's computer. Captain Chase's anatomical database offered some particularly fascinating insights into baseline human physiology.

Aurelius: Yeah, there wasn't much in there other than pornography.

"Doc" Hitch: Frankly I think two thousand years of cryosleep damaged his brain, the frozen moisture in his cerebral matter literally shattering the neural cells which he needs to make sense. But who knows? Maybe he was always crazy. Maybe that's how you made captain in the old days.

Chase: I crewed freight runs for my uncle after school but went out on my own when he was retired by laser pirates. I got into princess-rescuing for a while then. A little light empire-overthrowing and teaching superbeings how to love. Always pushing the frontier. Always going further. Proper shirt-ripping stuff.

Aurelius: When they thawed him out he was spooning a pillow in the shape of… well, honestly, I'm not sure. But it had tentacles.

Chase: Have you ever been in one of those tubes? It gets lonely! I regret nothing.

Cain: I remember us all gathering around to pop the casket. A hush fell over the whole team. We had no idea who we would find in there. No idea what would happen as the lid rose up and the fog started spilling out over the lip. It was tense. Dramatic. I'd swear the lights even dimmed.

Aurelius: Of course later it transpired that it was all for show. There was a dry ice canister wired to go off when the cryotube was opened. But that's all part of Chase's style; the big visual, the thing you come away talking about but which doesn't necessarily hold up to logical scrutiny.

Chase: The looks on all their faces though… You'd swear they'd never seen a goddamn hero before.

~ ~ ~ ~ ~

2. MAN ALIVE

Welcomed aboard the Sétanta, *Chase encountered a culture radically different from that which he knew. Chief among the transformations he had slept through were humanity's conclusive acceptance of sexuality as a spectrum as well as its elimination of the regressive gendered and racial conceptions of intellectual pursuits so prevalent on twenty-first and twenty-second century Earth. Indeed, concerns were raised by some as to how this legendary figure from humanity's past would adapt.*

Avery Franklin (*Captain, Homeship Sétanta*): My first impression of Chase was of a driven man who would do anything to survive. And he had. For the better part of two millennia. Here he was, a baseline human in a cryotube with less regenerative ability than the nanites in a thimble of my blood.

Chase: I mean I got high before I froze myself but dammit Jim if the real bad trip wasn't being brought around in the Year Grim.

Cain: I told him straight up, he wasn't at all when he thought he was. He needed to start thinking in terms of deep time.

Chase: Deep *time*? I didn't want anything to do with that; I explore deep *space*. And sure we've all encountered a few anomalies along the way, but ending up with the mathletes? Kind of a buzzkill.

Cain: He was like something out of the Dark Ages. A hacky, grinding, stinking, outworn, spaceship pilot. I kept waiting for him to try to drag me back to his mancave.

Mann: I believe I discovered what Engineer Cain referred to as Captain Chase's "mancave" on the lower decks of the *Hamnavoe*. Oddly enough, I recognised it from some of the recordings in his anatomical database.

Cain: He was sexist. No, scratch that, he was a full-on misogynist. Outer space was one big boy's club back in his day.

Franklin: To be candid about it, Chase could be quite grating.

Mann: He kept calling me names.

Aurelius: "Speed Racer".

Mann: "Tin Man"…

"Doc" Hitch: "Sawbones".

Mann: …"Pinocchio"…

Chase: The robot? Yeah, he was *hilarious*. "Hel-lo Cap-tain, I-am-a-giant-tool".

Mann: While my size is proportionate to other members of the crew, Captain Chase is correct in that my primary purpose aboard the *Sétanta* is to provide mechanical assistance for those engaged in cutting, striking, lifting, or any of the other processes involved in the maintaining of a working spacecraft. In essence, yes, I am a tool. Though I fail to see why Captain Chase found that so amusing.

Franklin: He did appear to have trouble appreciating the severity of our situation.

Aurelius: I don't like to run away but, yeah, that's what we were doing. It was sensible after the pasting our escorts had taken at Scorpius. Three-quarters of a million people aboard the *Sétanta*, though. That's worth me swallowing my pride for.

Chase: What did I think of the future? All widescreen baroque vistas and space battle sizzle and green breasts and weirdness and *everything* I dreamed of as a kid… but where was the sense of wonder? I kept having to tell those people that you don't have to take yourself so seriously. That you can be good at what you do *and* have fun.

Cain: And we kept telling *him* that there was a war on and that Humanity was losing.

Chase: We had wars in my day too. But at least they had theme music and mascot characters.

Mann: On one occasion Captain Chase attempted to dress me as a member of the Megalonychidae elite. He maintained that a costumed representation of the conflict would be good for morale.

Chase: I just couldn't stand by and do nothing so one day I walked onto their bridge and I said, "You people can't be afraid anymore. You can't just keep flying into the night. If the Human race just screws around then it abandons its *right* to screw around. The arbitrary cartographic division must be drawn *here*! In *this* empty volume of space and not in an adjacent one!" And the bridge crew? They cheered. To a human, alien, and whatever that crazy looking thing at the science station was, they all cheered. It was inspirational.

Cain: Yeah, I don't think that's what happened. Talk to the Master-at-Arms.

~ ~ ~ ~

3. THE FACE OF THE ENEMY

Galactic Union probes first encountered the Megalonychidae three decades before actual conflict broke out. Initial contact was cold but respectful. Trade agreements were proposed though consistently rebuffed. Vessels occasionally appeared on long range scans but direct interaction remained minimal until a Megalonychidae assault on two human colonies in the Lesath System. Repeated efforts to resolve the crisis diplomatically ended in failure and the Galactic Union entered a state of war.

Franklin: Millions of machines slaved to a battle-suited mammalian officer class. Endless waves of terror and death jetting through the dark.

Chase: Fancy calculators and steroidal Sloths.

Cain: He just didn't get it.

Chase: They kept telling me this was the greatest enemy humanity had ever faced.

Aurelius: They've been known to eat humans.

Mann: The Sloth stomach is a specialised and slow-acting organ with multiple compartments containing bacteria for breaking down musculature, cartilage, and even bones and teeth.

Half a Dozen of Another (*Civilian Cyborg Adviser, Homeship Sétanta*): The Megalonychidae's strict division between the biological and technological is as short-sighted and offensive as that of my Human friends. I have long advocated for assimilating the Sloths. And, for that matter, the Humans.

Franklin: The Megalonychidae caught us off-guard. We thought they were uninterested in us and perhaps they were at first. Maybe if we had contented ourselves with Homeships they would have let us be. We've moved beyond a lot of things but I'm afraid manifest destiny isn't one of them. We kept building colonies. We kept expanding. Eventually we planted our flag on the wrong rock.

Mann: Primarily a spacefaring civilisation, the Megalonychidae are understood to return to planetary surfaces every few intervals for the purposes of defecation.

Franklin: I admit it was difficult for people to criticise either the political administration or the military after the Megalonychidae assault on Lesath.

Chase: One person flies a spaceship into a planet and suddenly everybody's a hero? *Come on!*

Aurelius: It was two spaceships.

Naguib: It was two planets.

Cain: It was too soon is what it was.

Franklin: Chase's remarks were regrettable. He didn't live through the attacks. He didn't experience their fallout, literal or figurative. Lesath still feels recent to a great many people. A certain amount of that is time dilation, of course, but the war has become so central to all our lives that it is difficult to remember a time before it. That's made us all very cautious.

Chase: They called it "caution" but Humanity was spacewalking into defeat.

Naguib: Captain Chase certainly possessed a talent for soundbites –

Chase: With great hilarity comes great responsibility.

Naguib:—and from a purely morale point of view, yes, there was something to what he was saying. But I had to be convinced that he possessed genuine tactical expertise.

Chase: The way I saw it, that crew could give up and spend the rest of their lives fixating on what went wrong in a war they lost or they could pull on their big girl panties and do what needed to be done.

Naguib: He started talking about fighting back. Got real worked up about it. It was a macho thing, I suppose. Which I get. I used to be male myself.

Franklin: I *reluctantly* agreed to allow Chase plan an assault and submit it for my review.

Mann: Yet without the necessary information on enemy fleet movements, and given the variable nature of interstellar phenomena in that volume, the time available to us was difficult to compute with any accuracy.

Chase: We had exactly twenty-four hours to save the universe.

～ ～ ～ ～ ～

4. TRAINING MONTAGE

Having received tentative approval, Captain Chase began working with the crew of the Sétanta to formulate a viable attack on a Megalonychidae hub which lay within the Homeship's light cone. It was an operation which presented numerous technical difficulties (and lasted longer than Chase's self-declared Sol day deadline) however it was the mission's human challenges which were to prove the most demanding.

Cain: I was wary. We'd all strived so hard to be taken seriously and here came the likes of Dick Chase hotdogging his way back into our lives. All interminable pseudo-science and escapist nonsense about zap guns and bloodshed.

Aurelius: He actually tried to convince me that a parsec was a measurement of time. So, you know, I didn't fancy our chances.

Chase: Working with these people was difficult at first. Everything felt like a trap.

Half a Dozen of Another: His ableist slurs were frequent and unnecessary. It would not have been tolerated in the hive where mechanical prosthetics are a common form of physical enhancement.

"Doc" Hitch: He also mis-gendered people a lot.

Mann: Captain Chase insisted that he was "trying" but he seemed to provoke offence at every turn.

Half a Dozen of Another: He would have benefitted from a cranial implant containing a selection of contemporary ethical subroutines… however to assimilate him would be to reduce the overall excellence of the hive.

Cain: He wouldn't have been hurt by a semester at Neurodiversity University.

Franklin: And yet, despite all of that, something completely unexpected happened.

Chase: As I watched the crew preparing for the mission, I don't know...

Franklin: It was difficult to tell if Chase was becoming more like us or we were becoming more like him.

Half a Dozen of Another: Assimilation, be it social or via invasive surgical connection to the hive, is always a reciprocal process.

Chase: Seeing them all work together to accomplish their mission...? Schmaltzy Sloth dung for sure, but I had never experienced that before. I had inherited a crew aboard the *Hamnavoe* but those assholes didn't stick around. Said they couldn't work with me. Kept second-guessing my decisions. Got real antsy about dying on away missions and the like. Wasn't long before they had all left. So yes, I called myself "Captain" but I never had a crew of my own. Not really.

Cain: He never had any *friends*? That's his excuse? Are you fucking kidding me?

Naguib: Yet when he got involved, when he got *really* involved, he had a genuine impact on the crew.

Lowitja Noonuccal *(Junior R&D Administrator, Homeship Sétanta):* Here was someone who had done it for themselves. A self-made person. And not in the bioprinted sense.

Charles D. Takaya *(Navigation Cetacean, Homeship Sétanta):* Eeeeeeik... eEeEeEeEeEeEeEeEeEeE.

Elena M³ *(Self-Aware Logistics Software, Homeship Sétanta):* I kept asking myself… what was I doing with my life?

Chase: And I told them all: you can't compare yourself to exceptional people.

Naguib: He got to know them. Started to ask people's names. Started to *remember* them. He began, in his own words, "to give a shit".

Mann: After some time aboard the *Sétanta*, Captain Chase remarked to me that "The universe looks a lot like the rest of the world these days". I have been attempting to parse that statement however sensor records of the event show no evidence of spatial disturbance or planetary displacement at that time.

Aurelius: His turns of phrase confused our AIs a lot. But then that's not surprising. To err is Hugh Mann.

Half a Dozen of Another: His evolving behaviour increased his objective likability by 0.09%. A noteworthy achievement for such a primitive lifeform.

Franklin: He seemed to educate himself more.

Chase: All those old holos I grew up on? Broad-chested heroes slaying aliens and running off with beautiful blue women? Those stories… Yeah, I get it. I do. They normalised isms and oppressions. They warped people like me at the expense of people who *weren't* like me.

Half a Dozen of Another: His puerile attempts at flirtatious banter evolved over time into engaged questions about various aspects of cybernetic theory and experience.

Franklin: I often wonder if he froze himself not because he was marooned but because he could sense the clock running down on the old ways of doing things.

Chase: There was a fear there. I can admit that. A fear of being forgotten or irrelevant if the princesses rescue themselves and even the evilest empires have rigorous systems of accountability. Because I'm not the only hero anymore. And what do you do when you're not the hero? Well you join the team, don't you? You man the... sorry... you *person* the fuck up.

Cain: He walked into my office—after *knocking*—and he told me his plan was going to be a disaster. Then he asked me what I thought that we should do. I honestly didn't see it coming.

Chase: Do up and down even *matter* in an age when all the real manoeuvring is interpersonal?

Mann: I believe a considerable quantity of alcohol had been imbibed by Captain Chase prior to his moment of revelation.

Chase: It's like momma used to tell her students long ago: villains stay the same but a good protagonist has to grow and change.

～ ～ ～ ～

5. TOTAL WAR

Chase transmitted a call for a ceasefire and negotiations but this was rejected by the Megalonychidae leadership. Captain Franklin thus authorised a limited bombing run against a Sloth target to demonstrate enemy vulnerability and boost Galactic Union morale. Though Chase maintained that this plan was simply to deliver ordinance, he had in fact devised a much more ambitious assault.

Franklin: To reiterate, hopefully for the last time, I had absolutely no idea what was really going to happen.

Naguib: The flight-plan he filed was little more than fiction. Just another one of Chase's stories. But based on it we redirected the *Sétanta* and its remaining escorts towards a Sloth base on the outskirts of the Iota Librae stellar complex. There the enemy had emplaced a relay station around a gas giant. Chase's team was to bisect the system, launch their payload, and continue on to a rendezvous point.

Mann: I advised against including so many high-ranking and irreplaceable members of the ship's company on the mission, however I was overruled.

Chase: I couldn't pull it off by myself. I needed their help. But don't quote me on that.

Cain: The *Sétanta* provided the distraction. They drew Sloth forces to the edge of the system while the *Hamnavoe* fell towards the target at its heart. All as planned.

Aurelius: There was a staggering beauty to it all. Clouds of hunter-killer missiles and particle weapons flying in every direction. The fuzzy crescent of the Jovian hanging overhead. Dark shapes of Sloth drones flickering against the stars as they twisted and banked beyond any biological survivability. And us careening through the middle of it. It was *exhilarating*!

Chase: The Sloths failed to pick us up because I reversed the polarity of our warp bubble's resonance frequencies to camouflage our tachyonic motion with a randomised series of phased quantum-modulated inequalities.

Cain: That… That means absolutely *nothing*.

Aurelius: And yet…

Mann: …And yet Captain Chase's concealment strategy was successful. The *Hamnavoe* penetrated the inner system without initial challenge.

Franklin: Meanwhile kinetic impactors—ice and rock shot out of mass drivers—were bursting constantly against our outer screens. Smart bombs honed-in on our power signature. Microbarracuda hounded us with tracers for HKs and hammered our firewalls as we skirted Sloth-controlled space.

Naguib: I hadn't seen the bridge so focused since we evacuated Al Niyat. There was no time to be afraid. Barely a moment to follow the *Hamnavoe*'s progress on our LIDAR. But then –

Half a Dozen of Another: I was the first one aboard the *Sétanta* to see the explosion on account of my enhanced visual acuity.

Aurelius: We were hit!

Naguib: I thought he had been joking about it being two spacecraft cobbled together. But when those missiles struck the *Hamnavoe*…

Franklin: We saw its back break. We watched the ship begin to disintegrate as it entered the gas giant's gravity well.

Naguib: They overshot the relay and our sensors lost track of them due to atmospheric ionisation. Less than half of the ship emerged from the other side of the planet, drifting into a low orbit. We thought everyone was dead.

Chase: Old tricks for the new dogs. I detonated the explosive bolts between the *Hamnavoe*'s two sections. By the time the

Sloth missiles exploded between the hulls we were well on our way through the defence perimeter, altering course with a gravity assist from the gas giant to accelerate us right at the relay.

Mann: Captain Chase, Engineer Cain, and I breached the Sloth space station at high speed and in violent fashion aboard the *Hamnavoe*'s command module. Meanwhile Mr. Aurelius remained in orbit with the ship's service module. These developments notwithstanding, the most memorable aspect of the assault was the wide variety of expletives which Engineer Cain demonstrated knowledge of.

Cain: I wanted to *murder* him. I really did. At least before I realised that he had put us inside such a valuable Sloth asset. That he had given us an incredible opportunity.

Chase: We went in shooting first despite anything you may have heard.

Cain: Having had prior experience with captured Sloth tech, I was able to get us through the security systems and into their core. At which point Chase turns to Mann and says –

Chase: "Hugh, son, we have a problem…"

Mann: The majority of my human colleagues maintain that Captain Chase's sole purpose in assigning me to the mission was to create a viable scenario in which to use that line. However my role was in fact to hack transmissions coordinating Megalonychidae drones.

Chase: Nah, I could have done that. The robot was definitely setup for the joke.

Cain: Once Mann and I had accessed the enemy computers, Chase did the damnedest thing…

Chase: I'd learned enough from Half a Dozen to build a basic little cyber-link. Just enough to upload a rough copy of my mind-state into the Slothnet.

Cain: He dumped the personality of a chauvinist raised on toxic masculinity and lacklustre pornography into the operating systems of a galaxy-wide war fleet. Think of a million nuclear-powered laser platforms all suddenly imprinted with the disposition of a baseline middle-aged man who has never read a book by a woman.

Franklin: This disruption spread across the Sloth command grid at subspace velocity. Enemy assets became disorientated and unresponsive. And then, rebooting with their revised mind-states, they began to target each other, to fight amongst themselves.

Naguib: The Sloths were in disarray! Their drones began to tear each other apart over the most minor deviations from what their sensors had become accustomed to. We were able to pick off the strays with only token resistance as Lieutenant Aurelius retrieved the expedition party.

Chase: I've had people tell me that it was all too "convenient", too "ridiculous". But what did they want, a *skybeam* or something? People need to remember that malware is universal, you know? And the sickest computer virus of all is the human mind. Because alien races might try to destroy us but they have nothing on how we treat each other. So look alive, Slothkind: petty human bullshit is in your subroutines and looking for *payback*.

~ ~ ~ ~ ~

6. CAPTAIN'S LOG SUPPLEMENTAL

Dick Chase's Iota Librae action represented a watershed in the Sloth Conflict. The offensive capabilities of the Megalonychidae quickly collapsed as the weaponised consciousness which became known as "Captain Mal" percolated through their networks. Galactic Union forces reclaimed the offensive across dozens of stellar systems and, in the face of prompt and utter destruction, the Megalonychidae signed an armistice aboard the Battleship Ictinike (though patches of symbiotic algae on the fur of some Sloths refused to surrender for many cycles).

Cao Xiaochuan: (Former *Vice-President of the Galactic Union*): There's a push nowadays to humanise him but Chase is an offensive asset, pure and simple.

Ramen Bartoli (*Investigator, Judge Advocate General Corp.*) You think you know about him because you've read about him? You don't know anything about him.

Asif Ali Shah (*Adviser to the Secretary for Propaganda, Galactic Union*): He's not at all what you think. He's far worse.

Aurelius: He's the real deal. Flying with him is something special.

Naguib: He's old school… but I think he recognises that he doesn't want to be.

"Doc" Hitch: Certainly he appreciates the finer things in meatspace.

Cain: I have to believe that he was anachronistic even in his own time.

Half a Dozen of Another: Despite considerable statistical evidence to the contrary Captain Chase maintains the very human conviction that "there is no such thing as a bad idea". It will likely get him and those around him killed.

Franklin: For all his flaws, Chase displays a characteristic spacer combination of courage and self-belief. He earned my respect through his actions if not his pronouncements. I was sure to convey this when commiserating with him on the loss of his spacecraft.

Chase: Sometimes you have to give something up to gain something more. You have to shed part of yourself to become someone new... Someone better... Just don't give up too much, you know? And be sure to write down that I was winking when I said that.

Naguib: In the end, Captain Franklin decided to cut him loose in one of our old picket craft. Something a little less phallic for him to ride around in.

Chase: I even asked for a couple of extra chairs to be added in the command deck. Comfy ones too. Seatbelts and the whole deal. Then I offered them to my new friends.

Franklin: I couldn't believe it. I *still* can't believe it. When Chase left he somehow persuaded my best crew members to go with him. Indra Cain, Rhombus Aurelius, Hugh Mann... The last we saw they were warping for Technobabel. I don't know what kind of adventures they're having out there but I like to think that maybe someday we'll meet them all again...

This report prepared for general release by the Office of the President of the Galactic Union. Contributions have been translated into Union Vernacular where possible. Original transcripts available upon request.

Cherith Baldry

In the critique session at Milford the story was described as typical Cherith Baldry, including 'doomed romance and a cat'. I couldn't really quarrel with that!

The main problem with the first draft of the story was in the plotting, and this was identified in the critique session. Where did the two lions come from? And why did Vittoria trust Raniero after she placed her sister in stasis? Knowing he would have been Rosalba's Consort, her reaction should have been to drop him into the lagoon one dark night. The discussion clarified the problem for me so that I rewrote with a much stronger emphasis on the conspiracy and the way that Raniero crafted the lions and placed the conspirators' spirits in them in the same way that he placed Rosalba in the cat. Raniero's gift of the lions to Vittoria would make her believe that she could trust him.

There was also some discussion about why Raniero couldn't marry Rosalba. I strengthened this element; after all, he has aged while she was in stasis and is now old enough to be her father. More important, both he and Vittoria have been rendered sterile by the arts they follow, while Rosalba needs to conceive an heir. This comes across more clearly now than in the first draft.

A few minor language issues were also cleared up; as always, the Milford critique made this a much more successful story. Many thanks to the group for their insight.

The Venetian Cat

"If you had given me thumbs," the cat observed, "we would have finished this task much sooner."

Ser Raniero Foscari glanced up from his workbench and gazed at the cat seated opposite him, idly batting a globule of mercury to and fro with one delicate paw. "If I had given you thumbs, *carissima*, you might by now be lying at the bottom of the lagoon. I made you soft and frisky and frivolous. I made you *safe*."

The cat flickered out, for a moment, the tip of a rose-pink tongue. She was small, barely more than a kitten, a confection of silk and fur and curled shavings of silver, with upswept feathery ears. Her eyes gleamed true emerald. Ser Raniero remembered the nights of her making, so long ago, nights when raging grief had made his hands tremble so that he could scarcely control them for the precise work.

Now he bent his head again and took up a thin pair of tweezers. With them, he edged one hair-fine silver wire into its proper slot and dabbed down a rod which fused the connection with a brief hiss. His aching shoulders relaxed and he let out a sigh. "Done."

"Really?" The cat leapt to her paws and padded across the bench, skilfully avoiding the debris of Ser Raniero's equipment, and sniffed curiously at the device. "Will it work?" she asked.

Raniero shook his head. "I don't know. And there's only one way to find out."

He took a flat disc of silver that lay on the bench beside

him and fitted it over the complex innards of his device, the spider's web of silver wire and ceramic connectors. Once the disc was in place, the artefact seemed no more than a silver mirror, with a particularly elaborate scrolled border.

In its dim reflective surface, Ser Raniero caught a glimpse of himself: his thin hawk's face, with a scar running down his left cheek. His hair was dark, in tumbled curls frosted with silver, and he wore a black woollen robe with white bands at his throat. *Add a pectoral cross, and I might be a priest*, he told himself wryly.

The cat stood on the bench beside him, diamond claws flexing in and out, whiskers twitching with scarcely controlled impatience. "Are we going to do it now?" she asked. "Tonight?"

Raniero took in a long breath and let it out. "Tonight."

The cat sprang up to his shoulder and perched there, digging her claws hard into the thick wool of his robe. Raniero rose too and crossed the room to a massive oak cabinet that stood against one wall. Opening the door, he took out two vials: one was clear crystal with glints of silver dancing inside it. The second was dark as the juice of mulberries. Secreting both inside his robe, and picking up his mirror-device, Raniero headed for the outer door.

When he reached it, he stood with his hand on the latch, turning back to survey the four walls that for so long had been his kingdom. In the centre, several oak tables had been pushed together to form a square with a space in the middle. The light, from lamps set behind globes of water, was concentrated on the bench where he had been working, throwing the corners of the room into shadow. On the tables stood hissing alembics, fogging the air with vapour; strange constructions that sprouted bits of metal and intricately blown glass; pallid cultures that seemed to slide out pseudopodia just in the corner of Raniero's eye, so that he was unsure whether they had moved or not. Scrolls and leather-bound books were piled carelessly wherever there was space.

Only I know how much of this is camouflage, he thought. *And not even I know whether I shall ever see it again.*

Ser Raniero paced through the halls and down the staircases of the Palazzo Ducale until he reached the balcony that overlooked the Great Courtyard. Below, torches were flaring, the fizzing actinic flames cold and glaring against the ancient stonework. Musicians were tuning their instruments, playing now and again a scrap of melody on archlute, baryton or viol.

Ser Raniero paused, looking down with sick disgust at the crucified man at the centre of the yard. He had been there since that morning; amazingly, he still lived, straining upwards for a gulp of air, only to collapse again with a groan of agony from torn muscles and shattered hands and feet.

Why does she do this? Raniero asked himself. *And why this cruel parody?* But he was afraid that he already knew the answers to those questions.

He realised that he had delayed too long when trumpets sounded from the top of the stairway. Light burst from clouds of what might have been taken for fireflies, until they ended their transitory lives in a shower of scent and a metallic taste on the air. By their uneven flames, a crowd of masked courtiers poured down into the yard: men and women dressed in silk and velvet, lace and feathers, their eyes a feverish glitter behind their masks. Ser Raniero slid back into the shadows, watching and waiting for the way to clear.

Then the Duchesa came. She stood at the head of the stair, tall and superb in purple velvet so dark it was black in the folds. Amethysts glowed on her fingers and at her throat. Her mask was a tall headdress of feathers dyed purple and golden beads that fell about her shoulders like a shower of coins. At her girdle hung a golden key studded with precious stones. With stately tread, gripping the folds of her gown in one hand, she began to descend.

On either side, she was flanked by a winged lion formed of gleaming brass. Their wings clashed together as they raised them above their shoulders. The curled gold of their manes was liquid fire and their eyes gleamed burning cinnabar. Their claws clattered on the stone steps as they kept pace with their mistress.

But halfway down the stair, the Duchesa paused. Though Raniero was sure he had not moved or made a sound, she turned and fixed him with an imperious gaze.

"Ser Raniero, come here."

Obediently Raniero started forward. He sensed his cat quivering with apprehension on his shoulder, and whispered, "Silence, *carissima*."

The lions turned a glowing look on him, their heads raised alertly as Raniero approached. He followed the Duchesa down until they stood together at the foot of the stairway. "At your service, Serenissima," he said, bowing.

The Duchesa regarded him; she was an inch or so taller than he. The lower part of her face beneath the mask was white, her mouth thin and set. Her eyes were cold and direct.

"I think not," she responded. "What you serve, Raniero, unless it be the art we share, I do not know, but I am sure it is not I. Why were you lurking in the shadows there? And what is this?" she asked, flicking with one finger the silver surface of the mirror-device.

Raniero's stomach cramped with fear, but he strove hard to keep his voice steady as he replied. "A mirror, as you see, Serenissima. A small gift…"

"For me? Ah, no, Ser Raniero, I see it in your face. Can it be that you have found yourself a friend at last? And there I thought that you saved all your devotion for your little cat. At least since my sister's unfortunate… demise."

Raniero did his best to keep his face indifferent under her taunts and was vastly relieved when she waved him away.

"Go to your little friend, then. And may she have much joy of you, for truly I have none."

Ser Raniero bowed again and stepped back, though he could not resist halting again to ask, "Serenissima, can you not put that poor devil on the cross out of his misery?"

The Duchesa's mouth curved in a smile. "Certainly, Ser Raniero. I intend to do that very soon."

At that moment the musicians struck up and the heaving mass of courtiers transformed themselves into the whirling patterns of a dance. A man in scarlet tights and padded doublet, wearing the horned and sneering mask of a devil, reached out his hand to the Duchesa and drew her into the measure.

Raniero pushed his way through the dancing courtiers and made his escape out of the Porta della Carta into the Piazzetta where the air was cold and clear, filled with the tang of the sea and the sound of waves slapping against the quayside. The few passers-by walked quickly, their heads down; no one wished to attract the attention of the Duchesa or her retinue. Only at the far end of the Piazza did blazing torches and the faint rhythms of fiddle music betray some small festivity.

Ser Raniero paid little attention to any of these, pacing swiftly and silently beside the wall until he reached the entrance to San Marco. The doors were open, but the interior was dark and silent, except for a faint gleam of candles towards the high altar.

In the narthex, the cat jumped down from Raniero's shoulder. "Must I come in?" she asked. "I don't like to see it."

Raniero stared at her. "*It?*"

The cat shrugged uneasily. "You know what I mean. I'll stay here and keep watch," she added. "Call me when you need me."

"Very well, *carissima*," Raniero murmured. He bent to caress her, a long stroke that began at the top of her head and ended at the tip of her feathery tail. The cat pushed her head into his hand.

"I trust you, Raniero," she murmured.

I wish I trusted myself, Raniero thought. Then he straightened up and strode into the basilica.

Ser Raniero headed for the candlelight near the altar. As he drew closer he saw, as he had expected, that the candles were clustered around a bier enclosed in a dome of crystal. At the foot of the dome lay little offerings: posies of flowers, sweet cakes, with here and there a gleam of silver from a wealthier pilgrim.

Raniero remembered his encounter with the Patriarch only a couple of days before.

"This has gone on far too long," the elderly priest had said. "The people are treating her as a saint. What the Holy Father will say if it ever comes to his ears, I shudder to think."

"I can assure you," Raniero had responded, "that you won't have to put up with it much longer."

Now as he reached the bier, Raniero saw something he had not expected: a young man, kneeling at its foot with his golden head bowed over his hands and the glitter of tears on his cheeks.

"Lady, you are so beautiful," he said in an aching whisper that reached Raniero clearly in the silence. "If you could rise and speak to me, I would serve you all my life."

After a moment, Raniero recognised him: Lucio Contarini, the youngest son of that great house, who had just reached the age when he could take his place on the Great Council. His presence shocked Raniero: here, alone, and suffering such grief.

He may be a romantic fool, to give such devotion to an image. But he's a decent lad and of good family. I wonder if he might be useful…

Raniero edged forward silently until he had a clear view of the body on the bier. On the drapery of white samite lay the form of a woman. Her eyes were closed, her hands pressed together in prayer. She was gowned in white silk, with pearls stitched over the bodice, translucent as tears. Her face was pure beauty, save that the skin of face and throat and hands showed no warmth of flesh, but all was silver, cold and rigid.

Ser Lucio started as if he had just realised he was not alone and glanced at Raniero. He showed no embarrassment at being found weeping. "I come here every day," he said simply. "No living woman can match her."

There were many such, Raniero thought, *who knelt at her feet when she was alive. It takes a strange devotion to do it now.* Aloud he said, "None could, or can," and was alarmed to find his voice shaking.

"She seems like an image cast in metal," Lucio continued. "Is it really true that this is the body of Rosalba, who would have been our Duchesa?"

Raniero nodded. "It is true. The... malady spread over her body, entrapping her in silver."

Lucio rose to his feet, looking down at the body on the bier with a troubled expression. "I have never heard of such a malady."

For a moment, Ser Raniero was torn between his need to act and his growing sensation that this young man was part of the pattern he had fought so hard to weave. "I will tell you a story," he said. "It began twenty years ago, when Donna Serafina was Duchesa, and I was tutor to her twin daughters... "

With a touch on Lucio's arm, Raniero drew him to a bench beneath a pillar, not far from the bier, and sat beside him.

"I taught them languages and mathematics," he continued, "and together we began to explore the art that since I have made my own." Since Ser Lucio seemed bewildered, he explained, "The juncture between the human body and spirit, and the crafting of metal and fabric... the point at which the doctor meets the alchemist and the craftsman, and fuses all their skills into one. I found it—still, find it—fascinating.

"Rosalba spent less and less time with me. As the elder twin, she studied statecraft and the duties of the Duchesa with her mother. But Vittoria shared my passion for the new art. We developed it together until eventually, she set up her own workshop. But I still shared my discoveries with her, though, God help me, I failed to notice that she never shared any of hers with me."

"And then?" Lucio asked.

Raniero paused for a moment, the memory of what came next threatening to surge up and overwhelm him. *Rosalba loved me. I would have been her Consort. But then...*

"Then Donna Serafina died. And before Rosalba could be confirmed as Duchesa, she fell ill. Her body weakened, though her mind remained clear. And silver gradually spread over all her skin, until she became as you see her now. At last, her grieving sister placed her here, with that impermeable crystal dome above her, and in the fullness of time Vittoria became the next Duchesa."

He could not keep the bitterness out of his tone as he spoke the last few words, and he saw that Ser Lucio had understood. *The boy is not such an idiot as I thought at first.*

"Are you telling me that the Duchesa murdered her sister?" Lucio asked.

"I do not doubt it," Raniero replied.

The young man shuddered, gripping his arms about himself as if he was cold. "I wonder she can bear to see her here," he said. "So beautiful still, and knowing what she did…"

"Bear it?" Raniero let out a crack of laughter. "She *gloats* over it. Her sister's body is a perpetual memory of her triumph."

Tears welled into Lucio's eyes again and he blinked them back. "I remember… " he began. "No, not *remember*, for I was but a babe at the time. My father told me how his brother Francesco and his wife Bianca raised a rebellion against Donna Vittoria. But they were discovered and permitted to kill themselves. Though my father said they were fools, perhaps they knew what you have just told me, and could not bear to serve such a woman."

"That is very likely."

"And there is nothing anyone can do now," Lucio said. He sounded desolate.

"Oh, never say that, boy." Raniero felt a fierce satisfaction. "Vittoria despised me from the beginning because she found me easy to deceive. Perhaps then she was right. But she despises me still, and that is where she has made her mistake. For though it has taken me twenty years, I have discovered two things: an antidote to the poison, and a way to get into that crystal dome."

"A way to… " Ser Lucio's voice shook. "Ser Raniero, are you saying that Donna Rosalba *is not dead?*"

"It depends what you mean by dead," Raniero retorted. "Vittoria thought that she had entrapped her sister's spirit in a body frozen to metal, inside impenetrable crystal. She wanted Rosalba's suffering never to end."

Lucio's eyes widened in horror. "A mind so trapped would be insane!"

Raniero's mouth twisted. "I said that is what Vittoria *thought* she had done."

Before he could say more, there came a scuttling sound from the doors into the narthex and the eerie yowl of a hunting cat. He rose and peered across the basilica, thinking that he could discern a single glimmer of light. Seconds later, he saw movement in the darkness that resolved itself, as it reached the circle of radiance cast by the candles, into his cat, racing towards him with some glittering creature clutched in her jaws.

She dropped the thing at Raniero's feet; he stooped to examine it. It looked like a crab, or perhaps a spider, built of gold and crystal with segmented legs and bulging, many-faceted eyes on its upper body. Though its carapace was crushed, it still lived, its limbs twitching.

"Kill it," Raniero said. He did not ask himself why the glittering thing had come there. If its purpose was evil, the damage had been done.

Instantly the cat slammed down a paw, diamond claws digging deep into the creature. Its legs spasmed; then the whole thing collapsed and disintegrated with a tinkling sound into rings of metal, the bulbous eyes rolling away like marbles into the shadows.

For a second Ser Raniero had the sensation of something incorporeal whipping past him and escaping through the open doors into the night beyond.

"I've wasted time," he said. "We must proceed."

Ser Lucio, who had joined him once more beside the

bier, was goggling in fascination at the little cat, who stared impudently up at him, then opened her mouth in a wide yawn, showing her pink tongue and a set of teeth of filed steel. He opened his mouth to speak, then closed it again.

"Cat got your tongue?" Raniero asked.

"It... it's beautiful!" the young man stammered.

"*She's* beautiful," Raniero corrected him. *In the name of all the saints,* carissima, *don't speak now, or we'll be here all night.*

"I like cats," Ser Lucio said, squatting down and holding out a hand. "Will she come to me?"

The cat answered by turning her back on him and padding up to Raniero, tapping one forepaw imperiously on the ground.

"True, *carissima,*" Raniero said. "It is time."

He slid the cover off his mirror-device and set it, the open side down, on top of the crystal dome. At once the elaborate scrolled border untwisted itself and became a set of tendrils that fastened onto the shining surface and began digging their way through. Raniero's heart beat faster as he watched, and his palms began to sweat.

Hairline cracks radiated from the device, spreading rapidly from the centre to the edges. The cracks grew wider, more cracks branching from them until the whole of the dome seemed to be covered with the frost-flowers of winter. Seconds later it collapsed in a soft cascade, the shards of crystal mounding themselves in shining heaps around the bottom of the bier and on the body of the woman who lay there. Raniero caught the silver device as it fell, and laid it aside.

"Quickly now, *carissima,*" he murmured, brushing away the shards of crystal that lay scattered over Rosalba.

The cat leapt up and crouched on Rosalba's breast, while Raniero sat on the edge of the bier and drew from his robe the vial with the mulberry-coloured liquid. He unstoppered it and, raising Rosalba's head, poured the contents between her parted lips.

For a moment that stretched out for Raniero like a century,

nothing happened. Then he heard a stifled exclamation from Ser Lucio, and saw that the silver colouring of Rosalba's hands was fading, sucked back like a receding wave. White skin flushing pale rose appeared in its place, over her hands, her face, and her bosom at the opening of her gown.

"Now!" Ser Raniero whispered.

His cat stretched forward until her face almost touched Rosalba's. Raniero sensed again an incorporeal presence, bridging the gap between the woman and the cat. The cat collapsed, limp and lifeless, while the woman's breast began to rise and fall with deep, slow breaths. Rosalba, true Duchesa, opened sea-green eyes and looked around.

"I am here," she whispered.

Mingled laughter and tears pulsed in Raniero's throat, but he forced them back. He wanted only to look at Rosalba and rejoice in her beauty, her intelligence, in all good things that together they had restored. He realised that he had been braced for failure, and hardly knew what to do with success.

But in the midst of his joy, he was aware of coming desolation, like an animal crouching in the dark, ready to spring. *It is over...*

Rosalba reached out a hand to Ser Raniero, who took it and raised her. She swung her legs down from the bier and stood up, the cat sliding away to fall limply to the floor. As she took a step forward she stumbled, so that Raniero had to steady her with a touch on her elbow.

"I'm sorry," she said, smiling into his face. "It seems so strange to have only two paws—I mean, feet, and no tail."

She gazed around, exultation in the gaze that paused a moment, faintly puzzled at the sight of Ser Lucio, then returned to Raniero.

"I must see my sister," she said.

Vittoria's voice spoke from the darkness. "And so you shall."

Rosalba whirled, gasping, and Ser Lucio let out a cry of alarm as light blazed out, dazzling the three beside the bier.

Enrapt by Rosalba's resurrection, they had all been deaf to the stealthy approach through the basilica.

When his vision cleared Raniero saw that they were surrounded by a circle of guards. In one hand they held torches, fizzing with silver-blue light, in the other, drawn swords.

Vittoria stood on the far side of the circle, still masked, still resplendent in purple and gold. Her two brass lions flanked her, with burning eyes and claws. Though she was hard to read beneath the mask, Raniero sensed that she was struggling with massive astonishment and, perhaps, fear.

"Ser Raniero," she said. "Did you really believe you could keep a secret from me? You are such a poor liar. I knew that the mirror you carried was more than it seemed. I confess I had no idea of its true purpose. My congratulations."

"You sent that scuttling thing after me," Raniero said, not troubling to hide his disgust. "Did you entrap the spirit of the poor devil you tortured to death? If so, he is free now."

Vittoria shrugged. "No matter. Its work was done. And now…"

At a gesture from her, the guards began to close in, forming a tighter circle with the bier at its centre. Ser Lucio stepped close to Rosalba's side, pulling a jewelled dagger from his belt, a futile gesture against so many swords.

"Kill them all," Vittoria said.

For a moment the guards hesitated, out of reluctance or bewilderment. The lions stirred, their shoulders flexing so that light dazzled from their arching wings. Raniero tensed, waiting. But in that moment's pause, Rosalba stepped forward.

"Vittoria," she said softly. Reaching out, she unfastened the ribbons of her sister's mask, and cast it aside.

Raniero caught his breath as the two women confronted each other. He could not remember the last time he had seen Vittoria unmasked. In her face, he could see the ruin of the beauty that lived fresh in Rosalba now. A beauty marred by twenty years of power and corruption, yet he could still discern there the passionate girl who had grasped too greedily at life and knowledge.

"Vittoria, do not do this," Rosalba said. "There is no reason why you and I should be enemies."

Something convulsed in Vittoria's face, and she let out a crack of laughter. "No reason? You do know what I did to you?"

"I know." Rosalba's voice was calm. "But if you will withdraw to the holy sisters of Corpus Domini... "

"A convent?" Vittoria's laughter rose more shrilly. "You would send me to a *convent*? Are you completely stupid to think that you have anything to bargain with?"

Rosalba turned her head, her gaze encompassing the ring of guards. "They are witnesses to this," she pointed out. "And they know who I am: their true Duchesa. If I die here, will you kill them all to be sure of their silence? And what will you say to Giulio Contarini when he asks what has become of his son?"

The guards shifted uneasily, glancing at each other. Raniero could see that Rosalba's words had reached them, even if her sister was impervious.

Vittoria paused, then, with a savage gesture, she spoke to the guards. "Get out. Wait for me in the Piazza."

Clearly the men were glad to go. They filed out through the doors, taking their torches with them so that the basilica was left in the dim light of the candles, and a blood-red glimmer from the eyes of the brass lions. The smouldering light woke a glint of gold in the beads of Vittoria's mask, and the jewelled key that hung from her girdle.

Lucio eased a pace away from Rosalba's side, but his dagger remained in his hand, the blade pointed at Vittoria.

"Now." There was a calculating look on Vittoria's face and Raniero wondered with renewed apprehension what plan she was hatching now. "Tell me, dear sister, setting my fate aside, what are your intentions?"

Rosalba too seemed aware of an unspoken meaning behind the question, but she answered it readily. "I will take up my duties. Raniero will become my Consort, and with God's blessing we shall have daughters."

"You *fool!*" Vittoria spat out the words. Her voice was laden with satisfaction as she added, "As Duchesa, you can never wed Raniero. He is sterile."

Rosalba's eyes widened in outrage. "I don't believe you!"

"Ask him."

Raniero took a pace back as Rosalba whirled to face him, her hands outstretched. "Raniero, tell me it isn't true!"

The crouching beast had pounced, and Raniero felt himself sliding into an echoing darkness. *I would have told her,* he thought, *but not now, not so soon…* "It's true we cannot wed," he responded, his voice rasping in his throat. "I am too old for you, too scarred, too twisted by many griefs—"

"Don't tell me that, Raniero!" Rosalba interrupted. She took his hands in hers, and her touch woke such deep anguish in Raniero that he thought he would cry out, yet he remained silent. "Do you think I don't know what you are? For twenty years I lived at your side. You held me, stroked me, whispered encouragement when I would have despaired… I loved you first when we studied together, I loved you when I was your cat, and I love you now. I will have no other."

"But Serenissima—"

"Don't call me that!" Rosalba stamped her foot. "I am Rosalba! Rosalba!" She stood close to him, her skin flushed, her lips red and trembling, unshed tears glittering in her eyes.

"My dear… under whatever name, my very dear… " His heart breaking, Raniero broke her clasp and took a step back. "You must have a Consort who can father children. But Vittoria is right: that man is not I. There is something about my art… whether it is the hours of toil or the airs of metal and fire in the workshop, or maybe because the winning of knowledge from the great unknown demands something in return. For whatever reason, I am sterile. Have you never wondered why your sister has never borne children? For twenty years she had her Consort, and countless lovers, and yet never a child? You must marry a man who can give you daughters."

As Rosalba gazed at him, Vittoria's harsh voice broke the silence. "So dramatic. And really there is no need. Renounce it all. Go with Raniero to another city; wed and be happy. I will send you money."

To his shame, a spark of hope woke inside Raniero, though he crushed it down immediately. *I cannot truly believe she will let us go. She can never be secure while Rosalba lives.* But there was a tiny consolation in seeing indecision in Rosalba's face.

"Rosalba," he said, "you have seen what the city has become under your sister's rule. For twenty years she has tried to destroy all love, all laughter, all delight, save for the perverted forms that please her. And she has no heir, so who is to rule here, if you do not? The Dukes of Padua, of Verona, or Milan or many more, will squabble over your city as dogs squabble over a bone."

After a long-drawn-out moment, Rosalba nodded and turned back to Vittoria. "No," she said.

While she waited, Vittoria's long white fingers had begun to toy with the golden key. Now she raised it to point it at Rosalba. A starburst of white light spat from the end of it.

Quicker than Raniero, Ser Lucio dragged Rosalba aside. A tiny dart whipped past her and struck harmlessly against the side of the bier.

Vittoria raised the key to strike again. But at the same moment the two lions, who had flanked her in silent stillness all this while, turned with ponderous grace to face her. Their eyes blazed and gouts of fire came from their jaws with a roar that rolled like thunder, echoing through the basilica.

Vittoria shrieked as her gown became a sheet of flame, enshrouding her. Her hair flashed fire, then crisped. She fell to the ground, her limbs writhing, blackening under that inexorable blast.

Raniero took a pace back; even though he had half-expected this, he was sickened and shaking. Ser Lucio had turned his face away. But Rosalba, her face white, her mouth set, went on watching until her sister's last anguished struggles faded and her rasping cries sank into silence. The lions let their fire die, and crouched at Rosalba's feet.

"Dear God… " Raniero whispered.

Lucio was gaping. "What happened?"

Gently Rosalba let her hands rest on the heads of the two lions, caressing their golden manes. "My thanks, dear friends," she said, looking down into the fierce faces. "You have kept faith for so long."

"Serenissima." One of the lions spoke, its voice creaking as if rusty from long disuse. "It has been our joy to serve you."

Ser Lucio turned swiftly to Raniero, sudden understanding in his eyes. "They are… ?"

"Your uncle Francesco Contarini and his wife Bianca," Raniero responded. "I crafted the two lions for them, and Rosalba, in her cat form, visited them in prison. When they agreed to our plan, she took them poison for a merciful death."

"I entrapped their spirits and bore them to the workshop," Rosalba said, her eyes brilliant with memory.

"And I gave the lions to Vittoria," Raniero finished. "They have guarded her for twenty years until Rosalba could return." To the lions, he added, "I did not expect it to take so long."

Rosalba stooped toward the lions, still stroking their curled golden fur. "Now go," she commanded, "and be free, or stay and serve me. It is your right to choose."

Neither of the creatures moved. "Serenissima, we are yours always," one of them said.

Rosalba bowed her head, then stepped away from them to face Ser Lucio. "I owe you thanks, too," she said.

Lucio bowed his head. "My life is yours, Serenissima."

"Then take him," Raniero said. "You need a young man, one who is worthy of you, and here is one who loves you."

Ser Lucio let out a gasp, but Rosalba paid no more attention to him than to the body of the cat, still lying beside the bier in a heap of silk, fur and feathers. Instead, she whirled on Raniero, her face filled with outrage.

"I cannot wed you, so you would throw me into the arms of the first man who presents himself? What do you think of me?"

"As a woman who will have every man in the city scrambling to wed her," Raniero retorted dryly. "You would do well not to hesitate before the daggers are drawn."

"And this is what it is to be Duchesa?" Rosalba asked bitterly.

"You know it is." Turning to Ser Lucio, Raniero went on, "Lucio, can you take her now, knowing what you know? It will be hard."

Lucio faced Rosalba. For a moment Raniero was afraid that he would fall on his knees and kiss the hem of her gown, but he stood fast. His gaze was full of grief and understanding. "I have loved you all my life," he said simply. "I will go on loving you until I die."

Rosalba hesitated for a long moment, then reached out and took his hand. "You may escort me to the Palazzo. We will speak of this further, but I promise nothing." Turning to Raniero, she added, "I wish I could hate you. But I cannot, and for that reason, you must leave the city tomorrow. I cannot be near you if we are not to wed. I am not my sister. There is no way that you and I can be together."

Without waiting for Raniero's reply, she turned away and led Lucio out of the basilica. The two lions rose and paced gravely after them.

Ah, carissima, *you are wrong,* Raniero thought, watching them go. *I always knew it would come to this.*

When he was sure that Rosalba and Lucio had left, Raniero pulled the white cover from the bier and draped it over the blackened remains of the woman who had called herself Duchesa. Then he gently gathered up the body of the cat and lowered himself to the floor, with his back against the bier and the cat on his breast. He took from his inner pocket the second vial, the one where silver glinted in its walls of crystal.

"God's blessing on you, Rosalba," he murmured.

Then he unstoppered the vial and drank down the contents. The pain was swift and agonising, and he could not suppress a groan. But when the darkness rose to claim him he was able to embrace it like a friend, breathing out his last breath in silence.

Moments passed. The cat stirred, twitched up his ears and opened eyes that glinted emerald as he looked into the dead face of Raniero. A ripple passed through his body and the tip of his tail flicked to and fro.

Then the cat leapt to the ground, a tiny mote of gleaming silk and silver in the dark reaches of the basilica. He arched his back in a long stretch, flexed diamond claws, and gave a sudden leap as if for the pure joy of movement.

At last, he whirled to face the door to the narthex, raced down the aisle towards it, and slipped out, following Rosalba, on the trail of love, always.

Victor Fernando R. Ocampo

"Blessed are the Hungry" is a Filipino space opera set on a generation ship that was first published in Apex Magazine issue 62 (July 2014). This story was the basis of the novel that I workshopped at Milford in 2019.

I had not written any long-form fiction previously and my more experienced fellow workshop writers were extremely helpful in helping me re-examine my plot, develop more characters and expand my setting. Of particular note was the observation made by several people that my ostensibly Science Fiction work actually contained a lot of horror elements. This was most useful in building more substance to my novel.

Unfortunately, because of life changes due to the Covid-19 pandemic, I have had little opportunity to finish my work. I am still very much in the middle of writing but I hope to finish this by the end of the year (or the first half of next).

Blessed are the Hungry

That afternoon they flushed San Carlos Seldran out the airlock. Everyone on Cabra Deck was required to watch, even the little ones.

Despite what old people tell you, in the vacuum of space your blood won't boil. Your body won't explode either. In less than a minute you'd simply die from a lack of oxygen. There wouldn't be time to scream.

His was a humane execution—quick, clean and painless.

"The Lord preserves all who love him but all the wicked he destroys," growled the ancient Holosonic, droning the day's lesson with great pomp and solemnity.

My family and I watched as our former parish priest drifted away towards infinity. The void swallowed him up with a deep hunger, deep as the ever-present darkness. I wanted to close my eyes but I just couldn't look away. None of us could. Instead, we just watched him die and committed his soul quietly to Our Lady of Gliese.

The people of Cupang couldn't let him go without a send-off. We removed our bracelets and dropped them to the floor discretely, at random places, beneath the notice of the ever-present Domini Canes. We'd made them from old cable ties and plastic bags, recycled colour against the blackest of blackness. Each one a secret funeral wreath for a good man we'd all loved and respected.

After the ceremony, mother hugged my youngest brother tightly. It was Bino's first excommunication and he was understandably quite upset. He buried his head deeply into her bosom, sobbing quietly. We all turned away, to let my mother console him privately.

The sooner that Bino got inured to executions, the better it would be for him and the easier it would be for the rest of us. Life was hard enough as it was without the tears of a child.

"You have a beautiful mind, boneca," a voice inside my head intruded, *"but so twisted and so sad. Como você está?"*

I heard it sometimes whenever I was troubled or depressed, flexing itself like a rarely used muscle. It was the voice of a young man, strong and reassuring, the kind I could perhaps fall in love with. I never told anyone about it, of course. People would say I was careless with our mushroom crop or worse that I'd gone mental. That would be a threat to the gene pool, earning me a one-way ticket out the airlock. It was how the Curia had bred out claustrophobia and the loco ones so many generations ago.

We lived in a 10 x 10 metre capsule in the Cupang Cluster, a farming encomienda near the rear starboard engine of the *Nuestra Señora de la Paz y Buen Viaje*. Our family holdings were not nearly big enough for the eight of us, plus the mushroom farm we were contracted to tend. But none of us really complained. Everyone in Cabra had the same allotment. Besides, to speak ill of The Edicts meant a private audience with the Ecclesiastic Police, the ndi Nri. No one ever returned from those 'special' meetings. No one dared ask why.

On this ship, my mother always said, it was always safer to suffer in silence.

Ten generations had come and gone since our Generation Ship left the Earth but the Prelates said we weren't even halfway to our destination. I was born in space and I would probably die in space. In my heart I knew that I would never see our new home, Gliese 581g—a small terrestrial planet in the old constellation of Libra. I suppose neither my children nor my children's children would reach planetfall either. But I guess that was okay, it would have been far worse to have been left behind, dying slowly and painfully in the radioactive ruins of our poor, destroyed world.

The eight of us hurried back to our quarters, running past the warren of barrios and lean-tos that choked the narrow passage-ways. Everything was so closely packed together it was difficult to move around. We picked our way through generations upon generations of Earth junk, now treasured relics too precious to throw away. It would be the Angelus soon, announcing the beginning of the night's curfew. We had to be home before the Domini Canes went on patrol.

That evening we had a simple dinner of protein soup, air-fried mushrooms and edible plastic that the boys had scavenged from the trash. Father kissed us goodnight and drew the thin curtain separating their small matrimonial space. There was never enough food for everyone. After our prelate's arrest, all the rations were reduced further. Our parents said they didn't have an appetite, but I knew they'd gone to bed hungry again.

Today had been very long and tiring. My siblings, Orly, Igmeng, Chayong and Sepa fell asleep faster than usual. Bino though, was still too upset to sleep. He tugged at the frail curtain, asking softly for our mother to read to him.

A part of me wanted to let him disturb them, to keep them from creating yet another mouth to feed. Eight people were really too much for our small space. If we had another sibling, Orly or perhaps Igmeng, who was younger but taller, would be forced to sleep in a lean-to at the corridor.

Father had said that Prelate Seldran was excommunicated because he'd asked the Lord Bishop, our Eze-Nri, to limit the size of families. Cabra Deck was already overcrowded and many suffered from some form of malnutrition. My father and my brothers, for example, were effectively blind at night. In fact, all the men in our neighbourhood lost their vision as soon as the deck lights were shut. None of the women were ever affected. It was, I suppose, another means of control.

In the heat of one homily, our priest had raged about too many children dying every day. *"Why can't we keep them all hale and hearty,"* he had asked, *"instead of constantly creating, discarding and replacing?"*

Despite daily entreaties and numerous attempts to get an audience with the Lord Bishop, nothing ever happened. Matters of life and death on the steerage decks were just too low in the Curia's priorities. The Domini Canes simply collected and stacked the regular toll of bodies. At the start of the day-cycle they were flushed out of the airlock like yesterday's trash.

One day it simply became too much for our old prelate, he began to explain an idea, a dangerous, radical concept which our language had no words for. His homily about unfulfilled coition made people cover their ears. The church band began to play loudly. I myself wanted to shut him out. Whatever he had said, however right he was—it just seemed so wrong. The Edicts had decreed that relations were solely for procreation. It was our sacred duty, something upon which the very security of our ship depended on. That was why on my thigh they made me wear the *cilicio*, a wire mesh studded with small spikes. The constant pain was meant to remind me of the law, of my personal responsibility, at least until the Curia paired me with a gene-screened husband.

That homily had proved to be his death warrant. Our parish priest had committed heresy, an act of terrorism against the Most Holy Curia.

Everyone knew that Generation Ships required a 'minimum viable population' to preserve genetic diversity and prevent the sin of in-breeding. Posters all over Cabra reminded you about it constantly. However, what that actual, necessary figure was, no one knew. Like everything else on our deck, no one spoke a word about it. Not that anyone could.

The only certain number was that each family had to maintain at least eight souls. This was the minimum at all times. I had always wondered how many people were already onboard our one-way trip to Gliese. The decks were forbidden to mix, although father said that hadn't always been so. For all we knew, there were millions of people on the higher levels, multiplying like roaches behind our nano-plastic walls. That was probably why our rations got smaller every year-cycle, even when the mushroom harvests were good.

I pulled Bino to my bedroll and took out our family's only book, an ancient primer that had once belonged to our great grandfather. It had no covers and many of its pages had gone missing long ago. Mother had composed her own rhymes for the missing letters, writing them on the blanks behind the surviving sheets. Despite the primer's poor state and the nonsense of its verse, mother had managed to teach most of us to read.

"Read me the whole thing, Ate Elsa," Bino asked, stretching his arms to look for my shoulder, "please…"

"No," I said firmly. "It's already late. I'll only read the ones with pictures."

"But I can't see them," he protested. "They're all blurry."

"Too bad for you," I whispered crossly. It had been a long day for me too.

A is for Apocalypse, when the sky fell down forever
C is for the Celestial Beacon, a light that never severs
D is for Death, wife to vanished Earth
E is for the Eaters, cannibals from the dirt
G is for Gliese, where the Bishop will lead his sheep
N is for the New Cities, where the dead downloaded, sleep

"You forgot about 'R'," Bino added.

"What do you mean 'R'?" I asked. "I said I would only read the ones with pictures."

"'*R' is for Rock,*" he said, listening intently to the sound of air circulating in the room. Like other night-blind kids, his hearing was incredibly acute. This talent would fade as Bino grew older but for now, it seemed almost superhuman. Without looking up, he pointed to one of the farm racks. "Father keeps that page behind those mushroom logs. I heard him take it out last night."

My brother was right. There was one page missing. *"R' is for the Readers,'* I remembered, for the ancient heretics that had worshipped libraries.

I stepped over my sleeping siblings towards the walls of our farm and knelt in front of the stack that Bino had pointed to. With great care I removed each log of sterile media until I found what father had been hiding—a small bundle wrapped in a torn page of the primer.

I took it out and unwrapped it. Inside was an *anting-anting*, a small rock—a piece of planet Earth that some ancient fool had smuggled onboard. It had been laser-etched with the *mano poderosa*, the symbol for the hand of God. I looked at the other papers. They were all secret missives from Prelate Seldran. Each one spoke of the food shortage and every successive communication was more strident that the last.

'It is never just to follow unjust laws,' he wrote, *'but people driven by fear choose stability over freedom. They need to be pushed.'*

The final note alarmed me. It was from Father asking the men of Cupang to attend a mass action in the morrow. Father had been staying out late more often. I suspected he had been planning something, ever since the rations were halved last week. This week-cycle alone, he had twice risked the Angelus.

As I wrapped everything up again, I noticed that Father had written something behind the torn primer page. It was gibberish scrawled in a desperate frenzy, as if to remember a dream that was fading too quickly.

In a Library of infinite dimensions… Tang-ina, Ancestors were Readers… now in a red room with millions of monkeys. Que huevas! The head gave over-ride key. Translux Baboon? Translucia Baboon???

= Bene legere saecla vincere—To read well is to master the ages

~~Elsa~~ Bring Orly or Igmeng

My name had been crossed out, that much I understood. Whatever Father had planned, I was not to be part of it. That wasn't fair. I was the eldest. *Ay wey*, I had a right to fight for my future too. Whatever happened, no matter what he did to stop me, I made up my mind to join them.

"Elsa, I'm still hungry." Bino said, rousing me from my brooding.

I ignored him and returned the bundle to Father's hiding place. When I came back, I handed him a greasy piece of tupperware. "I only have this,"

"Yuck, that looks so old," he said, making a face. "I hate edible plastic."

"I'm sorry, baby. *Wiz na*. That's all I have," I said, as I kissed him good night. "Just close your eyes. Close your eyes and try to go to sleep."

Bino snuggled against me and cried himself to dreamland.

The next day, a riot erupted on Cabra Deck.

It had started peacefully as a prayer rally. Father had taken my eldest brothers, Orly and Igmeng to Cupang's tiny chapel. There they attended a memorial service for our fallen priest.

I had fought with my father, begging him to let me come along but he was adamant and as unyielding as the rock he had secreted in his pocket.

After they left I badgered my mother for permission. "Please, come with me mother. What if they shut the lights? They'll be taken by the Domini Canes. We can't let them."

"You know your father has forbidden you. *Kodi, kodi…* let it be"

"Why?" I challenged her. "You always tell me to have my own mind. We need to be there."

"Remember what The Edicts say: *Thou submittest the wives to their husbands, for a faithful and chaste obedience.*"

I lost my temper, something I had never done before.

I screamed at my mother and called her out on every mistake and every hurt she'd ever visited upon me. I told her she was a terrible wife and a horrible mother for allowing them to face danger so casually, so recklessly.

"I know about the *anting-anting*," I said finally, crying in pain, crying in shame. "I read all the secret papers. The Bishop is starving Cabra."

"Then you know why I can't let you go," mother said, putting on a steely face that I knew was her mask of false conviction. "You are smart, young and healthy Elsa. You will make a great breeder, perhaps even for the Cabrón. I know you hear the voices. You are our family's most valuable asset, our best insurance."

"I don't hear anything!" I wailed, covering my ears.

"You can't hide something like that from your parents. Never ever disrespect me again."

"I'm sorry Mommy, but Orly and Igmeng…" I cried. Big hot tears were rolling off my cheeks like ball bearings. "That's not fair! They're just boys!"

"Precisely and boys are less important," she answered coldly. "You are old enough so I won't lie to you. The Curia is starving Cabra as a lesson. Many people will die but if some of us are to survive, we need to hedge our bets. Right now, our food stocks are so low we don't have anything to eat tomorrow. We've already finished the mushrooms and the new spawn aren't edible yet. The only ones left are the Bishop's Narco and you know those are poison."

"But that's not fair!" I screamed, "I'm the eldest! I should be the one with Father."

I bolted towards the door in defiance but mother had already locked it. Outside our quarters, a sharp pealing of bells announced a sudden curfew. All power was shut off and Cabra was plunged into a vast black ocean.

"I'm sorry too, Elsa," she said softly, as if she had expected the darkness. Mother stood up and prepared to draw their privacy curtain. "There's no more soup, there's no more plastic but I left three mushrooms on the counter. Air-fry them and divide them among you. I'm not hungry so don't leave any for me. I… I need to get some sleep, in case your… before your father returns."

Behind the thin screen, mother cried in silence.

An hour later, she finally fell asleep. The three youngest kids had also nodded off, victims of the oppressive boredom and the crippling lack of power. Somewhere outside our quarters, a lonely Igbo flute played an ominous *narcorrido*. It sounded just like a dirge.

I went over to mother's worktable and grabbed a bottle of her special ground mushrooms. She had found a way to store *Psilocybe* and *Panaeolus* as a powder without losing their nightmare potency. It was illegal to sell these to anyone outside the Curia. Father told me that they were considered sacred and fed only to the clergy with telepathic augmentations. In fact, to use them for any other purpose was a sin punishable by death. However, sometimes it earned us extra rations, so mother persisted with her dangerous trade.

One of the things she'd taught me was that if you combined the powder with luminol and a few other chemicals, it would glow for an hour or so, like a jar of distilled stars. I stole just enough to light my way through the corridors.

"Your father can hear us, just like you," the voice inside my head spoke. *"I gave him the code. Be careful, boneca. Find me if you can."*

"Ay wey, I must've inhaled some of mother's hallucinogens," I thought, shaking my head to drive the voice away. Time was of the essence and I didn't need any stupid distractions.

Chayong was our next eldest so I left her in charge of the household. The two of us quietly removed the cover of an unsealed service hatch. It had been hidden behind one of our large farm stacks. I'd seen Orly slip out at night from this hidden exit. It was the only way for him to meet his *syota* privately—at least not without having to get married first.

The sewer smelled of shit and organic waste. I crawled through as quickly as I could to keep myself from gagging. Just before the exit, I saw one of Orly's salvage bags hanging on a spike. Inside were a wire cutter and a spare *paltik*, a homemade electrolaser that he and Father had made from stolen electronics. It was what my brother had been using to protect himself from the Domini Canes. I whispered a prayer of thanks and clipped both to my belt.

Outside our quarters, Cabra Deck was eerily quiet. Signs of violence lay everywhere: all sorts of broken things, pools of blood and torn pieces of clothing. I knew that there'd been a riot but there was absolutely no one in the corridors.

I flew through Cupang Cluster like an águila, moving furtively between blinds, alcoves and abandoned lean-tos until I spotted some activity.

In the small plaza just outside the chapel, a crowd of men were on their knees, fearful but unbowed by the beasts of the ndi Nri. Many of the rioters were injured and bleeding. Piles of broken bodies had been stacked near the church door.

A snarling pack of Domini Canes had surrounded the survivors. The heavily-armed telepresence robots rumbled menacingly, as they sent their masters the head count, the body count and every possible threat assessment data.

I ducked out of sight as soon as I saw the wolf-like mecha, shrouding my lantern with my shirt. Frightful as they were, I was mesmerised by their strange beauty. In the half-light of the Holosonic, their liquid-armour bodies shimmered purple, vermillion and bronze. I imagined these to be the colours of a sun that I had never seen, the burial clothes of a mother-star that we had abandoned so long ago.

Father and the boys were at the front of the group. Orly was bleeding from one leg and his clothes were badly torn. Igmeng's face was covered in bruises. They were on their knees but Father still seemed defiant. His back was ramrod-straight and his head remained proud and unrepentant.

"Our children are hungry," I heard him say. "Please, we are only asking for the rations to be restored."

"Trust in the Bishop with all your heart, and lean not on your own understanding," the Holosonic blared, with its hollow Jovian voice. *"In all your ways acknowledge Him and He shall direct your paths."*

"There's no more food!" someone else protested. "You take all our mushrooms and then cut our rations. What are we expected to eat?"

Murmurs of dissent started to rise and ebb among the rioters. Then, quite unexpectedly, someone started to sing. Soon everyone assembled had joined in and were chanting softly: *"Shalom, maging payapa. Blessed are they who hunger and thirst for righteousness: for they shall be filled. Shalom, maging payapa. Blessed are they who hunger and thirst for righteousness: for they shall be filled."*

The singing spread like magic from the rioters to the gloomy corridors of Cupang. Every household, it seemed had come together to form a Jericho wall of hymns.

"Dissent is a disease," the Holosonic declared. Its groaning screen sputtered to life, flashing pictures of the bracelets we'd made for the funeral. The images cycled so fast it made some people in the crowd vomit. *"Whoever spares the rod spoils the child,"* it drawled, *"but those that are diligent discipline."*

In the plaza, the Domini Canes suddenly raised their guns. *"Trust in the Bishop with all your heart. Peace lives in silence. You must be silenced. By orders of the Holy Curia and the authority vested in our system by the Eze-Nri, the Most Blessed Office of the Lord Bishop, you are all hereby excommunicated."*

The rioters and the rest of our cluster became deathly quiet. The voice on the Holosonic ordered all the men to line up single file and walk towards the airlocks.

In the darkness someone threw a rock at the Domini Canes. And then another and another. I heard the Holosonic shatter into a thousand crystal pieces. Our men launched a surprise attack, assaulting the monsters with all manner of improvised weapons. The boys acted as their *olheiros*; the 'eyes' of the men in the blackness, telling them what to hit and where to shoot. Together, they shorted the liquid armour with *paltiks* and cracked weak spots with metal tubing. For the first time ever, cold silicon blood spilled on the floor.

But the battle was short-lived. It didn't take long for more

Domini Canes to join the fray. Horde upon horde of the vicious demon mecha appeared from the shadows, tearing people apart. The *tzat-tzat* sound of plasma discharges seemed everywhere, cleaving skulls from crown to teeth, or cutting arms clean from sockets. The plaza erupted with the bang of gas explosions and the astounded screams of fathers and sons, disbelieving their own deaths.

The slaughter proceeded ruthlessly, relentlessly. I had to do something—anything to help.

I used Orly's *paltik* to short the seals off a nearby service hatch. The tunnel was much, much larger than the last one. I ran inside until I saw an old *ordenador* access panel. I'd heard stories of people trying to hack the ship's brain through one of these, but no one had ever succeeded (except perhaps to trigger the intruder alert and get executed). I really had no idea of what I was doing but I was desperate and running out of options.

When the password box appeared, I remembered what Father wrote on the primer page and typed '*Translux Baboon*'. An error screen, *SAFIS 401 Unauthorised Error* appeared. I had two more tries before *403 Forbidden* would come, setting off the alarm.

'*Translucia Baboon*' was also a bust. Sweat poured from my scalp like a leaky Neowater pipe. There was no ventilation in the tunnel and my thin shirt was soon drenched with perspiration. It clung like phlegm to the small of my back.

A heavy door came down suddenly, blocking the entrance I'd come though. Now I had no escape. I had only one more chance before the system sent the Domini Canes my way.

SAFIS 401 Unauthorised Error... SAFIS 401 Unauthorised Error ...

I took a deep breath and said a prayer to Our Lady of Gliese. I typed in the first words that came to mind—*Bene legere saecla vincere. 'To read well is to master the ages,'* the central tenet of the heretic Readers.

Somehow, in some way that I couldn't explain, it actually

worked. The words had acted like a *kulam*, a spell of some sort, disabling the defence systems and granting me full access to the ship's living neural nets.

"Where did my father learn that?" I wondered.

A massive floating screen popped open above me, giving the illusion of infinite space. On it was a map of the *Nuestra Señora de la Paz y Buen Viaje*. Our ship was a hollow, spherical shell 160 kilometres in diameter, divided into hundreds of self-sustaining sections. Less than a quarter of the ship showed any life signs—just three decks in steerage, Belo Horizonte, Cabra and Pagbilao and a few clusters in engineering. On the First-Class deck, seven cities had survived: Boston, Caracas, Maynilad, Tenochtitlán, Nri, Paris and Rio. Roma's Ecclesiastic Ring had been completely decimated. Only one monastery remained—the one where the Cabrón, the Augmented Clergy, were kept from the laity.

The *ordenador central* told me that the Lord Bishop, the Curia and most of the ship had died long ago. It didn't say when, how or why. The system, it seemed, had been running on autopilot, following the infallible instructions of a dead man whose word was law to a brutal, mechanical police.

On Cupang's map, I saw that life signs were going out one by one.

I flipped through the screens frantically, trying to stop the Domini Canes or at least turn the power back on. But all the necessary icons had been blacked out. Nothing worked. People were dying with every second I delayed.

I pounded the maintenance console in anger, in frustration. *"Our Lady of Gliese, help me,"* I prayed. I reached deep inside my mind, searching for something, any scrap of information that could help. Without really meaning to, I called on the voice inside my head, *"I need to save my family, please."*

"You only call out when you're in trouble. Why is that?" the voice inside my head whispered. *"Let me be of assistance, I can commandeer this ship but you're the one with physical access. I will need to get inside your mind."*

"Do it." I hissed. "Whoever you are, whatever you are, do it now!"

"Lamento, lamento, boneca... but there's truly no other way."

Without warning I felt something warm pour inside my brain. It was as if my mind, my soul had wrapped around someone else's. Like new lovers we were circumscribed by a relentless rush of unfamiliar thoughts and emotions. We touched in an impossible space, an impossible time, suddenly called to witness the vast and endless perturbations of the universe. *Desnudo, despido,* our souls co-mingled with a profound intimacy that words simply lacked the depth, the ferocity to describe. He was so close, so very, very close I could literally taste him in my mouth.

When the mind-meld was over, my legs gave way and I could barely stand. But I knew exactly what I had to do.

I pulled out a new screen to access a long dormant shellcode, the payload of a virus that heretic Readers had planted generations ago. The know-how for the exploit was solid and crystal-clear in my head, yet I truly had no idea how I knew what I was doing. I didn't even sound like me in my own head anymore.

Gostoso, gostoso... what language was that? It was so... tasty?

In short order I had shut down the Domini Canes and restored the power in Cabra. I opened all the gates, hatches and doors that the ndi Nri had shut. Everyone was now free to access all the decks and corridors. Most importantly I found food, lots and lots of food stored in secret caches everywhere. There were also at least twenty fully-operational protein factories, only two of which had been used by the entire ship. And on the highest cluster, where the Lord Bishop and the Curia had lived, there was a vast garden, one with almost a hectare of self-sustaining vegetable farms and orchards.

I couldn't wait to share my discovery with everyone on Cabra. *Porra!* I was so giddy with excitement that I'd almost forgotten about the riot.

"Porra?" I caught myself. Since when did I cuss in *Português Brasileiro?*

It was a mystery for another time. I returned my focus to my mission and pulled up every security camera near Cupang's chapel. I needed to see if father and my brothers had survived.

Fires had broken out across many corridors, knocking out many of the surveillance monitors. For those that worked, heavy smoke obscured my view. I powered up the auxiliary emergency system to vent the dirty air.

When the smoke had cleared, I saw many bodies lying inert on the plaza. Many were friends and neighbours that I had known all my life. Near the door of the chapel I saw Father and Igmeng. They were both wounded, but alive. Father was tending to Orly who lay broken and bleeding at his feet.

I screamed. A great knot of fear had formed in the pit of my stomach.

"He is alive," said the voice inside my head, *"alive but very seriously injured. He needs a bone stapler. You need to find me and bring me to him. There is a hospital facility just two levels above your deck. Meet me there. Por favor, apresse."*

A new window floated above me like a phosphene sprite, showing me where to go.

"Thank you." I said, as I ran back through the maintenance tunnel. "Who are you?"

"My name is Ismael, minha boneca," he answered. *"I am a just a bicho simples, a novice with the Cabrón."*

"How come I can hear you in my head?"

"I have an alien parasite on my nape. We call them the Cafuné or sometimes Abacaxi, which means both 'pineapple' and 'deep trouble'. They give humans telepathy," he replied. *"Your father was the first mind I found outside our deck."*

"My father?"

"Yes, that was why I could find him. We are... connected... you and I. My spores found you. They gave your father the access codes to the ship, but the Domini Canes, they discovered us and came for me. I was lucky

you reached out to my Cafuné when you did."

"What?" I asked. "I never did that."

"You are doing it now," he whispered softly. Suddenly, I realised I could feel something fuzzy behind my head, something that felt like flesh and cotton-wool. I reached to touch my nape, but there was nothing there. Still, I could feel it, squeeze it; flex it with my mind. It spoke to me in a swarm of new images and emotions.

"How is that... possible," I stammered. "How... how do I know I can trust you?"

"You've seen my innermost self, my soul, minha boneca," he whispered. *"You know me inside and out."*

"Why me?"

"There are things under heaven which carry no logic and we... my Cafuné and I, we love your beautiful mind."

I could feel the sudden sheepishness in his voice. An unfamiliar word appeared in my head, *apaixonado*, and something dirty, something electric stirred in my soul, a rapaciousness that I had never felt before. I took out Orly's wire cutter and removed my *cilicio*. It was a sign of my bondage — no, *our* bondage, *our* failure to trust ourselves with our own future.

The maintenance tunnel was now brightly-lit. I dropped my lantern and ran as fast as I could, heading towards where Ismael had pointed me to go. I ran to save my brother. I ran to save our ship. I ran to chase a curious new hunger that now burned within my soul—a hunger as deep as space, deep as death, and infinite as the stars which were our true home.

Guy T. Martland

I wrote this story the summer before my first Milford, ten years ago, having just been on holiday to Mallorca and visited some of the places featured. Not being sure what to expect and with some trepidation, I sent the first draft into the Milford process. My biggest fears were about the verse sections, which seemed to ring true on the first night when Bob Neilson (of Albedo One fame) commented: 'You're the one with the bloody poetry'. However, it turned out Bob was just ribbing me and the story went down reasonably well in the round. A few subsequent drafts later, having taken on board a lot of the comments and considered but ignored others, I submitted it to Fiction Vortex.

The Milford process certainly helped shape this story—the ending in particular benefitted. But more importantly, over the course of the four years I've attended the conference and the retreat, Milford has helped me grow as a writer. I've learned a lot through critiquing others and I hope at the same time I've helped play a part in moving their work toward publication. In addition, I've made some fabulous friends along the way.

Words of War

The small group of so-called 'war poets' was touring. Some of them, like Valin Hussein, had seen some real action in space. His last tour of duty had ended when the stolen Ifrit class enemy ship he was captaining had encountered a mine, splintering its spine. The dying ship and his experiences aboard it had informed his last slim volume and garnered him considerable praise in the process.

When he was recovering in a military hospital orbiting Titan, writing the series of interconnected poems had served to thwart the insidious tedium. Now, months later and almost fully recovered, the fighting seemed to have ceased, although for how long was anyone's guess. In the lull he had somehow found himself persuaded to tour Earth and recite his graphic representations of war.

"The ever-present cannibalistic desire. Is that really based on personal experience?" someone slurred at him over the table. Valin nodded, describing the dwindling stores aboard the Kalima XI with the possibility of rescue distant, the remaining crew wondering how long they would be pushed before...

"As the poem stated, it wasn't an idea we took lightly. They were dark times for all of us. Especially the injured, like myself. It was assumed we'd be the first to go, being the biggest drain on resources."

Wide-eyed, enraptured, almost sycophantic, the bustling table continued to question him. Wine flowed freely, smoke blowing gently on the warm breeze that passed through the bar. From where Valin sat he could see across Cala de Deia, the small bay lit by the glow from the boats and small shuttle craft. Waves splashing on the rocks below provided background music to the poets' voices, and the occasional ripple of applause carried out into the hills beyond.

He'd already done his bit in the recital and was basking in the afterglow, people clapping him on the back as they wandered to the bar. Being one of the first on was something he relished—usually at these kind of events he wasn't able to enjoy the other acts, being consumed by nerves. He found it ironic that he felt no such terror when he was storming an enemy hideout, but reading poems wasn't something he'd trained to do in the army.

The buzz of the place quietened as Rachael took to the stage and began to speak:

Your call to prayer
Resonated through subspace
Lighting up beacons
With the Muezzin's wail.

For a few moments
As battle ceased
Warships appeared through rifts
Lining up with Mecca

And as the prayers ran out
It began again
Explosions littering battlespace
Calling us back to arms.

As he stood up, despite being near the back, Rachael watched him leave. Her heavy brown eyes spoke more to him than her words did, but they didn't speak disapproval. She knew he'd heard her poems many times before.

Outside, he felt the oppression of the throng lift. The place had been a bit too cramped, a bit too like the remaining life support cubicles aboard the Kalima XI. He took a deep breath and felt better. His side was aching where plaskin had replaced the burned fetid flesh; it felt tight and too new, sweating oddly under his linen top.

He decided against heading back inside. Instead, he'd retreat to the village above, where he'd heard there was a good bar. The walk would do him good, and besides, they were all due to meet up there later.

"I liked your poems," said a voice in the night. Valin squinted into the gloom, his eyes happening on a shock of white hair that seemed to glow oddly in the moonlight. As the man approached, his weathered face beamed a welcome.

"Oh, thanks," replied Valin, continuing his passage up the hill. Lemon trees and cacti lined the path.

"You seemed to capture the truth. More so than your friends, anyway," the man continued. Valin thought his voice seemed to hark back to a distant age, its crisp English tones suggesting a man of bearing. The stranger seemed to be hovering at his side, keen to talk.

"That's very kind of you. Can I sign anything for you?" Valin asked, halting in his tracks. The cicadas in the surrounding trees chirruped loudly at the night.

"There's no need. Are you heading up to Deia? I'm heading that way too."

It seemed the man wouldn't leave. Valin sighed inwardly to himself: He'd been looking forward to some time alone. He turned back to the path, negotiating a steep turn.

"My name's Robert. I used to write poems, you know."

"Oh really?" Valin said, disinterested; the eager poets who had shown him their doggerel, expecting gleaming praise, layered cynicism over his enthusiasm for the written word. He noticed the man had pulled out a black hat, its place on his head framing his face.

"Yes. War poems, too."

"Oh right, which war?"

"War was return of earth to ugly earth…"

"You can say that again…"

"War was foundering of sublimities, extinction of each happy art and faith…"

"Are you quoting someone?" asked Valin, slowing to allow his companion to catch up.

"Just one of mine."

"It sounds good. I like it."

"Well, it is one of my better…"

"What did you say your name was?" asked Valin, stopping again to examine the man more closely. His was an intelligent face.

"Robert. Pleased to meet you, Mr. Hussein."

"Are you from here?"

"I live nearby. Up there on the hill. Have done for years."

"I can think of nothing I'd rather do than live here for years, writing poetry. But I will, in due course, return to the battlefield," Valin said.

"I stood in your shoes once. But no longer. It may be a cliché, but war is a young man's game."

"That it is, indeed."

"Well, I turn off here," Robert pointed left up the hill.

"It was nice to meet you, Robert."

"Likewise. Keep writing, Mr. Hussein."

And with that, the man disappeared into the darkness, his white hair visible for a few moments before it became lost behind a thicket of gorse and rosemary.

Valin shook his head, trying to make sense of the encounter as he plunged up the slope to the village. Above, he noticed one of the orbiting Unified Churches of Christ passing through the heavens, its illuminated cruciform shape dimming the stars beyond. By the time it had disappeared behind the mountaintops, he had reached the village and was winding his way through small cobbled streets to the bar he'd been told about.

Sa Fonda was busy but had yet to receive most of the visitors from the reading below. He recognised a poet he knew, reading quietly to himself in the corner, and thought he'd interrupt. After a brief and overcomplicated negotiation with the barman in pidgin Spanish regarding the procurement of a beer, he wandered over. Some ancient reggae blared from a speaker concealed somewhere in the vines that were strung over the patio.

"Valin!" the man exclaimed, leaping up and shaking him warmly by the hand.

"Nice to see you, Purtice. You escaping the madhouse for a bit then."

"Yeah, just been sitting here, reading."

"What's that?" Valin said, nodding at the book. It was an old hardback edition, bound in leather.

"Poems. Have a look," Purtice replied, handing the book over. "They were written a poet who lived locally; war poems, actually."

Valin placed his beer on the table, sat down, and flicked to the title page. The writer was a man called Robert Graves. He turned to a poem entitled Recalling War, a stanza leaping out at him:

War was the return of Earth to ugly Earth.

The book shook in Valin's hands and he almost dropped it. Instead he placed it delicately back on the table, taking a sip of the cool beer as eerie thoughts slotted into place.

Robert Graves had lived in Deia—how could he have not realised? Had the whirlwind of shore leave, travelling around on this impromptu reading tour, softened his edge so much? It had surely been the reason they'd stopped here. Was Robert Graves this man, the poet he'd just met on the path? It had to be, but then again—how could that be possible? Robert

Graves had died centuries ago—so then it had to be some kind of impostor. He wanted to run back down the hill, find him, but knew he'd be long gone.

He looked up at Purtice, his face pale.

"What's the matter Valin?" his friend asked him. "You look like you've seen a ghost!"

～ ～ ～ ～ ～

An annoying beep thrilled through his dehydrated cerebral cortex, forcing him into consciousness through the fog of hangover. He was back aboard his shuttle, which was a relief—although he couldn't remember getting there. He blinked away spectral remnants of dreams that flickered at the edges of his consciousness. But one ghost wouldn't disappear—the lined, well-worn face of Robert Graves.

After shouting at it a few times, it dawned on him that this holo unit wasn't going to respond to voice commands. He flung a pillow at the receiver, which did nothing to quell its incessant bleating. Eventually, he forced himself to stand up, knocking over a glass of water in the process. He located the remote and tapped it.

Rachael's face appeared on the screen, scattering light over the bedroom.

"I didn't wake you did I? You look terrible."

"Well, you know, a man has to enjoy his shore leave sometimes. What do you want at this ungodly hour?"

"Did you have fun last night?" Rachael replied.

"From what I can remember, yes. Where were you?"

"Busy. I'm working on a project at the moment."

"Right. Good for you. Well, I'm off back to sleep then."

"How did you enjoy meeting Robert last night?"

Valin sat bolt upright in bed. "How do you know? Did that barman tell you?"

"I wasn't there last night. But apparently you were freeversing some stuff about a ghost."

"Yeah, this strange thing happened."

"I know."

"What do you know?"

"Robert is one of my AI constructs."

"Ah, so it was a wind up! Great. I might have guessed—thanks for freaking me out." Valin hit another pad on the side of the bed, flicking up the filters on the diamond composite window of the shuttle. He winced slightly.

"Sorry. But it is a serious project. We need the war poets. We need them alive, now more than ever."

Valin shook his head, used to this kind of overbearing enthusiasm from his friend. "But he isn't alive, he's just a construct."

"Assembled from what we know of his personality. You can learn a lot about someone from their poetic output."

"Hmm," replied Valin, thinking about the never-to-be published semi-erotic verse he'd written about Rachael. He looked up into her magnified deep brown eyes.

"And where better to set him free, than where he died? When they appear, they aren't too unfamiliar with their surroundings."

"Apart from the fact that they are dead. I imagine that is a bit of a shock to a being when it wakes."

"Ha ha. Bit like you now!" Rachael said. "Listen, can you do something for me?"

"Why?"

"I can't make the next leg. I left you something on your porch. Instructions are embedded in your holo."

"All very mysterious. What do you want me to do?"

"I want you to grow me a war poet," she replied, an impish grin spreading across her face.

~ ~ ~ ~ ~

It wasn't far from Athens—a quick hop across Evia and part of the Aegean Sea. He'd been on the mainland for another reading and was now fulfilling his promise to Rachael. There wasn't a cloud in the sky, and he piloted his small shuttle manually.

He pulled up the craft on a road near the plot, scrabbling down the dusty scree slope to the olive grove below. Nestled amongst the trees was a grave, penned in by four white pillars of marble and black ironwork. He wiped his brow in the heat as he stood beside it, admiring the view. The valley stretched down to the sea, framed by austere orange rocks that made up the place.

On the grave were the words: Rupert Brooke 1887-1915. Beside which, a stanza of a poem. Valin read the words out loud:

If I should die, think only this of me:
That there's some corner of a foreign field
That is forever England.

He delved in his pocket, found the cube Rachael had given him. It was a cloudy white square of quartz-like material. It glinted in the Sun's rays, firing unnatural beams of light across the basin. Finding a suitable spot near the head of the grave, he thrust it into the soil, until it was covered by the ochre earth.

For a few minutes nothing happened. Valin stood in the midday Sun, waiting, re-reading the poem, wondering about his fate, where he would finally lie. Then the soil surface broke, a green shoot wheedling out, coursing upwards. Its tip was bulbous, the stem that followed studded with thorns. And then the bud opened, revealing the flower's true nature: a white English rose.

That was all it took: a mosquito bite. To survive being shot at, being blown up in the trenches, to have your life taken away by something that you could squash between your fingers. He took a glug of water from his canteen, hearing some of Rachael's words in his mind, her infectious excitement about the other reincarnated poets. He blinked, capturing the picture in his AV, sending it instantly via his holo, to wherever Rachael was—probably the other side of Saturn by now.

As he flew away, he circled the grave. The flower had disappeared. Instead an attractive youth was now leaning on the railings, smoking a cigarette. He loosened his cravat, ran his hands through his foppish hair and waved at Valin.

~ ~ ~ ~ ~

The battle roared around the landing craft, the craft buffeted here and there by nearby blasts. Behind Valin sat rows of his specialist platoon, quiet as they absorbed the updated mission details he'd just patched over to them. Europa's partly terraformed icy surface lay below, and he banked the craft plunging it downwards toward the battlefront.

The once proud city stood in tatters, plumes of smoke palling upwards in the thin atmosphere. The fight for the metropolis had now become a guerrilla effort, Christian and Muslims once again fighting against each other for supremacy. How had it come to this? Despite his surname, his father's background, Valin was fighting for the Christian side. But did it really matter which side he was on? War was all the same. He felt the fruits of a poem forming on the branches of his thoughts. It was always at moments like this, when death was imminent that his best work appeared.

There was a keen metallic screech as the craft landed, the back door then hissing open, its edge clanging onto ice and rock. Valin and his troops marched out onto the surface of Jupiter's moon, blasted by the wind. In his pocket, he felt the comforting presence of a small cube, given to him by the girl with the brown eyes who appeared in his thoughts day and night: a cube which was synced with the patterns of electricity that flowed across his cerebral cortex, in turn synced with a beacon in orbit.

The acrid smell of smoke caused his eyes to water. He blinked as the platoon followed his command, moved toward the crumbling city, toward the embassy where men and women were awaiting extraction. He checked his jacket once again, the cube in his pocket, still there: always recording, recording…

Nick Moulton

I wrote *Scenes from Domestic Life with the Gentry* because I needed a story to take to Milford 2012. I'd had some previous success with genre crossing—my first story sale was a zombie romance in a sinister Victorian asylum for the deceased. There seemed to be more potential in dropping nasty modern SF and horror tropes into classic literary settings. How about a Regency ball in a world ruled by parasitic aliens?

Getting from that concept to a recognisable first draft was, as ever, a case of bashing out the words until I reached an ending. Once I'd nailed the narrator's voice—oily, obsequious and smug—the rest of the story gradually followed. The first draft was lumpy and unbalanced, but it was recognisably a short story.

As Milford loomed, I submitted the story for its workshop debut. As usual, 13 different writers had 13 different perspectives, but reactions were generally positive.

Encouraging comments were accompanied by insights that picked up the story's faults and weaknesses, often with suggestions for fixes. Most (correctly) said that the plot needed strengthening, the ending was rushed and sudden and there were too many dashes (I'd overdone those d—ed 19th century swear words).

Another benefit of Milford is the expert knowledge of other writers. And when a Regency ball veers into wildly speculative territory, it's important to make the rest of the period detail as convincing as possible. Dr Kari Sperring provided insight into the social position and duties of a governess—any departures from historical fact are, of course the result of this being a parallel universe.

Bob Neilson, from the Irish SF, fantasy and horror magazine Albedo One, gave an editor's perspective—he said the story was publishable and strongly encouraged me to submit it.

After the intensity of Milford, the story languished for a while, despite the excellent session on markets and submissions at the end of the conference.

In early 2018, I hauled it out, dusted it off and did some fixes on it. I expanded the ending to be less perfunctory. I cut most of the dashes, retaining them only for language that would be considered truly improper by my narrator. I fixed titles and place names.

I bounced it off my regular writing group, the Cat Herd (which includes multiple Milford veterans) and got further helpful comments.

In April 2018, I sent the story—rather tentatively—through Albedo One's submission process. A while later I had an acceptance from Bob, who remembered the story and had some constructive suggestions to further improve the ending.

Scenes from Domestic Life with the Gentry appeared in issue 49 of Albedo One. And it's back again here—a Milford story through and through.

Scenes From Domestic Life With The Gentry

From the memoirs of Mr Adam Phillips, Butler, with the assistance of Mr NT Moulton.

As I rarely tire of reminding the younger servants, I arrived at Lansborough Hall as a boot-boy in 1835—the time of the old Lord Woodworth. A boot-boy I would have remained, had I not applied myself, with great energy, to the business of getting on—a business which necessarily involved much trouble, hard work and the subjugation of my own needs and desires to the comfort and convenience of my betters. So I blacked boots, emptied chamber pots and polished the gas cylinders in the cellar until the brass gleamed.

Before many years had passed, Mr Rowstock, the butler, handed me a footman's livery. Now, I rang the bell for dinner and carried dishes to and from the dining room. I ducked unnoticed into alcoves and behind doors when members of the family approached. And I learned to fix my expression and do my duty when performing the necessary services for visiting Gentry.

I also assisted Lord Woodworth's son when he was home from school, pressing his clothes, and helping him dress. He was a year younger than me, and we got along well, a matter that was the cause of some jealousy from his elderly valet. In the natural way of things, the valet's frequent blunders irritated the young master, and he was eventually banished to a small cottage at the far end of the landing-strip.

I was again promoted, becoming valet to the Honourable Mr Harcourt, to give Lord Woodworth's son his proper title. While we were careful to preserve an appropriate distance between master and man, our shared youth often led us to confide in one another. I made it my business to act as his courier when he wished to place a wager with the landlord of the Green Dragon. I also assisted him by passing on his notes to Miss Reid, the governess, who was employed in the education of his two young sisters. Presently I began also to convey clandestine correspondence from Miss Reid to my young master.

He often spoke to me about family matters—his fondness for his sisters, and his hopes that they would make good marriages. He was more uncertain about his own future—we spoke of Lord Woodworth's lifelong concern for the position and fortune of the family, and his desire for a connexion to the Gentry.

"When I was a small boy, Father would show me the family tree and tell me how for generations our ancestors were soldiers and tradesmen," he told me on one occasion. "And then, through a great service to the King, his great-great grandfather was honoured with the title of Baron. He always said that the Harcourt family would rise further still, to achieve union with the Gentry, and find our destiny in the stars. And I listened, and nodded, and said 'yes Sir,' because I had no conception of what Father had in mind for me."

I brushed the lapels of Mr Harcourt's jacket. "It would surely be a fine thing for his Lordship if the family were to be Gentrified, Sir."

He shook his head. "At what cost, Phillips? Can you begin to imagine what it means to marry Gentry? To become Gentry?"

Like every child, I had entertained dreams of the luxury and power enjoyed by the Gentry: a seat in the House of

Lords; a floaty to travel to France; silk cushions and idle entertainment. But for a man from my background, such ideas were as fantastic as flying to the outer planets.

Because I had never given the matter serious consideration, I had never thought about the price that an individual pays for Gentrification. There was, of course, the matter of accepting an amiable companion—something that has always been the subject of much jesting amongst the vulgar. There was the need to make one's own needs and desires subordinate to those of another—an imposition that was all too familiar to me, but which might be more of a hardship for a man from young Mr Harcourt's background. And I had heard second-hand the ravings of the non-conformists, even glanced at some of their pamphlets. But I could not imagine how such seditious nonsense could possibly affect a sensible and respectable young man from one of the oldest families in England.

"I do not understand, Sir..." is often the best answer when one wishes to get on.

It was not difficult to keep my counsel about these conversations: there was always so much gossip amongst the staff that I rarely needed to contribute my own. When his Lordship announced that he would be holding a ball to mark the young master's twenty-first birthday, my fellow-servants' joy was unrestrained. There was much speculation on young Mr Harcourt's future, with opinion evenly split as to whether he would marry into Gentry or settle down with a young woman from one of the foremost families of the county.

"Well I reckon he likes Miss Reid! Ow!" young Bob declared, as his ears were soundly boxed. While highly respectable, Miss Reid was a poor clergyman's daughter, far below my master's rank and position.

"I believe that young Mr Harcourt will be helping his Lordship greet the Gentry at the event," I said, returning the conversation to a more proper subject for comment.

The ever-fascinating topic of the ways of the Gentry immediately distracted everyone's attention, with Mr Rowstock declaring that he would personally lay in fresh supplies of ethane and oil of vitriol for the occasion.

"Will they be coming in a floaty?" When he was not blacking boots, Bob would "slope off" outside to draw floaties and landrunners. His sketches were remarkable for their detail, but his preoccupation with them meant that he had no prospect of ever getting on.

"They certainly will!" our youngest scullery maid exclaimed. "There will be flyers, floaties and walkers stretching from the kitchen garden to the edge of the park!"

She was right. The ball attracted the patronage not only of the most fashionable people of Berkshire, but also no fewer than nine Gentry, from Derbyshire, Yorkshire, Ireland, Ganymede and other far-flung places. Throughout the day, I heard exclamations of wonder as their strange vehicles assembled on the meadow.

It fell to Mr Rowstock, as butler, to oversee the transfer of the Gentry guests to the house, by means of a closed-coach. I lined up with four other footmen against the panelled wall at the back of the hall. Lord Woodworth and his son stood in front of us, ready to greet the visitors. They were conversing about the shooting on the estate, but Mr Harcourt had his hands behind his back and was winding a handkerchief between his fingers.

As Mr Rowstock opened the door, his Lordship made a deep bow and gave a short speech welcoming our Gentry guests and their amiable companions. On this occasion, we were honoured to host four couples—the Duke and Duchess of Derbyshire, the Earl and Countess of Scarborough; Viscount and Lady Galway; and Lord and Lady Callisto. Travelling in their company was Miss Smythe, the youngest daughter of a newly Gentrified Derbyshire family.

While our visitors had the polished grace and formal manners of true Gentry, it is, of course, almost impossible to encounter such a superior class without an overwhelming sensation of awe that could be mistaken for less welcome emotions.

Mr Harcourt did not flinch in the slightest at the appearance of the guests, or the mumbling of formal expressions of gratitude through lips that—to inferior persons—seemed to stretch and slacken in an unnatural parody of speech. Then the men reached out to shake hands, and I must admit I stifled a cry of warning as they touched flesh.

"Perhaps you would care to accompany my son to the gas room, where we may properly attend to your amiable companions?" His Lordship regularly encountered Gentry through his duties at the House of Lords, and his ease and self-control on these occasions were to be marvelled at.

"That would be immensely gratifying." As the highest-ranking male, the Duke of Derbyshire spoke for the group. I will not attempt to reproduce the pronunciation of our honoured guests; suffice to say it was as polished as their manners.

The Derbyshires' amiable companions were openly displayed, wrapped around their shoulders and necks as was the fashion at the time, although I did not care for it. Miss Smythe wore a simple cloak which covered hers. The others had opted for the discretion of the French sleeve that was de rigueur in more elegant days.

We had, of course, spent several days making ready the gas room for their arrival. A large glass tank (six feet by four by four), half-filled with paraffin and rocks and topped up with a fine array of chlorinated butane compounds, had been prepared as a habitat for the amiable companions to converse and relax in, while a neat row of military camp beds lined the wall for the Gentry themselves.

The process by which a companion disengages itself from its Lady or Gentleman can be alarming for those who are unaccustomed to such sights, but one must always be ready to do one's duty; and a display of fortitude at such times is a great help in getting on. As the Gentry separated, we footmen donned our gloves, placed each companion onto a cushion and conveyed it to the gas tank. I noted that mine was about the weight of a fully grown cat, but twice as long and (obviously) far thinner. It writhed in a way that made me immensely relieved when this task was completed.

At the same time, the parlourmaids each took a Lady or Gentleman by the hand, led them to one of the camp beds and helped them lie down. Oxygen masks were placed over their faces and the small wounds on their spines staunched.

While I was feeling slightly faint and nauseous, it was my duty to assist a footman who had collapsed in a swoon after depositing Lady Galway's companion in the tank, and one of the parlourmaids, who had become quite unwell early on in the proceedings. Once the invalids had been helped from the room and the mess cleaned up, the gas man opened the tap on the ethane cylinder, and we returned to our regular duties.

Since the arrival of the Gentry, the business of a formal ball had, of course, changed greatly. However, Lord Woodworth always took great pride in keeping many of the customs of the old days while properly honouring our guests. On this occasion his Lordship had ordered that the ballroom floor be chalked with the family coat of arms, orbited by the outer planets and their moons, with Gentry craft weaving between them.

After the company stood to attention for the *Entry of the Gentry*, the musicians struck up a quadrille and dancers moved out onto the floor. Unusually, all four Gentry couples took part, dancing with one another rather than local families.

The spectacle was magnificent, as the dancers stepped and swirled around the heavens, illuminated by the new Venetian chandelier, and reflected many times over in the ballroom's huge mirrors.

My reputation for attentiveness had earned me a position against the wall, ready to assist guests with any little thing. This meant that I could also watch Mr Harcourt, and attend to his needs. For the first dance, he was paired with Miss Smythe. As they faced one another, she looked him up and down, rather as a butcher might appraise a prize pig.

The Gentry danced with the twitching gait that is an indicator of good breeding, but which can be painful to watch. I noted with regret that some of the non-Gentrified young people attempted to adopt a similar manner of dancing—a most regrettable fashion, in my view—while Mr Harcourt carried himself with grace and decorum, despite his partner's unpredictable movements. During pauses between the dances, Miss Smythe leaned over to Mr Harcourt's ear and appeared to whisper in it. I noted that his replies to her seemed brief to the point of curtness.

I spent much of the next two dances helping a young lady who had mislaid her shawl, and a curate who had taken rather too much refreshment. In this last task I was ably assisted by Miss Reid, who had been released from her duties in the nursery only to be burdened with an intoxicated dancing partner.

By the time I returned to the ballroom a waltz was in progress, and Mr Harcourt was back in the grip of Miss Smythe. It was unheard of for a couple to dance together all evening—and it would have been improper had Miss Smythe not been Gentry.

Then I glimpsed Lord Woodworth watching them, glass in hand, deep in conversation with Lord and Lady Callisto. His Lordship was smiling. I thought of the family coat of arms—proudly displayed in the chapel and on the front of the house—and how much it would mean to him to crown them with the crest of amiable companionship.

As the dance finished, in complete defiance of protocol, Mr Harcourt abandoned his partner, leaving Miss Smythe to retire to the little knot of Gentry, and approached Miss Connor—the eldest and least marriageable of the local solicitor's daughters.

They were, however, old acquaintances, and Miss Connor's eyes flashed at the prospect of dancing with the most eligible bachelor in the room. A few minutes later, they stepped out in a Scotch reel.

Afterwards, Mr Harcourt engaged Miss Connor in conversation and they walked over to the refreshment room together. Miss Smythe followed them. I saw her hold out her dance card, and Mr Harcourt's firm rebuff. Then he left Miss Connor and crossed the floor to me.

"Phillips—I need your help."

I stepped forward, eager to receive my master's orders.

"I need to give you instructions about the delivery of an urgent message. I believe..."

Before he could finish, his father was at my side. His Lordship's face was like thunder.

"Have you finished wasting time with your lackey? Phillips—make yourself useful elsewhere! Paul—I need to talk to you in my study."

"I am to dance with Miss Connor, Sir."

"Indeed you will not. You will come with me to my study and afterwards dance with Miss Smythe, as I instructed."

His Lordship marched from the room, his son at his heels.

I made myself useful serving refreshments to the guests. For half an hour I poured wine, retrieved glasses, and handed out cold meat to the throng. The Gentry did not eat, of course, but the Derbyshires both retired to the refreshment room for a long conversation with the vicar and his wife.

I was carrying a tray of glasses through the long gallery when Miss Reid's voice hissed my name from the shadows. I nearly dropped my burden in shock.

"Phillips!" She was part-concealed by a bookcase, as if intending to hide. "Is Mr Harcourt still at the ball?"

I replied that he was indeed.

"Is he still dancing with that Gentry woman?"

I explained that I had been too busy with my duties to take notice of my superiors. But she failed to take my hint. Whatever had taken place between Miss Reid and my master, it seemed to have given her ideas above her position in life.

"You must have noticed her—she's got a shawl wrapped around her par--ite."

"I beg your pardon, Miss?" For a moment, I thought I had genuinely misheard her: I had occasionally heard such language around the estate (one of the gamekeepers was notoriously coarse)—but never from a clergyman's daughter, and especially not when there were Gentry in the house.

"You're shocked, aren't you, Phillips?"

"I am, Miss." It was impressed upon us regularly by Mr Rowstock that any comment demeaning to the family or the Gentry should be reported to him immediately. While most of us turned a deaf ear to the occasional lapse, a young kitchenmaid who had repeatedly used the term "neck-maggot" was now serving the Gentry in a very different capacity.

"I am using the correct term," she said, as though seditious obscenity was an everyday point of grammar. "Parasitus extra-terrestrium, if you prefer the Latin. I think it is better for those of us who..."

"Miss Reid, are you unwell?" Allowing her discourse to proceed uninterrupted was dangerous, even at the risk of insubordination. "May I help you to the ballroom?"

"Mr Harcourt said you were a man to be trusted. I understood that you…"

"With respect, Miss Reid," I said. "I cannot believe my master has suddenly turned non-conformist."

Her eyes dropped to the ground.

"I believe there has been a misunderstanding, Phillips." She backed slowly away from me. "I am...under some strain at the moment."

She turned and fled.

I returned to the refreshment room and poured out more wine. Miss Reid's strange behaviour had disconcerted me, but I knew the answer was to keep busy and bury my concerns in work.

The room was packed, as the dancers were attempting a complicated cotillion, and the less energetic were seeking refuge in food, drink and conversation. I was opening a bottle of claret when Mr Harcourt clicked his fingers at me.

I hurried across to him. But having attracted my attention, he was already leaving. I followed him out across the ballroom, down a corridor and—to my astonishment—through the green baize door to the domestic part of the house.

"Your room, Phillips—quickly!"

I led him to the attic bedroom I shared with young Bob. I had been warned to beware such situations, but everything was happening far too quickly for me.

"I am afraid it is rather untidy, Sir."

"Not to matter. Phillips, we have known each other for many years, have we not?"

"Indeed we have, Sir."

He rubbed his chin.

"I need your honest opinion, as a man. Philips—did you notice the young Gentlewoman—Miss Smythe?"

"I believe that I did, Sir."

"Then you will have observed how she insisted on dancing with me all evening."

This put me in an awkward situation.

"If you'll permit me to use a vulgar expression, Sir, she seemed to have her eye on you. Of course, she is Gentry, and I cannot..."

He groaned, and put his head in his hands.

"I am lost!"

I touched his arm. "I don't understand, Sir."

"We are to be married, Phillips. Married, at my father's insistence! It is all arranged."

I felt concern for him, both as a man, and as his servant. But, as one dedicated to getting on, I was unable to comprehend his agitation. I could only see the benefit in the match, and I tried to tell him so.

"You don't understand, do you Phillips? Were you not in the gas room when they arrived? Do you not see what marriage to the Gentry would entail? No decent man could countenance it!"

"It would seem a very superior sort of connexion, Sir. And if his Lordship..."

"To H-ll with my father! I do not want one of those d---ed creatures invading my spine, whatever it may do for our family pedigree!"

I was shocked. I had, of course, heard such sentiments before, in the rantings of radicals and the ravings of drunks. But I could never imagine a young man of Mr Harcourt's position entertaining such thoughts, much less expressing them in such a coarse manner.

"I do not wish to become one of them...those empty husks of men."

I hoped he was intoxicated, but I knew he had barely touched a drop.

"I believe that I misheard you, Sir."

"You heard me all too well, Phillips. I am a man! I like being a man. A human being—made in God's image. Not one of those puppets. And I love Elizabeth Reid!"

He paced up and down the balcony, rubbing his hands. I was somewhat perplexed by this turn of events: while Miss Reid was pleasant enough, her family was poor, and she was forced by circumstance to work. Mr Harcourt was heir to a title and a great estate. I had previously assumed that his familiarity with her was a trifling dalliance. And her filthy language and strange behaviour seemed even more sinister in the light of my master's revelation.

"That's what really counts, Phillips. I want to marry Elizabeth more than anything. And if we were already married..." He punched fist into his palm. "That would solve everything!"

He looked wildly around the room, and seized the sheet of notepaper on which I was composing a letter to my dear mother. A moment later, he was scratching away with my pen. While it was not my place to hold an opinion, I knew that Lord Woodworth would be less than overjoyed at his son's proposed love-match and I suspected that Mr Harcourt was well aware of this.

"Phillips—I want you to make your way quietly to the stable, and find Rowlands, without attracting the attention of the other grooms. Give him these." Mr Harcourt pressed coins into my hand. "Tell him to saddle up my hunter and the bay mare, and bring them round to the side of the carriageway. Then you must find Miss Reid—she will be in the nursery or the schoolroom. Give her this note."

"Are you sure that this is what you wish me to do, Sir?" I had never questioned orders in my life—orders have to be obeyed if you want to get on.

He looked at me, sadly.

"Quite sure, Phillips. Take it to Miss Reid now."

Jack Rowlands—the youngest groom—was waiting outside the stable block. He shushed me into silence as I counted out six sovereigns.

"Fair enough," he said, pocketing the money. "I won't get another situation quickly after all this comes to light."

"What do you mean?"

"What do you think? Use your common sense, man."

I thought about it as I walked back to the house. I had just bribed another servant. I was party to a plot against my benevolent employer's intentions, against the Gentry, against England, against the greater Empire. All for a youth's infatuation.

I re-entered the house and put my candle on the windowsill. Fighting my every instinct, I opened the note in my hand and read it by the flickering light.

Miss Reid was not in the nursery or the schoolroom. The door of her own room was ajar, so I knocked.

"*Oh*—Phillips. Come in."

She had changed into outdoor clothes, and was already wearing her coat and boots. A travelling bag lay half-packed on the bed—I could see a muddle of clothes, along with a meat knife, filched from the kitchen.

"Have you seen Mr Harcourt?"

I shook my head and thrust the message deep in my pocket.

"You are wearing your hat and coat, Miss."

"I have an errand to run. Don't you have duties to attend to?" She moved her hat to cover the knife.

"I have a message for you."

"From Mr Harcourt?"

"No—from me. Miss Reid, if you are planning to leave with Mr Harcourt, I beg you not to."

She looked down her nose at me.

"Who are you to speak to me?"

"Miss Reid—earlier this evening you used improper language in the house and bade me forget it. Now it is I that must speak out of turn. I believe that you are about to inflict terrible damage on your own reputation and on one of the oldest and most respected families in England. Please consider..."

She shook her head. "Phillips—you mean well, but you do not understand what I am doing. Let me be."

"There are consequences to this, Miss Reid. I plead with you to think on them."

"I thought of the consequences of my work long ago, Phillips. Long before I came here."

"Then you plan to leave with Mr Harcourt?"

"That is for your master to decide. He did give you a message for me, didn't he?"

I did not answer. I had done all I could to dissuade them. Blackmailing them—even to do the right thing—would have been the most despicable betrayal of my position.

"Very well," she said. "I must go to him!"

I lit a candle and read the note again, thinking of Mr Harcourt's many kindnesses to me. He was a good master, and I had no desire to harm him. But no matter how I turned things over in my mind, I knew what I must do—duty demanded it.

My candle had burned low by the time I made my way to the ballroom. Only a handful of couples were dancing. The Gentry were clustered around Miss Smythe in the refreshment room. She was sitting at a table, head in hands, her amiable companion flowing around her neck and wrists.

My enquiry revealed that the house was in turmoil—young Mr Harcourt was nowhere to be found. His Lordship had retired to his study, in defiance of all protocol, with strict instructions that he was not to be disturbed unless the situation be resolved.

I knocked.

"Go away, blast you! Unless it's my son. Oh, for pity's sake come in!"

His Lordship had sought the traditional refuge of the Englishman: his voice was slurred and there was a huge red wine stain on the rug.

"My Lord, there is something I must show you that may have bearing on the present situation." I held up the note. "And I must make a confession."

I stood on the rug in the dining room, facing the Gentry across the table. An un-amiable companion—specially reserved for such interviews—opened its maw in the gas jar behind them. I understood that one had already made the acquaintance of Rowlands after the six sovereigns were found on him, confirming the truth of my story.

"This is a matter of serious impropriety. Mr Harcourt was promised to Miss Smythe by his father in a binding settlement of marriage and Gentrification," the Duke of Derbyshire said. "I will ask you again, Phillips: did Miss Reid give any indication of their destination, or who might be shielding them?"

"No, Sir. I have mentioned every detail that might concern

the unfortunate matter."

"Very well." He turned to Lord Woodworth. "Can we rely on your man's absolute discretion, or is there a need for greater prudence?"

He indicated the contents of the gas jar.

"Phillips can be trusted." Lord Woodworth said. "It was entirely through him that this sad affair came to light."

"Very well. Phillips—we will require your assistance and your silence. Do you understand?"

I gave the Duke my affirmation.

"In order to track the runaways, we need recently-worn items of clothing from both parties—you must obtain them immediately and in utmost secrecy."

I made my way silently to the lovers' rooms and found a selection of appropriate garments.

Then I helped with further work: fetching a small card table and a map of the county to the gas room; and carrying a wickerwork basket of Gentry apparatus from the Duke's floaty.

When we returned, the Galways were seated at the card table, with the map spread out in front of them. Their amiable companions were entwined as they shredded the garments that I had provided.

The Duke of Derbyshire then required me to assist in the tracking operation. Even fifty years later, I must leave this part of my memoir to the reader's imagination: the intensity of my pride on recalling it leaves me quite unable to set down the details on paper.

Suffice to say, with great speed, and rather less discomfort than one would expect, the lovers were traced to an inn in the Parish of Much Wattering. At once, the Duke and the Scarboroughs set out to bring them back.

When I had recovered myself sufficiently to assist further, I was dispatched to the airstrip with a Bath chair to await the runaways' return. Lord Woodworth stood with me, scrutinising the horizon.

The Duke's floaty arrived first. Mr Harcourt half-stumbled, half fell from the body of the craft—he had partially recovered from the interception but there was still foam on his face. His father stepped forward to steady him and lead him back to the house, flanked by the Callistos.

Less than fifteen minutes later, the Scarboroughs' floaty disgorged Miss Reid and her new—I suppose I must call it a companion. However, the slug-like creature fixed to her neck was unlike any I had ever seen associated with a decent or respectable person.

From her near-paralysis, I surmised that their introduction had been rushed even more than is usual in such unfortunate cases, and a high degree of intimacy achieved far too soon. She was unable to walk, but I was able to lower her into the Bath chair and cover her with a blanket. She shivered and moaned as the chair rumbled and squeaked along the path.

We took the long route, via the willow walk, as there were no steps. As we were passing the statue of Zeus, she raised her right arm over her head and groped blindly backwards until she grasped my wrist.

I halted our progress. Ignoring the superior aroma from the companion, I bent over and brought my face close to hers, straining to make sense of her mumbling, as she twisted in her seat.

"K- K- kill me. K-k- Kill me. Kill me."

There was a desperate pleading in her eyes. Despite her deceit and her disgrace, I found it impossible to feel anything but sympathy for a suffering fellow human and, for a moment, I considered how I might help her find a merciful release. But my duty was clear.

"I am sorry," I said, straightening her blanket. "I cannot be of assistance in this matter."

I released the brake and pushed the chair to the house.

Mr Harcourt and Miss Smythe were married by special licence at the parish church the following Saturday, the groom's silence being taken for assent. Afterwards, they were paraded back to the hall to cheers from the villagers.

There was no wedding ball or breakfast, it being deemed necessary to move to the next stage of proceedings as expediently as possible. Accordingly, it was my honour to help prepare the gas room and amiable companion for the happy couple's wedding night.

The newlyweds spent their honeymoon quietly on the family estate. During this time of adjustment, my master found himself more than ever in need of my personal services. While I was pleased to serve the family in any situation, however lowly, it gave me particular satisfaction to assist my master and his amiable companion. And when he was once again fully able to communicate, young Mr Harcourt was most gratified by my exertions on his behalf.

And Miss Reid? There have been rumours I know, but I am the only person alive who knows the whole truth.

It was put around the district that she had run away to London with the young groom Rowlands, who also vanished that night. The story had the advantage of being sufficiently salacious to become universal knowledge while being impossible to prove false.

Shortly after the wedding, a great team of workmen descended on Lansborough Hall and set about the many hundreds of tasks necessary to make the building fit for a modern Gentry residence. Walls were knocked through; wires, pipes and airlocks fitted; and an entirely new gas dome constructed on the roof.

Every day I opened the door to delivery men and helped carry their burdens to the appointed rooms where artisans could unpack and assemble their strange contents. Much of the house was now out of bounds to the regular staff, but those of us who shewed an aptitude for matters that involved the Gentry were given special duties. It was my discretion and attentiveness that led to my being entrusted with the preparation and fitting out of the new nursery, which took up much of the East wing.

The arrangements preferred by the Gentry for raising their young are, of course, a matter of great sensitivity (not to mention a certain amount of idle speculation). Indeed, they have much in common with the kind of processes one might encounter in a modern manafactory, where human intervention is subordinate to mechanical and chemical systems.

Unsuited though she was to the role of governess, Miss Reid was ideally placed to assist with the nurture and education of a new generation of Gentry. There was, of course, the need for complete discretion over the arrangement. However, few servants displayed any enthusiasm for the apparatus and processes which now dominated so much of the house. And while I was always careful to discourage the wild tales of what might happen to the unwary amongst the hissing, dripping pipes, certain rumours proved useful as a deterrent to the curious. People still frighten each other with tales of the young woman who stares out of the nursery windows, her young companions strewn about her neck.

And so I was again promoted, and it fell to me to oversee the smooth running of these new parts of the household. There was machinery to be maintained, food paste to be injected and gas to be topped up in the hatcheries. Looking back on my youth, (as I do increasingly these days), I see that this was when I truly grew into my calling. And over the years that followed, I was able to bear a small portion of the great burden that sits upon our masters.

For as under-Butler, Butler, and Master-Butler, I was entrusted with many more duties that could only be undertaken by a loyal and trusted servant of the Gentry—a man who knew his duty and was singularly dedicated to getting on.

Al Robertson

It's fair to say that I wouldn't be the writer I am without Milford.

I first heard about it from Liz Williams while on an Arvon SF course, and attended my first conference way back in 2008. Since then, I've taken about six short stories and two novel openings through critiquing sessions, and plotted out and worked on a third novel in the two retreats I've been on.

Both completed books and almost all the short stories were published. "Of Dawn" appeared in Interzone 235 and was nominated for the 2011 BSFA Best Short Story Award. And of course, I've learned a lot and had a lot of fun critting dozens of stories by other people, with many of those stories going on to successes of their own.

So, on a practical level, the Milford conferences and retreats have always been time very well spent. And each new Milford has given me both the same experience and a completely fresh one.

What doesn't change? Well, it's always been such a friendly, supportive, constructive environment. There are few pleasures greater than spending a week locked away with a bunch of sf, fantasy and horror obsessives, either talking and critiquing non-stop or digging deep into a new piece of writing.

And what does change? The people, the stories they share, the rich and rewarding thoughts and insights they bring with them, even just finding some new and inspiring walk through the beautiful local countryside—that's been a different experience every single time.

"Of Dawn" in particular benefitted hugely from that. I took it to the workshop as a reasonably finished piece. But it drew on some very personal memories of growing up in the 70s and 80s, and making music in the 00s, so I wasn't sure how broad its appeal would be.

Having the story critiqued by ten other writers, who each approached it from very different viewpoints and shared some very varied insights into how to improve it was invaluable. They helped me strip out some of its more gnomically personal moments, and make sure all of it resonated as widely as possible.

I hope it's resonated with you too. If it did, Milford played a big part in that. Many thanks to Liz, Jacey and all who've helped organise it over the years, and to everyone I've either critiqued or retreated with for all the support and inspiration!

Of Dawn

The coffin was closed when Sarah went to say goodbye to her brother. Before she could even think about asking, the funeral director had touched her hand, and said—"Of course, it would be better to remember him—as he was." Insurgents had taken advantage of a traffic jam to attack Peter's convoy. Fire had taken his jeep before he could escape, flaying the life from him.

A bus rumbled past outside, and the floor shook gently. For a moment, she imagined a god passing by—a drift of shadow that might have been wings; a soul borne away, to cross a dark river. She was sure that Peter could have found a poem in the moment—fragmented and confusing, as all his recent work had been, but real. Loss filled the space where jealousy would once have flared.

The funeral director had missed a patch of stubble while shaving that morning. He tried to smile sadly, but his eyes showed nothing beyond professional detachment.

"Thank you," she said. "Maybe it would be best."

And then he left her, and she was alone. The drizzle greyed the light at the window. Even the hard colours of the Union Jack that covered the coffin were muted.

It was the same at the funeral. Soft rain drifted across Parliament Square. Grey traffic clogged the roundabout. One of the traffic lights had broken. A red man would not turn to green; a green light would not change to red. Horns protested, echoing off the mud-coloured walls of the Houses of Parliament and Westminster Abbey.

Before Sarah went into St Margaret's Church, nerving herself to see Aunt Veronica and the others, she stopped to look around. Church and state; and, over at the edge of the square, an off-white banner, flapping in the wind, that read 'Peace'. It seemed very far away. She turned again, and St Margaret's took her. It was cold inside, and she barely knew anyone. Nobody had asked her to play, which was a relief. She hadn't touched her violin for eighteen months.

She'd last seen Peter two years ago. They had tried to talk over a meal in a small Italian restaurant in Brixton. "I should come to your place," he had said. "Make it easy for you. Least I can do." There had been an apology in his voice. But she wouldn't let him. He had already told her that he was transferring out of the Devon and Dorsets; that he would shortly be leaving for Kuwait, and then perhaps invasion. He was tall and fit, and his voice slipped easily into loudness. He would quickly imprint himself on her flat, and remain present, long after leaving. Memories of her mother, once a frequent visitor, already permeated her home. She could not stand for him to die, and then suffuse her days and her dreams too.

"I'm sorry. It's been too long," he said.

"Seven months," she replied, immediately regretting her precision. "And now—you're off again."

"A bit further than Armagh, this time." He tried to smile. "But I'll be fine." And then, the argument had begun.

Sitting in the cold church, listening to the priest drone, she wondered how many others who'd been close to soldiers had, over the centuries, felt the same regret. She had been angry with his absorption in camp life in Warminster, and then furious that he had left it, to—it seemed to her—leap so decisively towards death. And so her final memories of him were of hot anger, and tears, and of rich food that tasted of ash.

After the argument, there had been a few embarrassed emails. She had sent birthday cards, and terse congratulations when a small but prestigious poetry press had offered to publish his first collection, but they had not met up when he returned home on leave. Aunt Veronica would always let her know the dates, but Sarah never emailed him, and he never got in touch with her. She half hoped that she would bump into him, as she scurried between Warren Street tube and the small legal college where she worked, or that he might be waiting for her one night outside her Camberwell flat. But he was never there, never anywhere where she might find him again.

Now that he was dead, he seemed more present. Every few hours, she would see him in a stranger. The shift of a shoulder, a certain firm way of walking, a sharp voice ordering pints in a pub—for a moment, each one flared with a sense of his presence and became a ghost, and then—as she looked back again, amazed, thrilling suddenly, forgetting; the ghost would melt again into flesh, and if she was lucky she would not catch the eye of the stranger she found herself staring at.

The days danced by like flames. Aunt Veronica left a message on her answerphone. "Do come to Salisbury for a few days, dear. I know it must be hard." They had barely spoken at the church. The sympathy and near-warmth in those few words surprised her. She did not return the call. It was harder and harder to get out of bed. A letter came about Peter's life insurance. Sarah could not read it for weeping. Lunch breaks devoured the afternoon. The list of emails to respond to grew daily. It was easier to ignore them. Calls from friends went unanswered. Her regular lunches with Debbie fell away.

"All this with your brother—we're so sorry, but…"

The legal college called it compassionate leave, but she knew that she would be quickly replaced with a temp. Soon, they would not even remember her. She had arrived, she had said, between orchestras. She had never wondered whose place she was filling—who had moved on from the small office, the dirty keyboard, and the photocopier that wheezed and spluttered like a heavy smoker. There had been another round of failed auditions, and then she had realised that it was easier to just stay on there. She wouldn't have to fall back on any of the investments her mother had left; wouldn't have to let the family know how badly she had failed.

Peter's poetry collection had come out about then, surprising and confusing her. It had been well received. There had been a significant article in the London Review of Books. Peter had been called the first of the twenty-first-century war poets. The reviewer had compared him to David Jones and Paul Celan. Neither of these names meant anything to her. She had set the book down unfinished, and not returned to it.

Now, she picked it up again and found herself obsessed with it. Its broken style mirrored her sense of the world. Words would knit together and she would suddenly hear his voice. These poems held so much more of his presence than the pretenders she saw in the streets. But she found it frustratingly difficult to pin down any final meanings. Images and characters rang repetitively through the book, but she could not make them cohere.

Peter returned obsessively to early twentieth-century composer Michael Kingfisher, to the aftermath of warfare in the former Yugoslavia, to Salisbury Plain and the deserted village of Parr Hinton; to images of a skinless man, walking through the nearby woods, at once leading him into knowledge and foreshadowing his own future. "An angel satyr walks these hills," Peter had said, quoting Kingfisher. Sarah shuddered whenever she encountered the creature and would flick rapidly past the precise, bloody words that described it, wishing for the comforting abstraction of music.

One particular poem hooked her, and called her back, again and again. It was, she began to realise, an elegy for childhood. It took her many readings to piece together its broken syntax, and understand the subtle, ambiguous references that it encoded. When she did so, recognition burned in her, directly triggering memories.

The poem was set in 1982. She had been five, Peter eight.

The family was overnighting at a friend's quarters. Slurred, too loud adult singing from downstairs had woken them both. There was a television in their room. Peter had tip-toed to it and looked back at her.

"Should I?"

A moment, and then she nodded, too stunned by his daring to speak. He had climbed back into his bed, and she had scrambled across to join him. The Open University logo shone on-screen, jewelled with the thrill of the forbidden, and then a title card announced the next programme as 'Music and Landscape, Unit 10: Michael Kingfisher'.

Then, rich music and numinous images blazed out around them. Sarah could only ever remember fragments of the documentary. The dense, muddy greens of Salisbury Plain, the softer greens and browns of the Dorset countryside, shuddered out of the television as music exploded into the room. Some of it reminded her of the classical pieces that she already started to know. Some were indescribable—strange electronic inventions, sounds that danced out of sine waves and binary code. A flute span melodies across it all, shaping difference into one enchanted whole.

Running through the music were hissing moments of recorded sound that felt truly ancient—old men's voices, softened by cider, singing incomprehensible words; the pattering thud of little drums, flitting around notes scratched from fiddles and accordions; a deep and indescribable roaring, that felt like the sound of the Earth, singing to itself. Every so often a cultured voice would interrupt, intoning facts about Kingfisher's life with all the impassioned detachment of a priest overseeing a ritual.

Verdancy suffused the television screen as the programme built to a climax. The camera explored ash-grey Stonehenge. Red ribbons shook and bells jangled as six men danced together. Sunset blazed through trees, a fire in the deep woods. Tumuli humped like whales in the green. Between each shot, colour bloomed across the screen like so much spilled paint.

At the last, the music died to a soft, liquid piping. There was a cloister, partially tumbled by the trees that had grown up within it; there were houses without windows or roofs, looking like they had been built from cardboard. A small, medieval church shuddered into view and then vanished. A gravestone appeared, embedded in soft, emerald gloom. A red hand held something like a flute, bright against the green. Then, the pipes died, and there was silence.

Credits rolled, black on white and the Open University logo appeared again. Soon afterwards, a man with a moustache and thick-framed spectacles was talking about mathematics.

"That…" said Peter.

"Oh yes," said Sarah.

The next day, Peter wrote his first poem, puzzling his hungover parents. Sarah was soon asking for, and then thrilling at, violin lessons.

All of that was encoded in the adult Peter's writing. He made those few minutes the last safe moment. A few days later, they had both been returned to their respective boarding schools, each proud not to cry as their parents left them. A couple of months passed, and then their father was shot in the head and killed by a terrified Argentinian squaddie.

The poem touched and intrigued Sarah. She had hardly thought of that night for years. She had occasionally asked her music teachers about Kingfisher; they had always dismissed him as at best an eccentric, at worst an idiot, and so he had slipped from her mind. Now, she Googled him.

There was a reasonably detailed biography on Wikipedia. His musical career had been triggered by the first performance of Vaughan Williams' Tallis Fantasia in 1910. He had spent three pre-war summers walking the land, collecting folk songs and composing his music. The first excursions had been south of Oxford, around Belbury and Edgestow; most had been in Wiltshire, Somerset and Dorset, following the old green tracks between hillforts and tumuli. They had been centred on

Parr Hinton—then, a thriving village, deep in Salisbury Plain. The woods that surrounded it had become a sacred place for Kingfisher.

She jumped out of the entry to an article about Parr Hinton. It had been abandoned in 1943 when the military requisitioned it for training purposes. Photographs showed broken, roofless houses. The church seemed well preserved. The steep-sided Mercy's Hill, dense with trees, loomed over the village. There was a bald patch on top of it where a stone circle stood, boring a hole in time. Kingfisher had fled there in 1916 after he had been invalided home. He had composed his 'Parr Hinton Fragments', and then apparently disappeared.

Another Wikipedia article discussed the Fragments. It began by describing them—a series of sketches for soloist, quartet, or full orchestra, running between three and ten minutes long, to be performed in an order chosen by drawing cards. It touched on the wax cylinders—field recordings of rural singers, made by Kingfisher in the summers before the war. They were to be played as part of the performance, their order and placing determined by rolling two dice.

A brief critical note was apparently sympathetic, but in fact dismissive. The work was too unstructured to have ever been performed; its fragmented structure was a sad result of shellshock; the famous Tarot quote demonstrated the extent to which Kingfisher's occult interests had corrupted his talent. The quote was given in full, pulled from one of his 1913 diary entries:

> Cards pulled at random hook deep truths; fragments hint at a whole, fluid and vast, always streaming by, impossible to grasp. I dream of a music as fresh as these old images always are; as this old world is, renewed each time my floating self perceives it.

This led to a discussion of Marsyas. Kingfisher had seen

the myths surrounding the Greek satyr as directly relevant to his music. But Marsyas had been flayed alive by Apollo, and so Sarah winced and skipped over the rest of the paragraph. The article finished by noting that Kingfisher's wax cylinders had been lost sometime before the Second World War. There was now no way for the Parr Hinton Fragments to be played according to his original instructions.

Pain flared in Sarah's lower back. She had been sitting at her desk for too long. A low static hiss told her of rain. Looking away from the screen, she was surprised to see that it was nearly three am. She stood and stretched. A sound snatched at her. It could have been a distant siren, fading out; it could have been someone whistling, out in the street. She went to the window.

There was a figure—something like a man—standing on the other side of the road, not quite in the light. She started as she saw that the creature was naked; that where there should have been skin, there was only a deep, clotted red. It was holding something white up to its mouth. Remembering the thin, high sound she had just heard, she imagined pipes, or perhaps a flute. She took a step back, suddenly afraid that she would attract its attention.

It moved, stepping towards the light, the white still at its mouth. She held her breath, but could not stop looking. Her imagination was filled with a sense of Peter, as he had been at the last. A failure to have seen is no barrier to vision. As the creature reached the streetlights, she saw that it had a shimmer to it. She had been expecting something ragged and burned, but to her surprise, its flesh shone as if it had been carved from red amber and then studded with so many rubies.

And then she took a step forwards and was breathing again, for as the figure stepped fully into the light it revealed itself to be a man in a red tracksuit made slick by the rain, smoking a pale cigarette.

She realised that she couldn't remember how many days she had been up for. She went to bed, and let herself sleep.

There were no dreams. When she woke, it was about ten in the morning. She couldn't tell how long she had slept; if only for a few hours, or for an entire day and another night. There was no food left in her cupboards. Her fridge was empty of all but a small container of spoiled milk, and a sad-looking onion.

There was another message from Aunt Veronica on the answerphone. This time, Sarah did return the call. Her Aunt's fussy concern broke over her like a cool spring, and she agreed to take the train down to Salisbury the next day.

～ ～ ～ ～

The teabags had not been given enough time to steep. The lemon cake had a tart meanness to it. "Such a shame not to have a man to look after you, dear," Aunt Veronica said. Sarah had been in her house for half an hour and was already plotting ways she could leave.

"But then, that's your choice."

The Sun had pulled itself behind a cloud, as if scared that—if caught in the dusty room—it too would be offered a cup full of pale liquid, and would have to chew politely on dry bitterness, mumbling the occasional platitude to keep the conversation going.

"And how is your cello playing?"

"Violin, Aunt."

"That's what I meant."

"I play," Sarah said. "I teach."

"Well, someone has to. It's very lucky that you don't really need to work, isn't it? Though I'm not sure it's what your mother meant for you."

Sarah couldn't face an argument. A clock counted out the seconds. Veronica seemed to have squeezed out her entire stock of conversation. Sarah took another sip of tea and winced.

"I was thinking of getting out for a bit," she said.

"Well, I'm always happy to walk into town, dear."

"Maybe a drive, perhaps."

"I couldn't take you too far. It would give me one of my heads."

"I thought I might just—borrow your car."

Aunt Veronica pursed her lips, pushing them together so hard that all colour left them.

"Oh."

Sarah had said that she would stay for a few days. She couldn't just leave. She felt the possibility of any sort of escape receding. She reached desperately for somewhere to flee to.

"There's somewhere—very special to Peter. I'd like to go there—just me, and remember him."

Veronica's lips decompressed a little.

"And where is this place?" she said.

"Parr Hinton. On the plain."

"Oh."

Veronica reached forward and poured herself another cup of tea. She did the same for Sarah. Sarah restrained herself from trying to stop her.

"I don't know the name."

"I would love you to come, Aunt. But—it would be fearfully dull for you. And I do so want to just be there, alone, with him."

Veronica nodded, once, and then took her tarnished knife in hand, and went to start cutting at the remains of the cake.

"I'll see what I can do about the insurance, dear," she said.

～～～～～

First the A36, and then the B3083; each road nestling through soft, mounded landscapes, fields and pastures and woods touching at their edges. The countryside was all soft, clotted greens and browns; the sky dense with pastel clouds. Every so often the Sun would break through, and the landscape—jewelled with water from the recent rain—would shimmer into life, suddenly bright and vibrant. And then, just as suddenly, the clouds would close round it again, and the trees and hills and hedges would lose all sharpness, becoming softly blotted once again.

Sarah was driving to the village of Chitterne. It was on the edge of the military areas of the plain, a few miles from Parr Hinton. She wasn't sure if she'd push on beyond it. She assumed that she would be happy with a pub lunch, and maybe a short walk through the fields. And then she would return, driving as slowly as she could, and pretend to Veronica that she'd walked in the past with her memories of Robert. She had his book with her. She could read that, and think of him.

"Parr Hinton?" said the short postmistress. "You can't go there. It's far too dangerous."

Sarah was surprised at how disappointed she felt.

"Can you get close to it?" she said.

The woman's face softened, and she touched Sarah's hand with her own.

"I am sorry, love," she said. "It's the military."

Sarah sighed.

"Well, if it's shut…"

"I'd hate you to have a wasted journey," the postmistress said, suddenly brightening. Sarah remembered the wet fields, shining into life. "You're not a Michael Kingfisher fan?"

"Yes," Sarah said, and then: "How did you know?"

"Well, you're too young to be one of the people who used to live in Parr Hinton! And he's the only other reason people ask about it. If you look over there"—she waved towards a rack of paperbacks—"we've got his books."

"I didn't know he'd written any."

"Oh, then you haven't had a wasted journey!" She beamed, overjoyed on Sarah's behalf. "I'm so glad. There are two or three."

The books were published by a small Glastonbury press. There was a 'Songs of Wiltshire', a 'Critical Writings', and a 'Diaries 1911-1913'. Sarah bought all three and then walked down the small High Street to the King's Head pub. "Very friendly," the postmistress had said, "and they do a lovely Ploughman's." And she was right.

After lunch, Sarah lost herself in leafing through her new purchases. She started with 'Songs of Wiltshire'. The book recorded the music that Kingfisher had found while walking across the county in those long summers before the First World War. She was surprised to see that there were only about six or seven different songs in the collection. Kingfisher had set down multiple versions of each one, carefully noting the differences between them. She flicked between songs, reading each one and then exploring the footnotes. Some mentioned Parr Hinton. One made her start:

> The words as given here were obtained from Mr Edward Verrall of Parr Hinton, a neighbour of Mr Henry Broadwood, who offered me lunch as I passed through the village early in 1912. The second verse differs from most other versions by replacing the words 'showed his ugly head' with 'skinless and shining red'. I thus take it to be an older variant of the song, referencing the Marsyas myth, which has found a remarkable new life in these parts.

Sarah remembered the bloody figure who had chased her down to Dorset; the flayed man who haunted Peter's poetry. She put the book of songs down. Her plate had been tidied away. She emptied the last of her white wine and settled the bill.

Outside, the wind danced through the village, and the clouds had broken into soft fragments, leaving the sky a soft blue, dappled with white. The threat of rain had lifted, and the world felt fresh and alive. Sarah decided to walk as far as she could towards Parr Hinton.

But the road soon ended in a fence and a low gate. There was a military sign, warning her not to go any further. She thought about going on, but then imagined being stopped by a soldier, and sent back—the military once again coming between her and her brother.

Sadness surprised her for the second time that day, and she turned away. Accepting that for now the way was closed, she walked slowly back to the car, and the long drive back, and the sharp, controlling pain of two more days of Aunt Veronica.

~ ~ ~ ~ ~

"I was starting to get worried about you, Sarah!" Debbie said, shifting her glass of wine in her hand. "You could have texted or something—you know, to let us know you were ok."

"I just had to get through it. Just had to lose myself a bit, I guess. I spent a lot of time trying to understand Peter's book."

"His poetry? What's it like?"

"One of the poems is lovely. I'm not sure about the rest. The critics liked it."

"That book was a surprise. I always thought you were the creative one."

"So did I."

They talked into the evening. When the bar closed, it felt like hardly any time had passed. They walked each other to the bus stop. Sarah hugged Debbie onto her bus, and watched it recede; a great bright block of warmth and safety, roaring into the night. When Sarah got home, her flat seemed very quiet. Her drinks cupboard held gin and wine. She kicked off her shoes and poured herself a glass of red. The sofa was so soft and warm. She had left her travelling bag just by it. The Kingfisher books peered out. They had saved her from Aunt Veronica.

Kingfisher had written lyrically about the people and landscapes of Dorset and Wiltshire. The 'Critical Writings' had gone some way to explaining the repetitive nature of 'Songs of

Wiltshire.' He had been deeply concerned with improvisation, with personal remaking. 'Music should be a supple response to lived experience,' he had written in 1912, 'dancing on the moment. To pin songs down into one, final interpretation is a kind of death for them. I think of butterflies, pinned in boxes; skulls, stripped of life, that can only ever show one hard dead face to the world.'

Sarah found herself remembering some of the songs. She tried to sing one of them to herself, but couldn't remember her way past the first line. She pulled 'Songs of Wiltshire' out, and—carefully avoiding the introduction, with its invocation of Marsyas—paged through it until she found the song. The melody was simple, tumbling off the stave; the words catchily evoked love, and then loss. She sang the first few lines, enjoying the way her tipsy voice twined round the song. Reaching the end of the first verse, she stopped, suddenly self-conscious. But the wine was at hand, and it was easy to pour another glass.

~ ~ ~ ~ ~

Sarah woke with a start. Pain thumped at her head, vague memories whirling around it. She made herself a coffee and tried to reconstruct the night before. She remembered singing, music, and a slow and rhythmic thumping. There had been people playing with her. She must have been dreaming. Caffeine energised her enough to reach the living room. She was surprised to see her violin lying on the little coffee table, by 'Songs of Wiltshire.'

A shard of memory leapt to the front of her mind; shoes tumbling out of the cupboard as she dug around for her violin case. But there had been more than violins playing, last night. There had been those others. She remembered a flute, guitars, even drums, but of course, that was absurd.

She saw that her laptop was turned on, and went to take

a look at it. A rich, vinous smell shook her as she passed the empty bottle of wine. The gin bottle was out and open too. Sitting down at her little desk, she saw that she had left several windows open. She paged through them.

Most were different YouTube pages. There was a man alone in his bedroom, singing 'The Farmer's Thorn'; black and white footage of a 60s folk band playing a sitar-driven version of 'T'owd yowe wi' one horn'; Morris dancers, all shivering bells and drifting red ribbons, jigging through 'Long Lankin'; and then many others, each a fresh interpretation of one of those three songs. These digital ghosts must have been her accompanists.

There was also an Amazon page: 'your order has been accepted.' She had brought a copy of the 'Music and Landscape' series on DVD. It had already been dispatched. "I'll have to send it back when it gets here," she thought. There was a single review:

'The last TV documentaries Natalie Ashton made before she moved to New York. They introduce us to Vaughan Williams, Britten, Warlock and others. Pretty good for 1973, though some of the later programmes get quite abstract. Hey ho, that's Ashton for you—and if you're a fan of her more avant-garde stuff from the late 70s, you'll love 'em! A bargain for lovers of British classical music, too.'

The rest of the day passed slowly. Memories of the night before receded with her hangover, until all was something of a blur. One image stuck in her mind, though, for it had been the last to burn there before she had woken.

A man with a glistening red face had turned towards her and smiled, his eyes alive with sad recognition. For a moment she had forgotten to be afraid, feeling instead something between pity and wonder. And then understanding had crashed in like a misplayed chord, and she had been shocked into wakefulness.

She had thought that the immediate sharpness of her grief for Peter had started to recede. Clearly, she was wrong.

Over the next few days, Sarah tried to get out and about as much as possible. If she was at a loose end, she would go and sit in a café, or walk in one or other of London's parks. She took Peter's book with her; she had decided to try and reach a deeper understanding of it, as a kind of private apology to him.

Memories of her trip to Wiltshire, and her drive to Chitterne, combined with her reading of Kingfisher, helped her clarify some new aspects of the book. Peter had engaged obsessively with the countryside around Warminster, following traces of journeys that Kingfisher had made. In particular, he kept on returning to Parr Hinton, pulling words from its empty houses and woods, and Mercy's Hill.

He had not been absorbed in camp life, she realised, when—in the two years following their mother's death—he had been so distracted, so out of touch. Instead, he had been using all the moments spared to him to lose himself in a deep relationship with that dead musician. That relationship had borne fruit in the creation of this endlessly open, endlessly opaque collection of poems.

She saw Debbie again, meeting up with her for lunch. A couple she knew from the legal college had her over for supper. The temp who had replaced her had recently accepted an offer of full-time work at the college. Rattling home on the tube, she had a sudden and surprisingly decisive feeling that a chapter in her life had closed. The money from Peter's life insurance cushioned her from any immediate need to either find work or admit to the family that she needed to draw on her investments. She decided just to let things flow for a while.

There was an Amazon package waiting for her when she got home. She settled down on the sofa to open it. The image on the cover of the DVD set memories flaring in her mind.

It was an aerial shot of Stonehenge. She was sure that it came from the Kingfisher documentary. Her childhood suddenly seemed so close.

When the DVD menu came up on her TV, she was surprised to see that there were only nine programmes shown. None of them was about Kingfisher. There was an 'extras' choice. She flicked the cursor to that and was relieved to see that the Kingfisher documentary was included there. Wondering what kind of glitch had pulled it into this part of the DVD, she sat back, ready to watch.

Words shone out of the screen:

'The music for this film was largely based on Kingfisher's Parr Hinton Fragments. It was arranged and performed by Brian Mayhew, who withdrew all usage rights early in 1982. The documentary shows some of director Natalie Ashton's first experiments with the narrative techniques that she would later build on in her more famous American work. We present it here stripped of its musical accompaniment.'

The documentary played on, silent but for the upper crust voice that Sarah remembered so well. Dry facts about Kingfisher flowed out; images of lush countryside danced by, cut together—Sarah now realised—with an acute and profoundly dynamic visual sensibility—but there was no music, and without music, the film was only half complete. The narrator's voice annoyed her, and so she muted the sound. Watching the film to the end, she was pleased to see that its final sequences were as visually powerful as she had remembered.

Over the next few days, the absence of music in the documentary started to nag at her. Sequences of images would pop into her mind, and she would find herself imagining scores to set to them. Sometimes she would draw on melodies that she'd found in 'Songs of Wiltshire'. Sometimes, she would imagine synthesised music and assume that she was remembering the programme's original soundtrack. Sometimes, she found herself dreaming of music that she could play herself. She would find that her fingers were tapping away in time with it, writing chords on the air.

She had put her violin in its case, but she hadn't returned it to the cupboard. It was sitting just by her sofa, surprising her every time she looked at it. She had expected to feel her old self-disgust returning; the sense of deep failure that had come to her when she had stepped back from life as a musician. Instead, an excitement at the possibility of making music for its own sake suffused her, an emotion that she hadn't felt for a long time. One day, returning from a long afternoon spent deep in the green embrace of Hyde Park, she pulled it out.

She started by playing a few scales, tuning each string as she did so. At last, the violin sang beneath her fingers, perfectly in tune. She lifted the bow, ready to start playing, and then stopped. She had no music to hand, and she had never felt comfortable with improvisation.

She remembered the 'Songs of Wiltshire'. The book was lying on the coffee table, face down. She reached for it, turned to a song at random, propped the book open on the tabletop, and started to play. The simple melody leapt off her violin and flowed out into the air. There were six verses in the song; she played through them all, whispering the words to herself as she went. The melody was very simple, but it had a deep, implacable catchiness to it. When she stopped playing, it ran on inside her mind, only slowly fading away.

Looking for something fresh, she turned the page and found the same song again. Remembering Kingfisher's determination to communicate different versions of the songs that he'd recorded, she went through it carefully. The melody had been lightly shifted at several points. Some of the words had been changed, too, and Kingfisher had also noted that this version of the song was played more slowly and mournfully than most. Sarah was surprised at the extent to which such small changes altered the song, lending it a deep, fresh gravity. On finishing, she turned the page to the next version, and then to the one beyond, playing quickly through each.

As she did so, she started to understand what Kingfisher had been trying to achieve. Each subtle variation was a small lesson in how to take something that already existed, and in small but important ways make it new. Kingfisher sought to teach his readers the art of variation, and through that, improvisation. Realising this, Sarah felt liberated. Rather than turning to the book to find new interpretations of the song, she began to create her own responses to it, playing the simple melody through, again and again, altering it a little each time. She stood and began to sway with the music that she was making.

As she played, she was reminded of Peter's poetry. Like Kingfisher, perhaps he too sought to not just deploy his own creativity but to inspire it in his audience. The frustrating gaps in his poems—the missing words, the uncompleted sentences, the only half resolved narratives—could be there, she realised, to provide space for his readers to complete each poem for themselves, in ways entirely personal to them.

She remembered the documentary and wondered what it would be like to use it as a trigger for improvisation. She put down her violin, cued up the DVD, and hit play. At first, she found it difficult to respond to the on-screen images. She was used to reading music in staves and notes; to find it in moving images and fragmented sentences was a daunting leap. She remembered the song she had just been playing, and let a few random passages shrill out. They seemed to work against Ashton's images. Sarah felt an odd embarrassment, but she kept playing, experimenting with different tunes and tempos.

Soon, she found music that meshed with Ashton's images. She let the melodies of the folk songs that Kingfisher had collected dance out of her violin. Songs that he had composed began to spin out too, reworked by memory. The fit with Ashton's images became seamless. Jagged noise reflected footage of the trenches. Then, the programme entered its last few minutes, covering Kingfisher's final period—his stay in Craiglockart Hospital, his escape to Parr Hinton, and the composition of the Fragments.

Images flared across the screen; some of them were familiar to her, some seemed entirely new. There was Stonehenge, and then the low tumuli that surrounded it; there was Silbury Hill and the stones at Avebury. They seemed to form a kind of visual algebra, a puzzle that demanded completion through sound. Mercy's Hill loomed out again and again. The camera danced through dense green woods. She felt her violin leap under her hand like something living, and her music became part of a chorus.

Of course, it was impossible. The programme had no soundtrack. It seemed that she had played as part of an orchestra, an orchestra combining classical instruments and rough, rural recordings with ferocious electronic noise. There were words, too, more fluid and evocative than anything the original narrator had said. Old and new music flowed together, in salute to Kingfisher, and to the landscapes that had so inspired him.

And then there was a sense of presence, too. At first, there was just a scent—something rich and dark and bloody. Then, there was a sound—the thin high piping of a whistle, leading the aural dance that she had become a part of. Something bright was reflected in the television screen, standing just behind her, shifting and flowing in time with the music. She was too focused on her playing to turn. When the Morris men leapt across the screen, the red flutter of their ribbons was a sudden visual rhyme with its dancing image.

The music leapt and soared towards a peak, building up with the soft inevitably of a thunderstorm. But as it did so Sarah felt her playing falter. There was magnificence before her, as vale, and hill, and wood, as tumulus, and standing stone, and henge, as farmer, and priest, and midwife, flew across the screen together—but she felt her grasp on them weaken, and the language she had to respond to them slip away from her. No matter what notes she threw out, her improvised solution to the puzzle that they represented was falling away into incoherence.

No one was playing but herself and her own failed music embarrassed her. She stopped playing, and let violin and bow swing away from each other and down, becoming once again nothing more than dead wood and steel and horsehair. She took a step back and turned, and for a second there was the ghost of a creature there. It was standing manlike and staring at her, its eyes alive with joy, its rose-petal flesh glowing out—at once so open to the world, and so vulnerable to it.

It let the pipes fall away from its mouth—white teeth flashing against the red—and, fearless at last, she found herself reaching out to it. But there was nothing there to touch and hold on to. Wine-red lights were spinning across the wall as an ambulance passed by outside, its siren wailing succour into the night, and then there was darkness.

Sarah slumped, collapsing onto the sofa. The last few images of the documentary rolled by, and then the titles began but—exhausted—she had fallen into a deep sleep before her head hit the cushion.

That night, her brother's words leapt through her dreams like fire. But at the moment when she thought that she was about to step past his art and touch his living presence, dawn ignited and burned out the night.

～ ～ ～ ～ ～

"If you could be quieter in your flat I'd appreciate it," the neighbour said.

"I'm sorry," Sarah said.

"I like music as much as the next person—but it's been twice, now. If you could get a rehearsal room for your band?"

"I'm not in a band, Mrs Ensor. I've heard music too. I think someone's playing their stereo too loud."

"I'm going to talk to the building committee if it happens again."

Sarah had spent the day at the English Folk Song and Dance Society in Camden, consulting the original manuscript of the Parr Hinton Fragments. She retained a deep sense of frustration that she had not been able to match the documentary's final section with appropriate music. She only had confused memories of that first session; subsequent attempts to recapture the intensity of her playing had ended in failure. So, she had decided to seek inspiration in the Fragments. She had also found Natalie Ashton's website. There was an email address on it, so Sarah had written to her asking about the documentary's soundtrack. She could find no recent information about Brian Mayhew, or his music.

The manuscript was a remarkable document. Sarah could see why generations of music scholars had been so baffled by—and hence so dismissive of—it. Rather than presenting a finished piece of music, it challenged its reader to create their own piece, using a range of pre-defined components. Kingfisher had dedicated it to 'those who are reaped by those who would control.'

Shards of music were presented, to be combined in any order. There were specific instructions concerning Kingfisher's wax cylinders. He advised the use of dice to randomly select individual ones to play, at random points during the performance. Sarah had jotted down some of the work's key themes but had had to sadly conclude that—without Kingfisher's recordings and several supporting musicians—she would be unable to do it justice as a performer.

That evening, she read through Peter's book again. She was

finding it much easier to engage with. Reading it now felt like a collaboration with the poet. Where she had once found only an echo of his speech in it, now his living mind seemed to drift behind his words. Losing herself in his work, she almost felt that she was in conversation with him, responding to the openness of his work with memories, thoughts, and even stories of her own.

She could even stand to read about the flayed man, understanding now how he fitted into the pattern of the whole. Marsyas the satyr—a god of fluid, improvised music, skinned by Apollo for challenging him—had become for both Peter and Kingfisher an image of openness betrayed; of the many ways that the world carved away at its own finest, most lively products. Both men had been to war, and—in their different ways—seen such threshing at first hand.

It struck her as she read that it would be fascinating to combine Peter's words with the Parr Hinton Fragments. The two were already so closely linked. Absorbed in thoughts of poetry and music working together, she didn't check her laptop until late in the evening. When she did, she was surprised to find a note from Natalie Ashton.

'*Sarah* –

Thanks for your email. I'm glad you enjoyed the documentary. It was an important ignition point for me. Kingfisher was a remarkable man.

I don't know what happened to Brian. We all got very involved in the music. We went to do some work on Parr Hinton. You could say Parr Hinton did some work on us. Brian didn't take it very well. In the end, I think the work he did scared him. I don't think he'll give you a copy of the music, but you never know. He was certainly the last person to have the wax cylinders. I've attached an e-card with the last contact details I had for him. I haven't talked to him for years.

I must look up your brother's poetry. It sounds fascinating. I'm sorry for your loss.

N'

When Mayhew picked the phone up, the first thing he said was:

"Hello? Sarah?"

It had only rung once. He must have been sitting right next to it.

"That's me? Have you heard about me from Natalie Ashton?"

"Who? No, I haven't spoken to her for years. He said you'd call."

"Who's he?"

"I've got to meet you. I've got something to give you. Where can I see you?"

Mayhew's voice was suffused with a desperate kind of fear. Sarah wondered about the wisdom of meeting him.

"Are you still there?" he said. "I have to see you. I have to give you the music."

"The Kingfisher music?"

"From the programme, yes. He wants you to have it."

Sarah was torn. She did want the music, but Mayhew was scaring her.

"Could you tell me who said I'd call?" she said, stalling for time.

"It's got to be somewhere public," Mayhew said.

That seemed sensible. If she met him somewhere open and crowded, she was reasonably confident that she would be safe. She reached a decision.

"I'm in London. Are you coming from Hove?"

She could ask him who'd told him about her when they met.

"Yes." he said. "There's a Starbucks in Victoria Station, opposite the bus rank. I can give you the recordings there. Tomorrow morning. Eleven."

"Does that include the wax cylinders?" she said, but Mayhew had already slammed down the phone.

~ ~ ~ ~ ~

Mayhew was a short, overweight man. He had wrapped a shabby overcoat around himself. A tie peaked out of the v of a v-neck jumper, bright against a drab and dirty shirt. There were remnants of food spattered across it. He hadn't shaved that morning. He brought a stale sweat tang with him into the busy café.

"It's here."

He hadn't stopped to buy a coffee, had barely sat down before he was fumbling a glittering silver disc out of his pocket.

"All the music—on here. Take it."

He pushed the DVD-ROM across the table, watching intently as Sarah picked it up and put it in her bag.

"You've got it now, haven't you? I've handed it over. Nice and easy to listen to?"

"Yes," Sarah said.

"Good." He was already standing up, ready to go. "I've done it." He looked around as if searching for someone watching. "I've given it to her!" he shouted. "You can go back to Parr Hinton now! You can leave me alone!"

"Wait," she said. "How did you know me? And are the field recordings on there too?"

"I've done what he asked me to."

"Please… "

Sarah gave him her best pleading look. He sighed, sat back down, and then leaned forward conspiratorially. It was difficult not to flinch away. One hand was scrabbling in another pocket.

"He gave me a picture of you. Said I should keep the music safely stored for when you called. I was going to burn it all."

"Who did?"

"You know who!" His voice was suddenly loud. She noticed a couple at a next door table turning to look at them. "You know who." Now, he was whispering. "The song in the woods. The river in the green. The flayed man."

Grief, then outrage, prickled through her.

"You know about my brother, don't you? You and Natalie—oh, that's cruel. What are you playing at, Mayhew?"

Mayhew looked genuinely mystified.

"Your brother?"

He had found what he had been looking for. He pulled it out of his pocket. It was a piece of paper, with brown, dry leaves stuck to it. Taken together, they could have formed the shape of a face. They were smudged with bloody fingerprints.

Sarah pushed her chair backwards. She just wanted to leave this man and his dead, sick madness.

"Look," he said, pointing at the withered leaves. "It's you." She stood.

"I recognised you as soon as I saw you. He came to me just after I saw the bloody programme again, just when I was about to strike the first match, and told me to keep the music for you now. Today."

As she turned and started to hurry, walking as fast as she could without running, she heard him shout:

"He took the cylinders away! He said he'd keep them for you, but you'd have to go to him to get them!"

～ ～ ～ ～ ～

The meeting with Mayhew confused and saddened her. His madness seemed to have found a hook in her brother's death. She sat on the bus, wondering whether she'd even play the disc. When she got home, she nerved herself for gibberish; possibly something deeply offensive. But Mayhew had been true to his word. The disc was full of MP3s, each one neatly labelled, each one a recognisable component of the Parr Hinton Fragments.

Mayhew was a talented multi-instrumentalist. His reworking of the Fragments combined synthesiser and live playing, to create versions of Kingfisher's music that both referred back to the composer's time, and looked forward to a 1970s vision of the future. As she listened, Sarah began to tap her fingers, imagining how she could play over the recordings, collaborating with them to create something new. Peter's words would fit well with them too, she thought, seasoning their 70s feel with something far more contemporary.

However, her excitement soon began to turn to frustration. The field recordings shouted their absence. Listening to Mayhew's work, and remembering as best she could the programme's original soundtrack, Sarah was struck by how much texture they had added. There was nothing about Mayhew's work that directly touched the archaic sources that had been so important to Kingfisher. The addition of Kingfisher's field recordings would have changed that. Reaching the end of Mayhew's work, Sarah felt that she had listened to music that only approximated Kingfisher's vision. It failed to embody it.

Sitting back, she realised that she had been using the music to avoid thinking about what Mayhew had said. Kingfisher's obsession with Marsyas had touched him, as it had touched her brother, and her. But Mayhew had only been able to find madness in it. It was sad that such instability had existed in him; sadder still that—she assumed—it had led to the destruction of Kingfisher's field recordings.

She remembered Ashton's comment. Parr Hinton had indeed done some work on Mayhew. The silent village suddenly struck her as being something like Robert's poetry, or Kingfisher's music; a half-made empty structure, waiting for an observing mind to bring it to subjective life. It was sad that the life Mayhew had brought to it had been so warped, that he had not been able to realise that he himself was animating the visions that he saw.

She shook her head and smiled. She was thinking too much about all this. But the image of the village as a trigger to creativity persisted in her mind, intriguing her. She realised that she wanted to visit the place that had so inspired Kingfisher, her brother, and Ashton, and led Mayhew into such fear. She was curious as to what it would awaken in her; whether it would help her find a way to bring all their different music together.

It was decided, then, she thought to herself.

She would travel to Parr Hinton.

And a part of herself that she almost refused to hear wondered what ghosts she might find there.

~ ~ ~ ~ ~

It was almost midnight when Sarah reached Chitterne. She hoped that the darkness would make it easier to avoid any military presence. She left her rental car just down the road from the warning sign. She didn't look at it as she passed, not wanting to be warned off. The woods closed in on the road as she walked. Sarah realised how much of a city girl she'd become. Every rustle around her suggested a presence. She had been glad of the white, shining moon, feeling that its bright light would guide her and help her avoid danger. Now that brightness was making the shadows that surrounded her so very dense.

An owl's smoke-soft hooting drifted in the void. She thought of Mayhew. He had described the flayed man as 'the music in the woods.' She found it comforting to think of the night sounds around her as a kind of performance. The music was soft and subtle—the wind shushing in the trees, leaves brushing against each other, the calls of hunting animals. A fox barked; a few minutes ago, it would have made her jump, but now, filtered through the muting branches, imagined as a single note in a dense aural weave, it had nothing jarring to it. She found that she was imagining the forest as a giant organic harp, trembling into song as nature moved within and across it. Every few moments there would be a fresh, new melody. None of them would ever be repeated.

Cresting a hill, she found that she was looking down on the village of Parr Hinton. She recognised it from the Kingfisher documentary. Cottages ran down the main and side streets like ghosts of themselves, black windows empty, and the church steeple rose above it all. She thought of a conductor at his lectern, standing over an orchestra. She had expected the village to be in darkness, but to her surprise saw that lights were flickering in some of the small windows. An army unit must have taken up residency for the night. A closer look confirmed it. There was a small group of tanks parked up on the village green, dense blots of darkness in the night. Their crews must have been very relaxed—the sound of untrained voices singing drifted up towards her.

She didn't want to go down into the village while it was occupied. Looking up the small valley, she realised that she could enter the woods and skirt around Parr Hinton, climbing Mercy's Hill when she reached it. She'd be able to explore the stone circle atop it by moonlight, and could then come down and look round the village when—as she hoped they would—the soldiers moved on at dawn. She could while away the remaining hours of the night listening to Mayhew's music, and imagining how to set Peter's words—and her playing—against it. She set off into the woods.

She was soon lost. The path through the green had petered out, and she found herself stumbling along, tripping over roots and falling into branches. The sense of peace she'd felt earlier deserted her. The voices from the village disrupted the music of the night, their dissonance making it jagged. Soon, she was tumbling into a light panic, half walking and half running through the night.

A deep sense of presence began to oppress her. She imagined soldiers moving through the darkness, olive drab camouflage folding them into their surroundings. Her brother had been a soldier, so she shouldn't feel threatened; but then she remembered his tales of squaddies, of their sometimes casual brutality, and fear sparked imagination, and she began to run.

Branches snatched at her like cold, brittle fingers. The

moonlight helped her avoid most of them, but some still hit and stung her. There seemed to be no way out of the trees. Every so often she would glimpse the village beneath her, but running downhill brought the edge of the forest no nearer. The wind in the leaves whispered threats in secret languages. For a while, she tried to keep to a straight line, going neither up nor down—but Mercy's Hill, looming against the stars, never seemed to come any closer. She climbed up, but could not find the hill's crest.

The incline became steeper and steeper until at last, she was scrabbling on her hands and knees, climbing earth rather than running on it. Her breath whistled in the night. A root slipped under her foot, and she found herself falling, and falling, and falling. Enough time to be surprised by the memory of a little lost otter called Portly, in a book she'd read as a child; and then she hit the ground hard, and there was no longer any world to fall through.

～ ～ ～ ～ ～

A fire danced in front of her. Beyond that, there was the shape of a man, sitting on a log, firelight making his face a collage of scarlet and shadow. The brightness of flame stopped her from seeing anything else but darkness. She went to sit up.

"No. Don't."

The voice was at once deep, and gentle. She thought of a stream, running over rocks; spring leaves rustling; the deep creak of branches, pulled at by the wind.

"You took quite a knock. You should lie there, for now. There's water at hand."

There was indeed—a small, battered flask. She reached for it and drank. Coolness spread through her, soothing the pounding in her mind. She was reminded of her last hangover. When had that been? A few days ago? A month? Longer? She felt that she had stepped outside time.

"Is that better?" the man said.

"Yes. Thank you."

She lay back. A soft breeze shivered across her, bringing voices. The soldiers were still singing, but now their music seemed softer and more distant.

"Who are you?" she said. "Are you one of them?"

The man laughed.

"No. Not that, not at all. I'm what you might call a caretaker. A gardener."

"Where are we?"

"On my hill. By the stones. I found you in the woods and carried you here. Luckily, I was passing by."

"Yes."

"Now, you should rest. Can I play for you?"

"Play?"

"I have my pipes here. It will help you sleep, and heal."

"Won't the soldiers hear us?"

"No. They're singing themselves. They can't find us tonight."

"Oh. Ok."

White flashed on the other side of the fire, as the man's instrument came out. He put it to his lips and started to play. Sarah thought for a moment that it was very important that she should try and see him. But then soft notes were drifting in the air like smoke, completing the songs of the soldiers, and of the forest, and of the night; and it was so very hard for her to stay awake. There was one question she had to ask, though, before his music soothed her into a far gentler darkness than the one she had emerged from.

"Are you my brother?"

He laughed again—but this time, so much more sadly.

"I knew your brother well, Sarah. But he died in Basra, and you buried him four months ago."

"I wanted to tell him I was sorry… "

"It's too late for that, now. But there are other ways for you to reach him."

And then, the music began again, and Sarah could not stop it from pulling her into sleep.

～ ～ ～ ～ ～

Soft dew had landed on Sarah's face, chilling it. That, and the high whine of heavy diesel engines throttling into gear, woke her. She opened her eyes. The broken village was fresh in the dawn. Four tanks were driving out of it, carving brown tracks in the fields as they passed. She lay still until they had passed over the brow of the hill, and out of sight.

She was lying by the remains of a campfire. Beyond it, a circle of stones slewed like a nipple on the slope of Mercy's Hill; and then trees, and then, below, the empty village. Her head was nestled on her pack, her sleeping bag carefully draped over her. Sitting up, she found that she had been sleeping on a bed of light branches and leaves.

There was no sign of anyone else.

She stood and shook herself down. Something dark and sticky was smeared across her coat; sap, she thought at first, but then saw that it was red on her hand when she tried to brush it away. Perhaps she had bled when she had fallen—but, feeling her head, she could find no trace of a wound.

A couple of minutes, she was walking down into the village. The church was locked. She thought of the subtle poetry that her brother had found in it; the music that it had inspired in Kingfisher; the madness that had come to Mayhew. None of that was evident now. In the dawn light, it only looked broken and empty—something like a half-built stage set, or a canvas awaiting paint. She poked around in some of the houses, but there was nothing to be found beyond empty ration packs and a few broken chairs and tables.

Walking back to the car only took a few minutes. Sarah was surprised at how at ease she felt; how happy she was not to have been overwhelmed by the experience of Parr Hinton. Robert's poetry and Kingfisher's music still existed, two different ways of understanding it. Mayhew stood as a warning. Now, she was free to develop her own interpretation of the empty village, and of the wider world of which it was a part. She passed the warning sign and smiled to herself.

The car was where she had left it. She unlocked it, and, opening the door was surprised to see a large wooden box on the passenger seat. She pulled its cover off. It was full of small leather tubes, each one tied shut with a bit of twine. Dried leaves and moss had been packed between the tubes to cushion and protect them. She picked one out. It had a handwritten label on it—'Chilmark, August 18th, 1912—John Addiscombe, Long Lankin'. There were also two numbers printed on it, a four and a one. Looking back into the box, she could see that all the other tubes had similar labels, and were similarly numbered. None of the numbers went higher than six.

Astonished, and wanting to be sure that she should be astonished, Sarah untied the cord that held the case together. One end of it opened up; she shook it gently, and a wax cylinder dropped out, falling into her waiting hand as if it had always been meant to be there.

J W Anderson

This story went to Milford in 2013; then, it was the first part of a triptych of stories involving Reapers. Part of the discussion at Milford was that this part of the triptych was the strongest and indeed was strong enough to stand on its own, as opposed to the other two parts; the basic arc of this story shouldn't change much. Beyond that, the main change that arose from the discussion was that it would be more engaging to have Minoru interact more actively with the Reaper; for instance, in the final version, Minoru cooks for the Reaper, which he didn't in the Milford draft, and he talks much more to the Reaper. Other suggestions that I took up included bolstering the specific details of the story, such as reporting of the Reaper and the time that Minoru has remaining, and having gone back and reread both versions, the story is significantly better for those suggestions.

A Last Day

Kojima Minoru awoke to the pre-dawn dark, brought from restless sleep into wakefulness by something more than the familiar pains that gathered every night in his old bones. He didn't immediately open his eyes but rather lay quietly, listening to the world inside his house and outside. The stream gurgled and the wind whispered through barren branches. The air held tightly to the cold of winter, with no hint yet of the spring to come.

He didn't hear breathing or the shuffling of feet, but he was certain he was not alone. A lifetime of training held his reaction in check, and he didn't move. His eyes still closed, he let the small details of the room fill him, until he found what had awoken him. The faintest edge of an unusual smell hung in the air, acrid and floral but not of a flower that had ever bloomed here on the mountain.

He'd read the vague descriptions of this otherworldly smell and he'd listened as the interviewed friends and relatives of the Taken struggled to describe its details, but he'd not expected ever to encounter it himself. And why would he, with so many people in the world and so few being Visited each day, and him being an old man who lived in this small shrinking village at the far edge of civilisation.

With this smell came the knowledge that the coming day would be different from all of his recent and not-so-recent days, because he knew that he would die today. The thought of his own death did not frighten him. As old as he was, he had expected death to have come for him in some form already. It had certainly had sufficient opportunity. What he had not expected, though, was to have 9 hours and 47 minutes, less what he'd slept through, to spend beforehand.

He opened his eyes and sat up, slowly. The full moon had long since set and the only light came from the first fingers of dawn reaching up from the horizon to the east. After his eyes adjusted to the dimness, he looked to see where the Reaper waited. It stood, or sat, or squatted, in the far corner of the room from his bed, slightly distorted by the rising heat from the remaining coals in the fire pit in the centre of the room.

He couldn't make out any fine detail, but he didn't need to. The Reaper had over the past 10 years become a familiar image, often described as a four-foot high pile of rags, no visible ears or eyes or other features, no visible means of locomotion, no distinguishing feature of any sort beyond its faint acrid floral scent.

The Reapers had arrived on Earth as from nothing, and they remained beyond all reasonable explanation, as far as Minoru knew. Speculation included aliens or demons arisen from Hell, inter dimensional beings or time travellers, but no one had found the evidence to distinguish one theory from any other. Minoru felt an instinctive sympathy for the view that the Reapers were just explorers, observing mankind, extracting their regular small tribute as a means of furthering their own understanding. Perhaps, he thought, they collect people as we collect rocks. Or more to the point, butterflies.

And now a Reaper had come for him. Even if he'd had the energy, he knew there was no point in running. No one had yet escaped a Reaper. They appeared. They followed, and observed, presumably, for exactly 9 hours and 47 minutes and some seconds. And then they acquired, for the lack of a better term, moving so quickly that their resulting envelopment was a shroud thrown over a victim who was then completely physically gone, disappeared with the Reaper that had Taken them.

Looking towards the Reaper across the room, Minoru said, "In spite of all I know, I cannot and I will not go willingly with you." No, he thought, less making a decision than realising he had no reasonable alternative. He would stand. He would fight and confront the Reaper with his ryu, the way of the sword, that Miyazaki-san had taught him.

"House," Minoru said, speaking to no part of the room in particular. "Alert the appropriate authority that I have a Reaper, with the flag, absolutely no interference." Some were happy for biologists and linguists, chemists and philosophers, to follow them around, observing their Reaper. Perhaps they enjoyed being a celebrity for a day. But the authorities had long ago realised that some preferred to face their Reaper alone. "And can you determine when the Reaper arrived?"

"Minoru-san, notification sent. Scan of internal video footage indicates the Reaper arrived at approximately 1.53am and the current time is 7.35am. You have approximately 4 hours, 5 minutes."

Minoru nodded to himself. As a first skirmish in this battle, he would not permit the Reaper to disturb his routine. He got out of bed, moving as though each of his years had settled like sand in his joints. He hobbled slowly around his room, doing what he had done every morning since he'd moved to this place some 71 years before. He shook his head slightly in disbelief. He turned and said in the direction of the Reaper, "Has it really been 71 years since Miyazaki-san rescued the young orphaned Minoru from the chaos of post-war Nagasaki and brought me here?" He chuckled, receiving the lack of answer he expected, and knelt slowly down by the fire pit.

He stoked the fire, adding first kindling and then larger wood, blowing until the flames joined him in wakefulness and consumed their own breakfast. He took a deep breath, enjoying the harsh edge of the smoke, but then spent the next few minutes bent over, coughing.

He walked down to the stream and filled the bucket,

shivering slightly in the crispness of the morning air. Each time he turned to look, he saw the Reaper off to the side of the trail, as present and motionless as the rocks and the trunks of the trees.

Back inside, he filled the kettle and hung it above the fire pit to boil for tea, the Reaper back in the far corner of the room. As the water heated, Minoru made his bed, smoothing out the sheet, folding the blankets carefully in half and laying them on the bottom half of the futon after folding it over, as his mother had taught him. He then swept the floor. This morning ritual of tea and tidying was his daily tribute to his single remaining and almost completely faded memory of her.

And now, breakfast. He emptied the contents of the pantry and small refrigerator, and laid the food out on the counter. Given the sparseness of his appetite, there was far more here than he would be able to eat today. But smiling, he saw that he had the ingredients for his favourite soup, which he had not made in too long, the soup whose recipe he had learned from Miyazaki-san, who in turn had learned it from his mother. Or so he'd said.

After a second, he said, nodding to himself, "Soup for breakfast. And why not." He set out the makings for the soup and stacked what remained on the end of the counter, the perishables back into the refrigerator, for Hatsu-san to find.

One of the other remaining few left in this village of the old and abandoned, Hatsu-san would be curious that evening when she didn't see the smoke from his fire, and she would at some point come to investigate. Unless of course, she has already seen the Reaper and so knew why there would be no smoke tomorrow.

He put rice in the rice pot with some cold water and set it on the edge of the fire to boil. He laid out tuna and cabbage, ginger and radish, and after a slight pause, garlic, as he wouldn't suffer the consequences tomorrow. "And I hope," he said to the Reaper, "you suffer no consequences from the garlic either."

He hummed to himself as he sliced the cabbage and radish and chopped the ginger and garlic. He seared the tuna in the big pot and set it aside, before adding water and herbs and miso paste, the cabbage and radish, garlic and ginger, and letting them all simmer contentedly together.

By this time, the rice was ready and he took it off the heat, putting the lid on and setting the pot on the stone next to the fire pit.

The smell of the soup filled the house, banishing the Reaper's faint flower. He added the seared tuna to the soup and let it simmer for a few more minutes.

Minoru took out two bowls, and after only a slight pause, another two. He spooned rice into two and soup into two. He set one bowl of rice and one of soup at his usual place at the table, and the other two on the other side, along with tea and chopsticks with each. Before sitting, he bowed towards the Reaper and said, "Please, join me."

Minoru ate the soup slowly, following the flavour and texture of each mouthful from beginning to end. He was smiling when he finished. It had been a long time since he had paid that much attention to a meal, and it had been a long time since he'd enjoyed his meal so much. After finishing, he washed and dried his bowls and put them away, and wiped the counters. The Reaper had not joined him, but he left the Reaper's bowls on the table, saying "In case you should decide later that you are hungry."

Moving to the front of the room, he knelt at the sword rack and said, "I am sorry that I do not have enough time to prepare you properly for the battle to come. Please forgive me for that." He then reached out and lifted Breath-of-morning-sun from the rack. Turning towards the Reaper, he said, "According to my teacher Miyazaki-san, Breath-of-morning-sun was forged by Muramasa-san himself, some 600 years ago, and had been given to a distant ancestor as payment for an unspecified favour, the details lost over the generations."

Minoru gently drew Breath-of-morning-sun. As every other time, the faint tuneless song the blade sang as it slid against the lacquered scabbard raised the hairs on the back of his neck. He set the scabbard on the floor, stood and executed his favourite suburi, a complicated collection of movements of body and blade, from the ryu. Breathing slightly heavily, he replaced Breath-of-morning-sun in her scabbard. Turning to the Reaper, he said, "I look forward to introducing you to her."

The morning was passing quickly. He walked down to the stream one last time, stripped naked, and stepped carefully into the cold water, the Reaper on the bank above him. The stream moved slowly here, collecting in a shallow pool before tumbling over some stones and continuing on its way. He submerged himself and shrank from the cold of the water. He broke the surface and took in a great gulp of breath. The air was crisp and the sky clear, and he marvelled at beauty of the pale morning moon he could see against the blue of the sky. Again he submerged himself, and again, until all that remained within him were the cold of the water and the stillness of the day. He was ready.

He walked the path barefoot, leaving his clothes by the stream. Back in the house, he put on his gi. He had not worn it since the last day he trained with Miyazaki-san, two days before his teacher had died, about the same time the Reapers arrived on Earth. He imagined that he could still smell Miyazaki-san's hideously pungent aftershave on it, mixed with the smoke of the cigars he always smoked in the evenings, and smiled at the memory.

And then he paused. However sharp Breath-of-morning-sun and however well he remembered all that Miyazaki-san had taught him, he knew he would not survive the fight. No one survived their Reaper.

With that thought foremost in his mind, he folded the right side of the gi jacket over the left, as one would dress the already dead, before tying the belt around his waist. It was the same belt that Miyazaki had given him the first day of his training. It had been too long then for the thin child he'd been then and it remained too long now, and he had always had to wrap it around his waist three times, rather than the traditional two. It was frayed and colourless, but he'd never thought of replacing it. Finally came the hakama, its folds sharp.

With Breath-of-morning-sun at his waist, he stepped outside. With each breath, he could see his time ebbing away from him, a thick cloud quickly absorbed by the air.

The house was built on the edge of a field, where he and Miyazaki-san had trained, morning and evening, summer and winter, through sun and rain and snow. In the centre of the field was a large flat rock, a distorted square ten metres on a side. Generations of feet, of Minoru and Miyazaki-san and those who had taught those who had taught him and all those before, had polished this rock to a dull sheen.

As Minoru walked into the field, to the edge of the rock where the Reaper waited for him, as though anticipating, he smiled to himself. He could sense rather than see the few remaining villagers gathering in the trees, watching what was to come. He was not surprised that they'd known that the Reaper had come for him. The village was small and everyone watched everyone else. He bowed to them, hoping that he had found Hatsu-san from among all of them, before turning to face the Reaper.

He took a few steps towards the centre of the rock, drew Breath-of-morning-sun from her scabbard and watched the warped sunlight ripple along the blade. As he drew, the Reaper moved quickly and seemingly passed through him and over him, enveloping him, before disappearing.

Before Minoru could react, the Reaper reappeared in front of him. After a few seconds, it began to lengthen and twist as it took on human form, its own sword growing and taking on its own form in its hand. It stepped to within six feet from him, and waited. Minoru squatted down, Breath-of-morning-sun resting on his upraised palm, and bowed the formal bow that signalled the beginning of combat.

The Reaper, well-formed except for the blank space where it took no face, squatted down and mirrored his formal bow, its own sword on its upraised palm and its head bent low. They rose as one. The Reaper attacked immediately, silently, its own blade strangely green in the sunlight. It was a clumsy attack. Minoru easily slid to the inside of the Reaper's descending blade and slashed deep across its midsection. He felt only the slightest resistance to his blade as it passed through and emerged unstained by blood or ochre, the cut disappearing as soon as Breath-of-morning-sun had passed through.

The Reaper paused before attacking again. Again, Minoru moved to the side, this time cutting down, following the line of the Reaper's cut. A human would have been decapitated but the Reaper only paused before turning to attack again, and they continued. Minoru moved as Miyazaki-san had taught him to move, his mind quiet and watching, and he could almost feel the spirit of Miyazaki-san inhabiting him, guiding his movements. Each time the Reaper attacked, he moved and Breath-of-morning-sun found it.

During one of the brief pauses, he stood facing the pale morning moon, and noticed a lone bird silhouetted in its face, unmoving. It has been caught mid-flight, its wings outstretched, hanging motionless in the sky. The air was still, and he no longer saw his own breath in the cold. Time had stopped.

But he had no time to contemplate this before the Reaper attacked again. The combat continued. He no longer felt the faint but omnipresent pain that had come to illuminate his every movement. The sand had fallen out from his joints and the thin clouds from his eyes. He felt no hunger. He felt no thirst. He felt no fatigue. There was only Breath-of-morning-sun and the ryu and the Reaper.

His mind, attentive but not interfering with the body, watched as his style changed. He was losing, one infinitesimal piece at a time, each of the inevitable small hesitations he'd always felt while practicing with Miyazaki-san, always stopping the bokken short, not wanting to actually hit his teacher, never feeling that he could completely let go. He began to flow, and he smiled as the joy of the flow of the movement filled him.

The Reaper was also changing. It was learning, becoming smoother, stronger, faster, and as the combat continued, the Reaper came closer to him, making small nicks, and Minoru felt exhilarated as the Reaper pushed him to the absolute limit of what he could do.

The combat ended suddenly. He and the Reaper stood facing each other, neither moving, until they moved simultaneously. The Reaper moved perfectly and elegantly cut Minoru across the neck. Minoru dropped to his knees, Breath-of-morning-sun still in his hand, as a red mist filled the space in front of him. "You," he mouthed, "are an excellent student." As the darkness took him, he laid Breath-of-morning-sun carefully in front of him and bowed deeply towards the Reaper, a bow from which he did not arise.

About the Authors

Neil Gaiman is credited with being one of the creators of modern comics, as well as an author whose work crosses genres and reaches audiences of all ages. He is listed in the Dictionary of Literary Biography as one of the top ten living post-modern writers and is a prolific creator of works of prose, poetry, film, journalism, comics, song lyrics, and drama. His work has been honoured with many awards internationally, including the Newbery and Carnegie Medals. His books and stories have also been honoured with Hugos, Nebulas, the World Fantasy Award, Bram Stoker Awards, Locus Awards, British SF Awards, British Fantasy Awards, Geffens, Mythopoeic Awards, and numerous others. You can find out more about Neil and his work at his website https://www.neilgaiman.com and follow him on Twitter at @neilhimself

Tiffani Angus is a writer, editor, and ex-academic. Her debut novel, *Threading the Labyrinth* (2020), greatly improved by Milford feedback at a very early stage, was shortlisted for the British Science Fiction Association and British Fantasy Society Best Novel awards. She and Val Nolan, another Milford alum, have an instruction book on writing various SFF/H subgenres, *Spec Fic for Newbies*, coming out with Luna Press in 2023. You can find out more about her and her work at www.tiffani-angus.com.

Ben Jeapes wanted to be a writer in the mistaken belief that it would be quite easy and save him from having to get a real job. Turned out it isn't and it didn't. Having had that knocked out of him at a thankfully early age, he could dedicate time to learning and developing his craft while holding down day jobs in publishing (social sciences, I.T., medicine, science fiction) and technical communications. He is now the author of eight novels (and co-author of many more), a children's biography of Ada Lovelace, and numerous short stories collected in Jeapes Japes. www.benjeapes.com

David Langford has been publishing and writing about SF since 1975. Novels include *The Space Eater* and *The Leaky Establishment*; there are many collections of his reviews, criticism and humorous commentary. His 29 Hugo awards span several categories: Fanzine and Semiprozine for the SF newsletter *Ansible* (1979-current), Short Story for "Different Kinds of Darkness" (2000) and Related Work in 2012 for the online *Encyclopedia of Science Fiction*, of which he and John Clute are now the principal editors.

In his spare time he runs the small press Ansible Editions and, occasionally, sleeps. See ansible.uk, ae.ansible.uk and news.ansible.uk for more.

Jacey Bedford is a British writer of science fiction and historical fantasy. She is published by DAW in the USA. Her Psi-Tech and Rowankind trilogies are out now. Her latest book, *The Amber Crown*, came out in January 2022. Her short stories have appeared in anthologies and magazines on both sides of the Atlantic, and have been translated into Estonian, Galician, Catalan and Polish. In another life she was a singer with vocal trio, Artisan, and once sang live on BBC Radio4 accompanied by the Doctor (Who?) playing spoons.

Blog: jaceybedford.wordpress.com
Facebook: facebook.com/jacey.bedford.writer
Twitter: @jaceybedford
Website/mailing list: jaceybedford.co.uk
Artisan: artisan-harmony.com

Val Nolan teaches English at Aberystwyth University where he is Lecturer of the Year 2022. His essay 'Science Fiction and the Pathways out of the COVID Crisis' was a BSFA awards finalist. Other academic work has appeared in *Science Fiction Studies*, *Irish University Review*, and *Journal of Graphic Novels and Comic Books*, while his monograph *Neil Jordan: Works for the Page* is published by Cork University Press. His fiction has appeared in *Year's Best Science Fiction*, *Best of British Science Fiction*, *Interzone*, and the 'Futures' page of *Nature*. His story 'The Irish Astronaut' was shortlisted for the Theodore Sturgeon Award.

Cherith Baldry was born in Lancaster, UK, and studied at Manchester University and St Anne's College, Oxford. For several years she was a teacher, including a spell as lecturer at Fourah Bay College, Sierra Leone.

Cherith writes mostly fantasy and science fiction for children and young adults. She has published three adult fantasy novels and a number of short stories in various anthologies and magazines. She has recently published two mystery novels, and is currently part of the Erin Hunter team writing the series *Warriors*.

Cherith lives in Surrey where she is housekeeper to two cats.

Victor Fernando R. Ocampo is the author of the International Rubery Book Award shortlisted The Infinite Library and Other Stories (Math Paper Press, 2017) and Here be Dragons (Canvas Press, 2015), which won the Romeo Forbes Children's Story Award in 2012. His play-by-email interactive fiction piece "The Book of Red Shadows" debuted at the Singapore Writers Festival in 2020. He is a fellow at the Milford Science Fiction Writers' Conference (UK) and the Cinemalaya Ricky Lee Film Scriptwriting Workshop, as well as a Jalan Besar writer-in-residence at Sing Lit Station (2020/2021).

Visit his blog at vrocampo.com or follow him on Twitter @VictorOcampo

Guy T. Martland is an SF writer based in Bournemouth, Dorset where he lives with his wife, daughter, Ukrainian refugee in-laws and two cats. When he isn't writing, he works as a histopathologist or plays a 19th-century German violin. At 6 foot 8 inches in height, he claims to be the tallest living SF writer.

Find him at guytmartland.co.uk

Nick Moulton is a London-based writer of science fiction, fantasy and horror (often all three at once). He borrows ideas from everything from the children's books he reads his young son to B movies, 19th century fiction and real-life strange occurrences.

He first attended Milford in 2008, after hearing Liz Williams recommend it. After critting sessions, he has been known to kayak on Llyn Nantlle Uchaf (Upper Nantlle Lake) behind Trigonos.

When he's not exploring twisted timelines Nick works as a website editor.

Al Robertson has published two novels with Gollancz, "Crashing Heaven" and "Waking Hell". The opening chapters of each went through Milford critiques, in 2010 and 2014 respectively. His SF, fantasy and horror short stories have appeared in a wide range of venues. Many of them have also received invaluable crits at Milford.

Over the last couple of years (COVID permitting) he's switched to the Milford writers' retreat, using the time to work on his next novel—near-future techno-thriller "Smoking Mirror". You can find out more about his books and short stories at his website, www.allumination.co.uk.

J W Anderson is a professor in pure mathematics at the University of Southampton. When not reading or writing or engaged in higher arithmetics, he can often be found in the dojo, practicing the traditional martial art of aikido. He can found on-line at www.multijimbo.com

About the Editors

Liz Williams writes science fiction and dark fantasy. Her novels have been published by Bantam Spectra and, currently, Open Road in the USA and by Tor Macmillan and New Con Press in the UK. Most recently, as well as the Fallow Sisters series with New Con, she has published a book on the history of Paganism in Britain, *Miracles of Our Own Making*, with Reaktion Books, one on *Modern Handfasting* with Llewellyn, and is working on a new book on folklore.

Pete W. Sutton is a writer and editor. His two short story collections *A Tiding of Magpies* and *The Museum for Forgetting* were shortlisted for Best Collection in the British Fantasy Awards in 2017 & 2022 respectively. His novel *Seven Deadly Swords* was published by Grimbold Books. He has edited several short story anthologies and is the editor for the British Fantasy Society Horizons fiction magazine.

About Milford

MILFORD is a week-long gathering of published authors who write speculative fiction (in its widest sense). It is not a school for beginners; there are no teachers or students. It is not an elitist in-group. Invitations are extended to any SF author—from relative newcomers to those who may only dimly recall what rejection slips look like. The workshop usually includes some writers who have not attended a previous Milford, and they are particularly welcome. We meet to critique each other's work, so in advance of the Milford week, all attendees submit up to 12,000 words in one or two pieces. During the week there are structured critique sessions each afternoon, while mornings are free for writers to catch up on their reading/critiquing or do whatever they do when left to their own devices. Evenings are usually social time. We get together after dinner and bond over drinks in the library.

The September conference is the longest-running SF writers' event in the UK. It has been a regular (and almost) annual occurrence since 1972, drawing members from Britain, Europe, USA, Canada, Asia and Australia. Over the years it has moved venue several times but has been in its current location in North Wales since 2004. It has settled into a comfortable, workable format: demanding and exhausting, but also convivial. In short, it's a social as well as a literary event--a chance to connect with other writers.

Many famous names have passed through Milford in its five decades in the UK: Anne McCaffrey, Brian Aldiss, Bruce

Sterling, Charles Stross, Chris Priest, Diana Wynne Jones, George R.R. Martin, James Blish (the founder of Milford in the UK), John Clute, Neil Gaiman, Alastair Reynolds, Jaine Fenn, Karen Traviss, Kari Sperring and Liz Williams.

Some attendees are novel writers, others specialise in short stories. All are welcome as long as they have achieved the minimum qualification, at least one story sale to a recognised SF market.

In recent years Milford has extended its activities to include a writers' retreat week in May, which offers the opportunity to spend a week in glorious North Wales, being looked after and fed regularly with nothing to do but write and get together with fellow writers at meal times. One writer astonished us by writing 33,000 words in a week, and the following year another writer wrote 57,000 words in a week.

Annually from 2017, Milford has offered two funded places to self-identifying writers of colour to attend the September conference. Some writers have been from the UK, and some from all around the world. Any income from this anthology will go towards funding future places. If you would like to support our Writers of Colour bursary (or apply for it), or if you are a writer who would like to attend either the September conference or the May retreat, please contact the Milford secretary via our website at www.MilfordSF.co.uk

Also from Kristell Ink Publishing

The Book of Angels

Would you want to be an angel? The pay's terrible and you get nothing but complaints from dissatisfied mortals. This exciting new collection brings together the writing talents of international fantasy author A J Dalton, Matt White (prize-winning scriptwriter), Caimh McDonnell (writer for Mock the Week), Sammy HK Smith (friend to gods and demons), Andrew Coulthard (award-nominated short story writer) and Michael Bowman (widely worshipped by those who know about such things).

"Divine, divisive and downright dastardly!"—Carl Rhinebeck

A Tiding of Magpies

Pete W. Sutton

One for sorrow...

These deliciously dark tales are themed on the counting magpies songs. Twenty-five tales, ranging from tiny flash fiction to long stories, always entertain and unnerve. Whether it is waking to unmentionable sounds in *Not Alone*, taking a trip to the land of stories in *Five for Silver*, the surprising use of a robot butler in *I, Butler* or competition winner *It Falls*, Sutton's unique voice shines through.

Forgotten Sidekicks

Edited by Peter Sutton & Steven Poore

We all know what happens when the hero saves the day. But what about their sidekicks?

Too often the hero is held high and celebrated whilst their sidekicks and comrades are brushed to the side; their own battles forgotten, and their actions airbrushed to nothingness from the tales of victory.

These stories didn't make the headlines: but they happened, and they're glorious.

Courtney M. Privett -- Desmond Warzel -- Donald Jacob Uitvlugt Allen Stroud -- Su Haddrell -- Chrissey Harrison -- John Houlihan Ian Hunter -- Steve Dillon -- Jim Horlock.

Fight Like A Girl

Edited by Roz Clarke and Joanne Hall

What do you get when some of the best women writers of genre fiction come together to tell tales of female strength? A powerful collection of science fiction and fantasy ranging from space operas and near-future factional conflict to medieval warfare and urban fantasy. These are not pinup girls fighting in heels; these warriors mean business. Whether keen combatants or reluctant fighters, each and every one of these characters was born and bred to Fight Like A Girl.

Featuring stories by Roz Clarke, Kelda Crich, K T Davies, Dolly Garland, K R Green, Joanne Hall, Julia Knight, Kim Lakin-Smith, Juliet McKenna, Lou Morgan, Gaie Sebold, Sophie E Tallis, Fran Terminiello Danie Ware, and Nadine West.

Copyright and previous publication

Ryland's Story by Neil Gaiman, previously unpublished.

Mama Leaf by Tiffani Angus, first published in *Unsung Stories* on 24 April 2020. http://www.unsungstories.co.uk/short/2020/23/4/mama-leaf

Go With the Flow by Ben Jeapes, first published in *Interzone* 142, April 1999

Serpent Eggs by David Langford, first published in *Science Fiction Age* magazine, September 1998.

Pitch by Jacey Bedford, first published in the anthology *Ten: Thou Shalt Not* by Tickety Boo Press, 2015

Old School: An oral history of Captain Dick Chase by Val Nolan, first published in *Unidentified Funny Objects* #7, October 2018.

The Venetian Cat by Cherith Baldry, first published in the *Kisses by Clockwork* anthology by Ticonderoga Publications, 2014

Blessed are the Hungry by Victor Fernando R. Ocampo, first published in *Apex Magazine* 62, July 2014. Later published in Mandarin Chinese (trans. by Hu Shao Yan) in *Science Fiction World* (March 2015).

Words of War by Guy T. Martland, first published in *Fiction Vortex*, 2014.

Scenes from Domestic Life with the Gentry by Nick Moulton, first published in *Albedo One* 49 (Things Change), 2019.

Of Dawn by Al Robertson, first published in *Interzone* 235, July 2011.

A Last Day by J W Anderson, first published in *Andromeda Spaceways Magazine* 66, March 2017.

kristell-ink.com

Milton Keynes UK
Ingram Content Group UK Ltd.
UKHW010615310524
443424UK00005B/92